Yours in mystery
and intrigue,

Rhett
12/13/12

The
Precipice

Penny Goetjen

NEW YORK

The
Precipice

Ithaca Press
3 Kimberly Drive, Suite B
Dryden, New York 13053 USA
www.IthacaPress.com

Cover Design   Penny Goetjen
Book Design   Gary Hoffman
Cover Photo   ©Sapsiwai

Manufactured in the United States of America

9 8 7 6 5 4 3 2 1

Library of Congress Cataloging-in-Data Available

First Edition

Printed in the United States of America

ISBN 978-0-9839121-4-9

www.PennyGoetjen.com

To Kent, who has always supported me through all my

endeavors, including this one.

Chapter 1

Elizabeth sank down into the upholstered, swivel chair, leaning forward with her forearms against the cold, hard edge of the mahogany conference room table. She took a deep breath and exhaled what could have been interpreted as a sigh of relief. She was desperately trying to catch her breath. A wave of excitement and exhaustion coursed through her veins. Her boss had just escorted their largest client out to the elevators leaving Elizabeth to her thoughts in the quiet of the room. Only the coffee pot in the corner kept her company. The remnants of the day's java were slowing starting to burn on the bottom of the pot, emanating its tell-tale, acrid stench.

Their largest client had just become even larger. During her seven years in interior design and her college years at NYU, she had only dreamed of the opportunity Jack Drescher had just presented. Jack was a fairly good looking man in his mid-forties, a bit stocky with piercing blue eyes, complete with laugh lines and wavy, dirty blond hair. He usually used too much after shave, but he probably couldn't tell he overdid it. It reminded Elizabeth of Pig Pen in the Peanuts comic strip. She pictured him with his own cloud of his scent that traveled around with him. During his visit, he had looked a little uncomfortable in his dark blue Armani suit that belied his humble beginnings. He was a self-starter who had made a name for himself and a fortune to match in real estate in New York

City. Starting in the Bronx where he grew up, Jack purchased neglected properties or buildings in foreclosure and renovated them before putting them back up for sale. Before long he had amassed an impressive net worth and soon moved on to acquiring properties in Manhattan. Most recently, he had been acquiring properties throughout New England, particularly in Connecticut and Massachusetts.

He was a powerful and well-connected man who enjoyed living a life of luxury, yet never tired of the pursuit of the next acquisition. Known for his business savvy, he seemed to know the right people in the right places that could make annoying complications go away. He travelled in impressive circles of politicians, wealthy investors, and dignitaries. Drescher had made his share of adversaries over the years, though, as he demonstrated his determination to get whatever he went after and a temper to match.

Drescher's latest acquisition was near Battery Park, a block west of Ground Zero. It was an empty twenty-four story foreclosed commercial building that he had purchased from a bank. Previously used for office space, the front of the property gazed across the Hudson River to the sprawling expanse of New Jersey. A glance to the southwest from the front of the building offered a view of the majestic and proud Statue of Liberty, still standing, unwavering after the dust settled from 9/11. Reconstruction efforts were currently underway in the area surrounding Drescher's new building. He was confident that the resurgence of building would mean a rebirth in lower Manhattan. His plans were to be a part of this growth by reconfiguring his building into a luxury downtown hotel. He was planning to gut the first three stories of the building and, enlisting the help of Elizabeth and her boss, Vera Loran, transform it into the lobby of the hotel; an exquisite, unforgettable focal point that would be the trademark of this and future hotels to be owned by Drescher. Accommodations would be luxury suites, complete with fine furnishings and amenities.

Rumors had circulated recently that Drescher was leveraged beyond his means and having serious financial problems, but

Elizabeth didn't see how that was possible if he was actively planning this new hotel project. She hoped that when she was finally brave enough to launch out on her own and open her own design studio one day, that she was able to acquire powerful, successful clients like Drescher.

Elizabeth spun her chair around from the end of the table, toward the wall of windows behind her, high above the busy streets of Manhattan. Rain gently spattered the glass. Florescent lights from neighboring office buildings glittered through the raindrops. With the late afternoon light melting into the grayness of the rain clouds, Elizabeth became mesmerized by the rhythm of the rain and gave in to the fatigue washing over her.

Holding onto the cold, brass railing that traveled waist high along the inside of the wall, Elizabeth gazed out of the windows through the sheets of rain to the ocean waves crashing against the rocky breakwater below. The thunderstorm was particularly violent, the remnants of the hurricane that had worked its way up the East Coast, thrashing parts of Maine before exiting out to the open sea. Tiny bits of sleet pitted against the windows and were blown away just as quickly by the gusts of wind.

She loved climbing the tall, spiral staircase to the old Pennington Point Lighthouse counting each step as she went, lingering on the treads that creaked. The only thing she loved more was watching a storm come in from the sea from within the solid, hundred year old walls. As a child, she would steal away from the house and head for the beacon at the first sign of an impending storm, feeling very secure and protected once inside the lighthouse.

Elizabeth was lost in the midst of the storm so she didn't hear anyone approaching from behind. A hand was placed on her shoulder. She sprang out of her chair, spinning around in mid-air, landing on her feet with arms flailing, desperately trying to grab onto an arm of the chair to steady her, and then flopped awkwardly back into the chair. Her face turned red when she looked up and saw the amused look on Vera's face. "Sorry, Liz. Didn't mean to startle you." Her voice was rough and raspy from decades of smoking cigarettes. She preferred the long skinny brown type that looked more like cigars than cigarettes.

Elizabeth quickly tried to gather her composure in front of her boss. She could feel her face turning red. She hated when that happened. Her boss seemed to have a knack for catching her in uncomfortable situations, or rather putting her in them. "No, n-no. That's all right. I just...I just got lost in my thoughts. That was quite a proposition, wasn't it?" switching the focus back to the excitement at hand.

Vera leaned her back side against the end of the table next to Elizabeth's chair and folded her arms as if keeping a measured distance from one of her staff. Elizabeth took that as a sign that she should stay seated. She looked up submissively at Vera. There was a package of smokes jammed into the pocket on the lower right side of Vera's teal blue linen suit jacket with part of the plastic wrapping poking above the top of the pocket. Elizabeth didn't have a visual on her boss's lighter, but the bulge in the pocket on the left side of her jacket told her it was tucked in there.

"Drescher has big plans for the future and he wants Loran Design to be a big part of it, *you* to be a big part of it," she added the last part for clarification and emphasis. It wasn't lost on Vera that Jack had a twinkle in his eye when he gazed toward Elizabeth, fifteen years his junior. Who could blame him? She was an attractive, intelligent, yet shy, woman in her late twenties who usually dressed quite conservatively. Her shoulder length, silky dark brown hair had a slight bounce to it when she walked. She was tall, thin, and proportionately shaped with warm, blue eyes that had a way of smiling at you, while hiding pain that had been buried so long ago. A couple of small, slash-like scars on the side of her face near her chin were the only detectible imperfections.

Vera, on the other hand, was not so tall and usually wore three-inch spiked heels to compensate for her lack of height. She was a thin, very stylish woman with short, almost masculine, coarse blond hair, the color of which originated from a bottle. Although the years had taken their toll and the lines on her face gave away her fifty-something age, she was always dressed as if the next client through the door was going to be from Cosmopolitan Magazine. The design studio had been engaged by its share of clients that Vera could name drop with, but Cosmo hadn't been one of them.

Loran Design had grown with its clients, both residential and commercial, but it had been a long, hard fight for Vera to transform her company into one of the top design firms in the city. The battle came with a price. While her friends were marrying and raising children, Vera was burning the midnight oil preparing presentations for prospective clients, trying to build a name for herself and a business to sustain her. Men had come and gone in her life, having different priorities than her at the time. Eventually the men stopped entering her life on a personal level, so she was just grateful when they became clients. Her work had become her life. So if her biggest client kept coming back for more and her top staffer was part of the reason, so be it. It was good for business even if Elizabeth was oblivious to it.

Vera barely stifled a sinister chuckle as she looked down at Elizabeth. Reaching her right hand into her pocket she pulled out a small package wrapped in clear plastic. Her hand with its pale, wrinkled skin, protruding blue veins, and fingers bent into a seemingly permanent clutching position, looked like a vulture's claws grasping its next meal. Vera skillfully tapped the package against the side of her left hand. A single cigarette emerged. Raising the package to her mouth, she pursed her lips, accentuating the wrinkles encircling her mouth, around the lone cigarette and pulled it out. By the time she had returned the remaining cigarettes to her pocket, she had already retrieved the lighter from the other pocket with her left hand. In a single, flawless motion that comes from many years of repetition, Vera pressed down on the red tab on the lighter, inhaled deeply while looking up toward the ceiling, lit the end of the cigarette, and then released the tab and shoved the lighter back into her pocket. Turning back to Elizabeth, she exhaled the smoke into her face. As on many occasions, Elizabeth just held her breath as long as she could to minimize the second-hand smoke she breathed in.

Elizabeth despised her boss's smoking habit. She considered it quite disgusting. Filthy. Maybe it fitted her personality. She found it tiresome to have her clothes reek of cigarette smoke at the end of each work day. Realizing she was still holding her breath to avoid breathing in the smoke from Vera's cigarette, Elizabeth exhaled a long, deliberate breath. She wished she didn't have to breathe in again. She blinked and tried hard not to cough as she took a shallow breath.

"Sometimes I wonder about you." Vera shook her head slightly. Standing up, she turned away from her and walked half the length of the table before she turned around to face Elizabeth again, motioning with her left hand while grasping the cigarette, "Are you really that naïve?" Her tone was beginning to sound condescending.

Elizabeth tried to control her reaction, but inadvertently furrowed her brow.

Vera's voice suddenly became much quieter. "You do realize that Jack finds you attractive, don't you? And I'm not saying there is anything wrong with that. In fact, that could really be to our advantage." She looked into Elizabeth's eyes for a reaction.

Elizabeth could feel her face turning red again. She shifted uncomfortably in her chair.

Vera's hands rested on her hips, the cigarette sticking out like an extension from her left hip. The cigarette ash was hanging precariously in danger of falling off. She appeared to be carefully choosing her words before she spoke again. "You need to be more aware of what's going on around you." She started making her way back toward Elizabeth, stopping at the last chair and leaning her right side against the padded chair, hands still on her hips.

Elizabeth watched in horror as a large clump of ash fell toward the floor, landing on the black floral Oriental rug next to the pointed toes of Vera's shoes. Her boss was unaware of her indiscretion, but Elizabeth couldn't tear her eyes away from the glowing ember until it died out. She returned her gaze to her boss who stepped closer for effect and continued.

"For a young woman, who is talented and shows a lot of potential, you sure don't have any street smarts." Vera was hovering uncomfortably close to her at the end of the conference room table. "But you need to figure out how to do everything in your power to make sure Jack is happy. He is a major client and we need to cater to him, to his needs. Whatever they might be."

Elizabeth cringed. She wasn't exactly sure what Vera had meant by her last comment but wondered how much more of Vera's berating she was going to have to endure. Looking carefully into her boss's face, into her eyes, she thought she had the look of someone who was desperate enough to do almost anything to keep herself from becoming a has-been. Her eyes were red and blood-shot. The skin on her face was pale and drawn. She tended to go heavier on the eye liner and mascara than Elizabeth cared for. And the worst part of it all was that her breath smelled like an ash tray. It was hard to imagine anyone wanting to kiss her.

They were interrupted by Sara, the office receptionist, a young perky woman with a blond page boy hair style, who stuck her head into the conference room far enough to tell Elizabeth that her grandmother was on line one. Liz did her best to stifle a gasp at the announcement. Her grandmother usually only called when something was amiss. Elizabeth switched her gaze from Sara to Vera to catch her reaction. It was well known that Vera vehemently opposed personal calls on the company clock. Elizabeth watched as Vera's eyes widened as she shook her head slightly. Vera stood up from her resting spot on the conference room table, turned her back to Elizabeth, and then flicked her cigarette over her shoulder as she walked toward the door. Elizabeth watched again in hor-ror as a lump of glowing grey mass fell into her lap. She jumped to her feet in time for the ashes to roll off her skirt and fall to the floor. Elizabeth's nostrils flared. She looked toward Vera as she reached the conference room door. Vera turned back toward her and struck an authoritative pose with one hand on her hip and the other poised with palm toward the ceiling and her cigarette caught securely in the "v" between two fingers. She asked Elizabeth to stop into her office before she headed out for the weekend. Elizabeth cringed on the inside. Her blood pressure was escalating. She knew what that meant; Vera wanted to get started on developing ideas and making preliminary sketches for Jack's project. *No time to waste!* Instead, Elizabeth really wanted to just enjoy some R & R this long weekend. The whole office had been working hard lately. That never seemed to bother Vera. It was as if she had nowhere else to go and nothing else to do.

She took a deep breath and reached for the receiver to speak to her grandmother.

Chapter 2

Elizabeth rode down in the elevator with two middle-aged men in dark suits. She recognized them as attorneys from the firm of Mendelson, Jenkins, and Leate. They had entered on the nineteenth floor and stood next to her, self-absorbed in their own conversation, without so much as a nod or a word. They didn't seem to notice she was even in the elevator. She was entertained by their chatter, though, tossing client names around like confetti, bantering back and forth about this judge and that judge. *Amazing how unprofessional two guys can be.*

The elevator doors opened to the lobby and the two men pushed forward to exit before Elizabeth. She stood back. A smirk spread across her face as she watched them enter the bustle of the lobby and stride swiftly across the broad room, their egos in tow. She shook her head. "Jerks." Her voice was barely audible. She stepped out into the flurry of activity.

It was a grand room with a high ceiling, antique brass chandeliers, and dark marble pillars spaced evenly throughout. Warm burgundy carpet with a stylized oriental pattern anchored the large space. It was furnished with traditional mahogany side and coffee tables, paired with stately wingback chairs, and set in small groupings. Since the location was a popular meeting place after work on a Friday afternoon, many of the chairs were occupied by other young professionals, with glasses in hand. Located on the far left side of the lobby was a rather large, European style bistro that catered to the lunch and dinner crowds. Happy hour was in full swing with a noisy crowd of young urban movers and shakers. On the opposite side of the lobby were a newspaper stand, a shoe shine booth, and a modest flower shop.

Elizabeth noticed a small group of men in suits gathered just ahead and to the left of her path to the exit. She recognized the one gesturing with his hands while he talked as the mayor of New York City. The rest were probably aides and a handful of the city's well connected.

Elizabeth walked halfway across the lobby when someone stepped out from behind one of the grand pillars from her left, startling her. "Elizabeth, so good to see you again." It was Drescher and he was right in her face, smiling with a strange look in his eyes. She wasn't surprised that he was among the mayor's entourage at happy hour.

"Mr. Drescher!" She stepped back to put more space between the two of them, but looked him directly in the eyes, trying to figure out what he was up to. The smell of his cologne made her nose wrinkle slightly. She rubbed her nose with a couple fingers to try to stifle a sneeze.

"Elizabeth, please call me Jack." His voice was sickening sweet. He stepped closer to her and gently touched her forearm with his hand. "Elizabeth, why don't we go grab a drink?" He motioned with his head toward the lively bistro. "Then we can talk further about this new project."

He leaned in toward her. His face was so close to hers that she could feel his breath. She was so uncomfortable that she desperately wanted to back away. She could hear Vera's voice in her head reminding her to keep Drescher happy. His happiness was going to have to wait.

He looked into her eyes and seemed to be able to tell that she was not going to acquiesce. "It's the weekend," he implored.

"Mr. Drescher, I'm sorry. I'm on my way out for the weekend. I can't really stay." She was polite, but firm. "I'm sorry." The two stood there for a moment looking at each other in the awkwardness of the situation gone sour. Elizabeth turned away from him and headed directly for the revolving doors, leaving him standing alone by the pillar. She could feel her stomach becoming nauseous. Too many times over the last couple of years, Jack had gotten too close for comfort with Elizabeth. She had turned him down on several occasions when he asked her out for drinks or dinner. Although she had to admit to herself that there was something about his self-confidence and his powerful presence that attracted her to him, she had no intention of jeopardizing her career by making a mistake like that. It concerned her, though, that he appeared very frustrated each time she declined his offer. Clearly he was not used to having to take "no" for an answer. Sensing his eyes following her out, she tried to shake off her uneasiness and lengthened her strides.

When she reached the sidewalk in front of the building along Lexington Avenue, the rain had slowed to a fine mist. She barely noticed it. Delayed by the encounter with Drescher and distracted by the phone call from her grandmother, she had some things to sort through in her head. Nana, as Elizabeth referred to her, did not go into a lot of details but was obviously concerned about some things that were happening at the inn that she ran in Pennington Point, Maine. The inn had been in the family for several generations. It was originally built as a private school for girls and run successfully for decades. That is, until the mysterious disappearance and presumed death of a student under questionable circumstances. The case was never solved which forced the permanent closure of Pennington School and still haunts the family to this day. It was later reopened, after extensive renovations, as a charming New England seaside inn.

Nana seemed to think that one of the handymen for the inn had turned up missing. Elizabeth didn't take this news too seriously. Girard was a forgetful sort of man who was diligent and hard-working, but could easily misplace tools or supplies and be looking for them for days before they turned up in a most unusual place. Perhaps he had headed out for an errand and forgot why and where he was going. All in all, Girard was a pleasant guy and seemed to be an asset to the inn. His brother, Renard, on the other hand, who also worked around the inn doing odd jobs, was a bit of a nuisance to Elizabeth. He seemed to be infatuated with her and often went out of his way to be near her and speak to her during her occasional visits.

Elizabeth switched the portfolio she was carrying to her other hand and pulled her taupe trench coat closer to her neckline. Before heading out the door she had grabbed drawing supplies and sketch pads, not knowing how long she would be out of the office. She had deliberately neglected to stop into Vera's office. No telling how long she would have been delayed if she hadn't. Vera tended to get a little long winded when she is excited about a new project and this one would certainly be no exception.

She was on her way to Maine. Her grandmother, Amelia Pennington, had asked if she could come up and spend a little time at the inn. That was all Elizabeth needed to hear. It was a three day holiday weekend and she loved to have an excuse to go help Nana. She loved the city very much, but the rugged, rocky coast of Maine with the salty sea air blowing in her face was in her blood, having grown up in the inn.

It wasn't the best of childhoods, but Elizabeth chose to dwell on the positives from it. She was very close to her grandmother; she loved her very much. Her grandmother had raised little Lizzi after her parents died when she was very young. No one ever really talked about what had happened to them and Elizabeth had left it that way as a child. As an adult, however, she struggled with a nagging urge to find out. And the older Amelia gets, there is a very real possibility of her taking the story to her grave.

Besides Elizabeth and Amelia, the Pennington family also included Cecelia, Amelia's husband's younger sister, who had never married. Elizabeth remembered her great aunt as an angry woman who seemed to spend a lot of time in the upper rooms where the family kept house, often erupting in fits of rage toward little Lizzi. A bedroom closet was her refuge when Cecelia was particularly ornery. She felt safe in the small, dark space. When the air had cleared, Elizabeth emerged cautiously and quickly searched out her grandmother. She never spoke of her great aunt to anyone, but often wondered why she contributed so little to the day-to-day operations of the inn.

Amelia had done the best she could balancing the responsibilities of running the inn with raising her granddaughter. As a young child, Lizzi looked for ways to help out, longing to be at her grandmother's side. It seemed as though Amelia was always working her fingers to the bone. In spite of her hardship, she was a warm, loving individual who ran the inn as efficiently as a ship captain. Her husband of twenty-nine years had been the captain of a large fishing vessel that had succumbed to Mother Nature while trying to outrun an approaching storm. He had widowed Amelia when she was only forty-nine. The girls' school and subsequent inn had been in his family as long as anyone could remember. It was believed to have been built by his great, great grandfather, with additions and outbuildings added over the years.

Amelia treated the staff and guests as family. She had a soft voice and a gentle touch and a way of looking into your eyes with the experience and knowledge the years have afforded her, all the while touching your heart. Elizabeth would do anything for her grandmother, including dropping everything at work to go to her aid. But, at the moment, she was feeling a bit uncomfortable because she had just given her boss the slip. She would have to catch up later with Vera by cell in the car and try to explain.

Elizabeth was so engrossed in her thoughts that she did not notice the man who had fallen in behind her, several strides back but keeping the same pace as her. He kept her in his sights. She was walking the three blocks to the parking garage on East 45th Street to retrieve her car, a prized, silver BMW Z4. It had been a recent splurge that she justified as a reward for all the late nights and weekends that had become the norm at Loran Design. Elizabeth was heading for what she hoped would be a relaxing couple of days off but she wondered exactly what she would find when she got to Pennington Point.

The mist turned back into a light rain, but Elizabeth didn't bother with her compact umbrella. Only one more block to go. She quickened her pace and the man in the wind breaker and baseball cap behind her followed suit. She reached the garage and headed straight for the elevators. A set of doors opened as soon as she pressed the button. She slipped in and quickly pressed the button to close the doors. The man behind her was not quick enough to catch the elevator with her. Elizabeth reached the top floor of the garage and stepped out onto the roof. As usual, there were only a few cars parked on this level on a Friday afternoon, particularly since it was just before Labor Day Weekend. Late August/ early September seemed to be a popular vacation time so traffic was slightly lighter and the parking garage was a little less crowded than usual. A smile spread across her face when she saw her car, backed neatly into a corner parking space that allowed ample room on either side. It wasn't easy to protect that car in the city the way she wanted to, the way she should, but she did her best to care for it. She couldn't wait to get in, start the powerful little engine, and shift into first gear. She was itching to get out of the city and onto the open road heading northeast.

Elizabeth skillfully negotiated the downward spiral of the parking garage ramp, pressing the button to lower the driver's side window at the precise moment on the last curve. Reaching the ticket booth, she slipped her monthly parking card into the slot and the gate retreated slowly toward the low ceiling. She pressed the button to close the car window. Slowly releasing the clutch, she pressed the gas pedal. As the car started forward, a man lunged from the left and banged his left hand onto the hood of the car, his face pressed up to the driver's side window. Elizabeth shrieked and hit the brake and clutch simultaneously. Then she caught her breath. It was just Lenny from the mail room, standing there, towering over her car looking a bit pitiful, like something the cat dragged in after a rainstorm. He looked wetter than the past few minutes of light rain could possibly have caused. Tufts of his chestnut brown, curly hair were poking out from underneath his baseball cap, flipping up and partially obscuring the bottom edge. His bushy brown eyebrows were touching the brim. Water was dripping off his hair and cap. Raindrops glistened on his navy blue jacket. She started to feel sorry for him and a bit foolish for overreacting. Lenny seemed like a harmless guy, probably the only one who had been working at Loran Design longer than Elizabeth. No one really knew. No one seemed to know him. He was quiet, kept to himself. Tried to keep his nose clean and avoid Vera as much as possible. Elizabeth wondered how old he was. Hard to tell. She guessed late twenties or could it be early thirties? She couldn't be sure.

As Elizabeth lowered the window, she noticed he was clutching a package tightly in both hands. Lenny didn't wait until the window was completely down before he started babbling about Sara and the package that she thought Miss Pennington needed. Elizabeth didn't remember ever being so close to his face before. He had sad brown puppy eyes. His face was covered in red splotches of acne. Some areas looked particularly red and irritated, perhaps infected. Her stomach started to turn. Elizabeth thanked him and relieved him of the damp and dog-eared, manila envelope. She was sure it had not looked this way when the receptionist had sent him on his errand. It appeared to be something that one of the courier services delivered. There was no return address. One thing was sure, though. If Sara knew Elizabeth had left the office, Vera would know soon, too. Sara runs the front desk like a control center and keeps her boss informed. Not much gets past either one of them.

Elizabeth took a cleansing breath, tossed the package on the seat beside her, pressed the button for the window one final time, and set out onto the rain soaked streets of New York, giving Lenny one final wave. She was finally on her way. A pit stop at her apartment to pick up the essentials was all that stood between her and her long, Labor Day weekend in Maine.

Chapter 3

The drive from New York City to Pennington Point could take anywhere from five and a half to six hours, depending upon the traffic, but Elizabeth usually cut the trip down to just under five hours in her little sports car. She spent the time alone with her thoughts, focusing only on the radio when a station started to fade out, compelling her to tune in a new one. With the impending phone call that Elizabeth would have to make, her thoughts drifted to what she had just left behind.

Vera was difficult to work for. Her staff turnover rate was quite high. She had high standards, *very* high standards, and expected a lot from her employees as well as herself. Elizabeth thought that Vera could use an executive coach to help her soften the edges of her caustic personality. Of course, Vera undoubtedly had never considered such professional guidance. She probably figured she didn't need anything of the sort. It was her business and she would run it the way she saw fit. Elizabeth seemed to be the only one of the design staff who had lasted very long with her, going on seven years. Seven long years. There had been moments when she wondered why she continued to endure Vera's wrath. She could be totally irrational with her expectations, erupting in fits of rage. Yet, she was a design genius with a head for business, an unusual combination to be sure. Elizabeth's plan was to bide her time, hang on as long as she could and learn as much as possible before launching out on her own. That kind of aspiration, however, was not something she could share with Vera. Elizabeth was not really sure of their relationship. On a day-to-day basis, she just felt like a lowly staff person that Vera enjoyed stepping on. Other times they were adversaries, disagreeing on design approaches. Still other times, though, they almost seemed, in a twisted, surreal sort of way, like mother and daughter. Of course, that was usually when they went out after work and had a couple of drinks together. Vera would pry a bit, trying to find out what made her tick, while offering alcohol-induced career advice. Vera was a manipulator. She played with Elizabeth's head, trying to get inside. Elizabeth was careful how many drinks she had while with her and was selective in what she revealed to her boss, not knowing what she might do with any information she might extract. It wasn't a matter of trust…well, yes it was. But, even so, she suspected there had to be a vulnerable side to Vera.

The demands of the job, with Vera setting the tone for the office ambience, led to stress-filled, often long, and arduous days. Elizabeth had become skillful at escaping this environment, whether it was getting away for the weekend or just hitting the streets of New York City for a brisk walk. She loved the city. She loved the aromas wafting from the street vendors' carts as she passed; the steamed hot dogs with sour kraut and the burning smell of roasting chestnuts. She loved the roar of the taxis as they rushed their fares to their destinations, honking their horns and maneuvering through congestion; the rumble of the subway below her feet, through the sidewalk grates. She loved the throngs of people she walked shoulder to shoulder with and the ones who brushed past on their way. She could get lost in all of that, not from herself because she always had her own thoughts, but from everyone else. She could be absolutely anonymous among the tall buildings. She liked it that way. Elizabeth would walk for blocks, even in inclement weather, to clear her head before re-entering the quagmire commonly referred to as the offices of Loran Design. This was her survival technique and it had served her well.

Elizabeth had fallen in love with New York City when she had visited colleges, years ago, while trying to decide where to further her education after high school. The city was nothing like her home state of Maine, any part of it. It had a life of its own, an electricity that was contagious. After all, it is called the "city that never sleeps." There was always something to do. So much to see. With what little time she had off from work, she tried to get out and explore her city. Central Park was one of her favorites. Located in the middle of Manhattan, it was like an oasis in a desert of asphalt, steel, and concrete, with its green grass, trees, walkways and ponds, and extended nearly three miles long. In warm weather, you could rent bikes to ride on the paths or remote control boats to navigate around a pond. Many people rollerbladed, played tennis or used the jogging trail. The Central Park Zoo offered an impressive array of wild animals including an aviary that was home to an extensive collection of rain forest birds. The carousel was a perennial favorite for park goers of all ages, but if soaring on a wooden horse wasn't your style, there were many benches scattered throughout the park. People-watching was always an interesting pastime. Elizabeth loved to watch all the lucky pooches that were getting walked in such a beautiful place. It made her yearn for a small pup of her own. She had once considered getting a little dog, but decided that it really wouldn't be fair to leave a four-legged pal alone in an apartment for long periods of time. And she was sure Vera would never allow her to bring a critter to work. She didn't seem to be the type to be fond of dogs. Maybe if Elizabeth had her own design studio someday, she could bring her little dog to work. She smiled at the thought. Someday...

Elizabeth also enjoyed the museums in the city. There were so many to choose from and several were situated within walking distance of each other. Her personal favorite was the Metropolitan Museum of Art. The Met was located on the east side of Central Park on 5th Avenue and was surrounded on three sides by the park. The Frick Collection was a stone's throw away, just off 5th Avenue on East 70th street. Elizabeth also enjoyed the Guggenheim which was further north on 5th Avenue, overlooking the park, and the Museum of Modern Art which was near Rockefeller Center.

When you tired of the museums, 5th Avenue had everything you could want in a shopping excursion. All the major stores were located along this main thoroughfare and many popular smaller ones occupied the side streets. During the holidays, the city shined even more brightly, all decked out in extra lights and festive trimmings.

Some people say that New Yorkers are not the friendliest of folks. In fact, there were friends back in Maine who expressed concern over how Elizabeth would get along in the city when she was preparing to set off for college at NYU. Elizabeth found New Yorkers to be very friendly. She thought there was a further softening that occurred after 9/11 that actually brought New Yorkers closer together and made them a much more caring people.

Glancing at the green highway signs passing overhead, Elizabeth realized she was just outside of Boston. The jazz station she had been listening to since Hartford was starting to fade out so she pressed the seek button until she found something with a Latin beat to help keep her awake. She found herself moving her shoulders to the tempo of the new music. Her friend Rashelle Harper had introduced her to Latin music while they were in college together where they had become fast friends. While Elizabeth had focused her attention on interior design, Shelle majored in hotel management and hospitality. She now greeted the guests at Pennington Point Inn as their newest hire ever since Elizabeth convinced her grandmother to delegate part of the day-to-day operations. Rashelle had become a wonderful addition at the inn, fitting in with the atmosphere of warm, Down East hospitality, even if her Brooklyn accent revealed her roots. Amelia embraced her like her own granddaughter, visibly relieved to have such reliable and qualified help. She didn't hand over the reins outright to Rashelle, but she was gradually entrusting her with more and more responsibility.

One of Shelle's first tasks this summer was to hire a new tennis instructor. The last one had to be fired because he spent more time trying to improve his relations with the female guests than actually teaching tennis. Complaints of sexual harassment were rampant, not the sort of activity management could tolerate. Unfortunately, Aaron did not take the news of his firing very well. He insisted he was an innocent bystander and that the complaints were unfounded. His denials escalated into threats and he had to be physically removed from the property.

Just north of Portland, Elizabeth hopped off of Interstate 95 onto Route 1. Years ago, Route 1 was the main road to travel along the coast of Maine. It meanders through delightful small New England towns, twisting and turning along the rugged shoreline, past local lobster shacks and wild blueberry stands. These days, most people stayed on I 95 or the Maine Turnpike as far as they can go before getting off onto Route 1, as they hurry to get to their destination as quickly as possible. Route 1 had become congested with tourist traps and the accompanying traffic, suitable only to those with all kinds of time on their hands. Elizabeth had only a short distance to travel on Route 1 before she turned onto Route 72, a winding, hilly road that wound its way through seven miles or so of pine trees and the occasional dirt or gravel road that led to a residential dwelling. A knitting shop was located on the corner of Routes 1 and 72 and had been in the same location for as long as she could remember, probably longer. She thought it was called Dolly's Woolery. It was across the street from Ronnie's Clam Shack, a favorite of summer tourists as well as locals.

Elizabeth slowed down to turn right onto Route 72. The past several hours of driving were starting to take their toll. She yawned and picked up her empty Dunkin Donuts cup hoping for more caffeine to keep her going. She had already drained the last drop before Kennebunkport. It was getting late and the lack of street lights and oncoming cars created a very dark, back road. Travel had become much slower. Replacing her cup in the cup holder, she reached for her package of Twizzlers from the passenger seat only to discover it was completely empty, too. She pressed on. It wasn't much further. After the last familiar curve, Elizabeth turned off 72 onto Pennington Road. She was nearly there. She cracked the windows for her first sniff of the salty sea air. A warm smile spread across her face as she felt welcomed home.

Pennington Road was even darker than 72, if that was possible, and snaked its way through an expanse of pines that were part of the state forest, ending in a clearing on a precipice, high above the crashing waves below. Pennington Point Inn was situated on 125 wooded acres of unspoiled Maine coastline. The main building was an impressive, stately looking structure, set back from the edge of the cliff above the water. It was like many New England inns, with white clapboard siding and multi-paned windows with black shutters. An open porch, where wicker furniture sported worn floral cushions, ran across the front of the inn and wrapped around both ends. Double width steps were set left of center of the porch; ornate carved wooden railings framed either side. The inn hadn't changed much over the years. It stood strong, proud, and almost defiant against the tumultuous ocean, very much like its captain, Elizabeth's grandmother, Amelia Pennington. The property included nearly a mile of unspoiled, sandy beach and, in its entirety, is quite a piece of coastal Maine real estate. Any real estate developer would salivate at the possibility of acquiring a piece of land like this. For the Pennington family, it was simply home. Over the years, rumors had surfaced from time to time that the gracious, old inn was haunted. Elizabeth found this quite amusing since she had grown up there and never experienced anything of the sort. She often wondered if those rumors actually attracted some people to stay there.

At the top of the last hill, the Z4 emerged from the woods into a small clearing where Elizabeth came upon a fork. She slowed the car to a stop, shifting it into neutral. She smiled a crooked smile as a couple of clichés came to mind; "the road less traveled," and "the crossroads of life." There was a wooden sign pointing to the left for Pennington Point Inn and one pointing to the right for

Pennington Point Lighthouse. She resisted the temptation to follow the right fork. Not a good place to be in the dark near the rocks. Elizabeth put the car back into first gear and started to ease off of the clutch when she noticed lights coming down the road on the left toward her. Gently, she pressed the brake again to hold steady long enough for the oncoming car to pass. The road to the inn wasn't really wide enough for two cars. Shortly a small car appeared from the pines so she glanced into the driver's side just as her headlights shined in. The driver was male, approximately 25 to 30 years of age, with short, dark hair. He looked familiar to her, but she couldn't quite place him. His name would probably come to her later. He didn't try to make eye contact, just looked straight ahead. The car was one of those sports car wannabees; probably a Mazda Miata. Couldn't really make out the color. Something dark. Maybe dark blue or green.

After the car passed, Elizabeth steered onto the left fork that meandered through more pine trees for about a hundred yards until she came to another, larger clearing. In front of her was the open sea. She followed the drive to the left toward the inn, passing the entrance to the guest parking lot on the left and continuing on to the circular gravel driveway in the front of the inn. The placement of the parking lot behind the main building of the inn was quite deliberate, maximizing the view of the sea from inside the inn. Her headlights carved a swath in the fog that was beginning to roll in from the water as she rounded the circular driveway. She could just make out the outline of boxwood bushes near the edge of the cliff that had been planted to keep guests from doing anything foolish.

The sight of the inn sent a tingling sensation through her body. Elizabeth was so glad to be back. It had been too long. She pulled the car as close to the front door as possible along the circular drive. Relief coursed through her. She turned off the engine, inhaling deeply, and exhaling a long cleansing breath. A myriad of emotions swelled up inside of her. She was glad to be here, but wondered what was in store. Elizabeth jumped out of the car leaving everything behind. As she gently closed the driver's side door, she stepped backwards to admire her prized possession, bathed in the lights of the front porch. A smile spread across her face in spite of her fatigue. "God, I love that car." She laughed to herself when she realized she had said it out loud and had sounded just like a television commercial. It was just after ten o'clock, but she hoped that her grandmother would still be up. She paused to look south-east, out over the water, listening for the waves crashing against the rocks below. The moon was nearly full and was directly in front of her, casting its light across the shimmering water, from so far away. Turning back toward the inn, she glanced at the porch and noticed the familiar sight of a couple of Schwinn bikes leaning against the railing, a light brown wicker basket hanging from the handle bars of the ladies' version. She shuffled up the front steps; her feet sounded like sandpaper on the wooden steps dusted with sand from the beach. She was too far away to hear her cell phone ringing. A disappointed Vera would have to leave a message.

Elizabeth burst through the front doors into the lobby. Oriental rugs fashioned in warm, rich colors greeted guests of the Pennington Point Inn. Situated halfway between the front door and the front desk was a substantial round wooden table with a magnificent fresh floral arrangement displaying the waning colors of summer. This was Amelia's signature. She felt strongly that guests and visitors should be greeted with this display of simple opulence. Elsewhere in the inn, fresh flowers were also presented, but in a much more understated, yet still elegant, manner. All of the flowers used in the inn during the warmer months came from Amelia's garden that was her pride and joy. She looked forward to tending the garden and it gave her an excuse to step away from the stressful day-to-day operations of the inn, providing a form of therapy for her. In the off seasons, she used flowers she had me-ticulously dried to create similar artful arrangements.

A travel weary couple was checking in at the front desk so Elizabeth slowed her pace and remained behind the urn of flow-ers to allow time for them to finish. She was thrilled to see that they were speaking with Rashelle. She must have known she was arriving and gave the night manager the night off. Rashelle was an energetic young woman of Elizabeth's age. She had dark brown, almost black hair that she sported in a retro-shag look. It suited her spunky personality perfectly. She was of average height and build, but her outstanding characteristic was her high energy level that could not be squelched.

The lobby was centered between a sitting room to the right and the dining room and lounge to the left. Glowing coals in the sitting room fireplace and the lingering smell of smoke in the air were all that remained of an earlier fire, an unexpected yet welcome treat to ward off the chill of a cool summer evening by the sea. Old built-in wooden bookshelves on either side of the fireplace were filled with well-worn hardcover novels, just beckoning anyone entering the room to pluck one off the shelf and sink down into one of the oversized chairs arranged in conversation circles around the room.

The dining room was located toward the back of the building on the left side. It was closed for the evening and quite dark at the moment, but was set up for the hustle and bustle of the morning brunch. Weekend brunches at the inn had become popular, not only for Pennington guests, but for guests of other hotels and locals as well. A long standing favorite was Amelia's famous orange-macadamia nut French toast served with warm maple syrup.

The lounge, located next to the dining room toward the front of the inn, was alive with a spirited card game going on between a foursome of older gentlemen. An imposing wooden bar, with dark leather stools pushed up to it, anchored the far end of the room. A large mirror occupied the wall behind it. A half a dozen square tables were spaced evenly throughout the bar with four chairs set neatly at each. The card game was occupying the table closest to the bar on the left side of the lounge.

Elizabeth glanced into the sitting room and noticed an elderly lady sitting in one of the wing chairs, her back to the front of the inn and the sea, her left profile visible from the lobby. She seemed to be the only occupant of the room and looked eerily familiar. Her head was bowed as if reading a book on her lap.

Rashelle finished with the couple checking in and looked up to see Elizabeth. Her eyes opened wide; she clasped her hands together and squealed in delight. Turned to her right, she disappeared through a door to the left of the front desk and reappeared through a door to the lobby marked "Staff Only." She flung her arms around Elizabeth and they embraced. It felt so good to see her again. Emails and texts didn't quite have the same warmth as her hugs. Elizabeth detected the scent of alcohol. Some things never change. Rashelle was quite the party girl in college, always looking for a good time, even if it wasn't the weekend. There were many times that Elizabeth had to drag Rashelle back to her dormitory at two or three o'clock in the morning with Rashelle protesting that it was too early to go home. Once she had to rescue her out of the bed of some guy Rashelle didn't even know. The next day Rashelle did not confront her for embarrassing her so Elizabeth figured she had no memory of the incident. Elizabeth had a hard time understanding that kind of behavior but she assumed it was a result of the alcohol. Somehow she passed her classes and graduated with a degree. Toward the end of their four years together, Rashelle seemed to be inebriated more than she was sober. Elizabeth wrote that off as senioritis. She had hoped Rashelle would be a little more responsible with her drinking as an adult, especially on the job. Apparently not.

"You made it! So glad you're here. Your grandmother will be pleased. How long are you staying?" She didn't give her a chance to respond. "We'll twist your arm to stay longer, no matter how long it is. Oh, I am so glad you are here!" Rashelle couldn't hide her excitement. Her Brooklyn accent came through loud and clear. "Let's find Amelia. She will want to know right away that you have arrived." She grabbed Elizabeth by the arm and started leading her toward the carpeted stairway, which was to the left of the guest reception desk and led to the second floor, where the family and staff kept rooms. Rashelle stopped mid-step, rethinking her direction.

"I think she may still be talking with Tony. She wanted to be sure that everything was all set for brunch in the morning." Anthony had been the chef at the inn for fifteen years, but Amelia still kept her hand in running the kitchen from time to time. Tony, as everyone at the inn referred to him, was a rather short man in his forties, with short brown wavy hair, a slight build, a French Canadian accent and a fiery temper to match. His cooking had been reviewed by some of the most prestigious gastronomic magazines. Having Tony at the helm of the kitchen was a real feather in the inn's cap.

The girlfriends' arms were linked together as they headed toward the dark dining room. On their way, they by-passed a short hallway to the right that led to the back porch. One flick of Rashelle's right hand, as they crossed the threshold into the room, produced a path of light to the kitchen.

Elizabeth suddenly remembered the woman sitting in the wing chair near the fireplace and she paused to wonder why her friend was leaving the front desk unattended. A glance over her shoulder told her the woman was no longer there. A puzzled look crossed her face. She didn't remember seeing the woman leave and she couldn't shake the feeling that she should know who she was.

Their footsteps were quite pronounced on the old wooden, planked floor that was the original flooring for the school's dining room. It creaked loudly. A wall of windows along the right side of the room offered a beautiful northeastern view in daylight. There was a wooden bar stretched out along the wall in front of them, to the left of the swinging door into the kitchen, which was a smaller version of the bar in the lounge. Empty bar stools lined the counter in silence. Voices emanating from the kitchen assured Elizabeth and Rashelle that they had found Amelia and Tony. The girls burst through the spring-hinged, double doors into the kitchen, and caught Tony mid-sentence. Warm smiles spread across their faces; they were glad to see Elizabeth.

"Hey, Nana!" There was Amelia, standing in the middle of the kitchen, with a crisp white chef's apron folded in half and tied at her waist. Wire-rimmed half glasses were down at the end of her nose. Her white, wavy hair was neatly styled to frame her face and accentuated her bright blue eyes. Smile lines punctuated the sides of her mouth. At times, Amelia had a way of looking like Mrs. Claus without the extra weight. She certainly had the warm personality to fill the shoes of such an icon.

"Elizabeth! It's wonderful to see you." They both reached out spontaneously to each other and hugged until the silence became awkward for the non-participants. It had been several months since she had made the trip up from the big city. Work seemed to get in the way of long weekends or any vacations plans, for that matter. A twinge of guilt pinched her in the gut, but the warmth of Nana's arms washed away the tentative, negative feelings. She wondered if this is what it would have felt like in her mother's arms. Elizabeth was only four or five when her parents died.

Elizabeth breathed in deeply as she hugged her grandmother. The familiar scent of Obsession, mixed with whatever hair spray had been on sale when she ran to the store, permeated her nostrils. She smiled. She loved that smell. It was great to be back in her grandmother's arms. Finally she pulled away and turned toward the head chef.

"Hi, Tony. How's it going?"

"Great to see you, Elizabeth." He smiled like a proud father gazing upon his own daughter.

The squeak of the swinging kitchen door announced a new face that Elizabeth had not seen around the inn before. His all white attire and the selection of racquets slung over his shoulder revealed that he was the new tennis instructor. Nice looking guy in his thirties with dirty blond hair pushed to one side. A Denis Leary type, who looked more like an NYPD detective than a tennis pro. His eyes surveyed the small kitchen; cramped quarters with two large commercial stoves and large, weathered, aluminum pots and pans hanging from the ceiling on a rectangular rack. His eyes came to rest on Elizabeth.

"You must be Elizabeth. I've heard so much about you." He extended his right arm and shook her hand, clasping her forearm in his left hand. He looked deeply into her eyes. It was her turn to feel uncomfortable. She pulled away and stepped backwards from him.

Rashelle jumped in to smooth things over. "Oh, this is Kurt Mitchell, our new tennis instructor." Pleasantries and nods were exchanged. Rashelle quickly moved on. "Hey, Liz, let's grab a glass of Pinot, shall we?" dismissing Kurt with her shoulder.

Elizabeth thought a glass of wine sounded divine after that long drive. Then she realized they would have to venture down to the wine cellar and she shuddered at the thought. It was located below the kitchen in what used to be part of the tunnel system for the school. Maine winters can be bitterly cold and stormy, particularly so close to the ocean, so a system of rudimentary tunnels was constructed so that the girls could move from building to building without enduring the elements. Most of the tunnels had been sealed off once the school was converted to an inn. The wine cellar was one exception. Elizabeth was relieved to see Rashelle making her way to the small wine cooler that Anthony kept filled with a nice selection of whites. After pulling out a couple of bottles and examining the labels, she selected a magnum of Pinot Grigio, Elizabeth's favorite. Then she crossed the creaky wood floor to the utility closet and pulled out a wine bucket, which she filled with ice from the ice bin next to the closet. A cork screw was lying on the counter so Rashelle placed the bucket on the counter and skillfully uncorked the bottle. She then nestled the opened bottle into the ice bucket and headed back across the kitchen grabbing Elizabeth by the arm. Glancing at Amelia and Tony, she asked, "Anyone care to join us?"

Both declined the offer, citing the late hour and the early hour they would be up in the morning for brunch. Kurt smiled and just shook his head. Amelia added, "I'll catch up with you in the morning, Elizabeth. Oh, and you can sleep in the front room this weekend, or however long you are staying."

Elizabeth stopped in her tracks and turned back, giving her grandmother a puzzled, almost startled look. "The front room? Isn't that…Cecelia's room?"

"Well, yes," she chuckled. "I don't think she'll mind. I know how much you like an ocean view."

Elizabeth couldn't shake the feeling that she would be stirring up a hornets' nest by sleeping there. She really didn't want to displace anyone, particularly her ornery, miserable great aunt. Elizabeth took a deep breath and tried to stand straighter. She was an adult now and should be able to handle her great aunt.

Bidding everyone a good evening, the two linked arms and headed back through the swinging doors and into the dining room. Rashelle's arm unlocked from Elizabeth's long enough to slip behind the bar and grab a couple of wine glasses from the overhead rack. They clinked together as she pulled them down. She rejoined Elizabeth at the end of the bar and they linked arms together again and headed across the room. Before they reached the lobby, Amelia poked her head out of the kitchen.

"You girls are going to stay inside tonight, aren't you? Probably not a good night for a walk anyway."

"Don't worry, Amelia. We're going to find a couple of cozy chairs in front of the fireplace," Rashelle reassured her. Elizabeth had a puzzled look on her face again and wondered what she was missing, but was too tired to care enough to ask.

"Feel free to put another log on, if you're going to be up for a while."

"Okay. Thanks, Amelia. Goodnight."

"Goodnight, Nana."

"Goodnight."

They crossed the lobby and entered the sitting room. Elizabeth surveyed the room and made a mental note to speak to her grandmother about a redecorating project. It was a warm and cozy room, very comfortable for the guests to relax in. But they needed to be careful that the shabby chic décor didn't evolve into a worn and dated look over time.

Then Elizabeth remembered the lady who had been sitting in the wing chair by the window. "So, you are officially off-duty or am I taking you away from something you should be doing?"

"Oh, heavens. I'm done for today. We're not expecting any more arrivals and all the current guests seemed to have turned in early."

Elizabeth glanced back toward the lounge and noticed that the gentlemen had finished their card game. The room was dark and quiet. "What about the elderly woman who was sitting there when I first arrived?" She gestured to the right.

Rashelle furrowed her brow. "I don't remember anyone in the sitting room. I thought everyone had cleared out by then."

Elizabeth let it go and sank down into an overstuffed upholstered arm chair close to the fireplace and facing a matching chair. Rashelle placed the wine bucket and glasses on the oval wooden coffee table in front of them. She approached the fireplace and retrieved a log from the pile on the left of the hearth and tossed it in. They both watched as the sparks burst out from under the new log into a gentle explosion and settled back down again. Rashelle rejoined Elizabeth who had begun filling the glasses. They sat back, enjoyed each other's company, catching up on all the small stuff, carefully avoiding anything heavier. It felt so good to both of them to just sit and relax. Finally, Elizabeth couldn't resist pursuing a less comfortable topic.

"So, how is the new tennis pro working out?"

"Oh, Kurt? Well, okay. I mean, I don't know how much tennis he is teaching, but he does arrange round robin tournaments and does some clinics for the guests. There haven't been any complaints so far, which is an improvement. To tell you the truth, there weren't a lot of candidates to choose from with the paltry salary we were offering. Amelia liked him so I went along with it." She paused to examine Elizabeth's face to see if she had taken offense at the salary comment. When it appeared she had not, Rashelle continued. "I think he is bored at times, though, because I do find him poking around, sticking his nose in peculiar places. Says he's just interested in the history of the inn, claims to enjoy old buildings. He seems very interested in the old tunnel system."

A shiver ran down Elizabeth's back at the thought of the tunnels. They were cold, damp, and dark and they just gave her the creeps. She couldn't imagine anyone wanting to explore them and did her best to push that thought from her mind.

After finishing the first round, Rashelle reached over and refilled their glasses. The wine was starting to take effect and Elizabeth was enjoying its warmth. They had been catching up for a lengthy period of time, what seemed like only minutes to them, when the last giggle faded to silence. Only the crackling of the fire in the fireplace was audible. Rashelle decided it was time to fill her in on what had been going on at the inn. Her face turned serious and she leaned over to place her wine glass on the table. She scooted ever so slightly forward in her chair, folded her arms as if in a hug, and looked deeply into Elizabeth's eyes. Suddenly Lizzi became very uncomfortable. It wasn't as bad as when Kurt was holding her hand because she knew Rashelle. But it was as if they were both searching for something inside of her. Obviously something was awry. Rashelle began in whispers.

"Elizabeth, I need to tell you what's been going on here. I'm sure your grandmother hasn't told you much, if anything. And this probably shouldn't come from me, but you really need to know."

Elizabeth sat perfectly still, not breathing. She wondered what she going to reveal; what had her grandmother kept from her? She finally found her voice, "Girard's disappearance?"

"No. We're not really concerned that that will turn into anything. Apparently it's happened before. Actually, what is worrying Amelia is some attorney—I think he's from New Jersey—who is pressuring her to sell."

"Sell what...the inn?" She was incredulous. Her voice rising with each word.

Rashelle tried to bring the volume back down. "Yes! I don't think she would ever do it. It would break her heart to see this place fall out of the family holdings. But this guy has been relentless. But that's not even the worst of it."

"...It's not?" Elizabeth held her breath again, this time freeing her hand of the wine glass by placing it on the table next to Rashelle's. She pressed her hands together as if about to pray and wedged them between her legs near her knees. She looked expectantly into Rashelle's eyes.

The creaking wooden foyer floor announced the arrival of Amelia and Anthony into the lobby. Amelia bid goodnight to her head chef as he headed out the front door and she headed toward the sitting room. Kurt must have left through a different door. "Well, girls, it's getting late. I'm going to turn in. You might think about doing the same."

"We will, Nana. We're almost caught up." Elizabeth didn't dare look at Rashelle. They both wished Amelia a good night. After watching her ascend the carpeted stairs to the left of the front desk, they turned and looked at each other.

Elizabeth spoke first. "Okay...Go on," she pressed her.

"Oh, Elizabeth. I don't know if I should—"

"What! You've gone this far. If she asks, just tell my grandmother that I dragged it out of you. Now, spill."

"Okay, okay. The worst of it...is that the fourteen-year-old daughter of one of our guests is missing. The parents didn't say anything right away because they thought she had taken a longer walk around the grounds than expected. When she didn't show up for dinner last night, they thought she just made other plans. By noon today, they asked to speak to Amelia. She called Chief Austin who was tied up and didn't show up until dinner time. He left just before you got here. He had his men searching the property, walking through the woods, but couldn't accomplish a lot in the waning light. He said he'll come back in the morning. Just between you and me, I think the parents are afraid she ran away."

That wasn't the only possibility of what could have happened to her around here.

There were many other possibilities, including getting swept off the rocks by the lighthouse by a rogue wave. Elizabeth recalled a story that surfaced periodically about a little girl and her father who were swept away by just such a wave. It's not all that common, yet warnings are posted near danger areas, such as the Pennington Point Lighthouse, specifically for the unsuspecting tourist. The tragic story of the little girl and her father must have happened quite a while ago because Elizabeth didn't remember it happening; only the stories people have told since. Of course, as a lot of stories go, the details change along the way. Sometimes it was a little girl and her mother. Either way, it was a tragic story.

Elizabeth sank back in her chair and took a deep breath. This was all Nana needed. The daily stress of running the inn was taking its toll, but the latest couple of developments could prove to be too much for her. The last thing she needed was the bad publicity from a police investigation. This could also feed into this attorney's intentions.

They finished off the bottle of wine well after midnight and decided to call it a night. Elizabeth thought she had never felt this tired before. It took everything she had to hoist herself out of her chair. Hopefully things would look better in the morning light.

Elizabeth headed to her car out in front of the inn to retrieve her belongings. She was not going to bother moving her little Z4 until morning. The only thing she could think about right now was getting some much needed sleep. When she reached in from the driver's side she noticed her cell phone on the passenger seat next to her overnight bag. "Shit!" She had forgotten to call Vera. Somehow it had never crossed her mind during the long drive up. Picking up the phone, she noticed that she had missed two calls. They were probably both Vera. Well, she would have to deal with her in the morning.

With the strap of her overnight bag slung over her left shoulder, Elizabeth eased open the door to her great aunt's room. She paused in the doorway and peered into the dark room, fully expecting to see Cecelia fast asleep under the covers. She winced as she flipped the switch on the wall inside the door that illuminated the small ceramic floral lamp on the table next to the bed on the left side of the room. She felt herself breathing a sigh of relief. Her great aunt would have been in bed long before now so she must have taken a different room after all. That was uncharacteristically nice of her. Certainly not the Aunt Cecelia she remembered from her childhood.

Elizabeth stepped inside the room, closing the door behind her. She was so completely exhausted, and feeling the effects of too much wine, that she decided not to bother changing into the comfortable sweats she usually sported at bed time. She tossed her bag onto a small chair with a woven cane seat next to the window looking out to sea on the right side of the room. A faint creaking sound emanated from the obvious antique. It was one of a pair of chairs placed like bookends on either side of the small round table in front of the large picture window. It was the perfect spot to enjoy the start of the day with a strong cup of Earl Grey or to watch dusk creep over the estate with a glass of dry merlot before heading downstairs for a late dinner.

Elizabeth grabbed her toothbrush and toothpaste from the side pocket of her bag and quickly made her way to the bathroom, tucked to the left of the bed. After freshening up, she headed straight for the bed, pulling her shirt out of her slacks and unbuttoning the French cuffs of the white cotton shirt, to give herself more wiggle room while she was sleeping. She turned off the table lamp next to the bed. Slipping quietly under the covers, she felt her whole body starting to relax. She breathed in the faint lilac scent that was ironed into the bed linens for that extra special touch for which the inn was famous. Her eyes closed and she quickly started to drift off. She didn't notice her great aunt open her door and peek in as if checking on her. The door made a soft click when it closed. Elizabeth opened her eyes for a moment, but was too tired to move, so she closed them again until morning.

Chapter 4

After a restless night's sleep, Elizabeth awoke to the annoying ring of her cell phone. She was groggy from the long drive and one too many glasses of wine the night before, but she knew who it was. Elizabeth reached for the phone on the bed side table where she had tossed it in the wee hours of the morning. She sat straight up as she read the caller ID.

"Hey, Vera," trying to sound up-beat and positive. She cringed in anticipation of what was coming.

"ELIZABETH! WHERE ARE YOU?" Her voice sent a shiver down her spine. "We have a lot of work to do! I expected to see you in the office first thing this morning so we could get started."

Elizabeth had the strange feeling that Vera knew where she was already. She took a deep breath, gathering her thoughts. *Stay calm.* She struggled to keep from getting sucked into Vera's emotions. "Vera, I'm sorry." She spoke slowly and deliberately. "I forgot to call you last night. My grandmother asked me to come up and give her a hand with some things—"

"ELIZABETH! Where is your sense of priority? Drescher is our biggest client and a real power broker in this city. This is not someone you ever want to disappoint. He knows how to make things happen and he can make things happen for us. He is entrusting us with one of his biggest projects ever. How can you run off at a time like this?"

Run off? She is heading for the deep end. She needs a lifeline before she goes over the edge. "Vera. I brought supplies with me to get started—"

"Get started? You know how we operate. We brainstorm together. We sit in the same room and think out loud together. That's how we work best. What were you thinking?!" Her voice was loud and grating on her nerves. Elizabeth struggled to remain calm. A tension headache was creeping up the back of her neck. She stood up and started pacing around the room. She could think better on her feet.

"Vera. We can work separately first, and then get together to hash through some ideas. Our time could be better spent if we came up with some original concepts on our own." *Uh-oh.* Elizabeth was afraid she had just overstepped an invisible line. Was Vera worried she wouldn't come up with anything fresh? "I can fax you what I come up with from here." She was throwing her a bone. Would she grab it or leave it right where it had landed?

"…Alright, but I want you to keep in touch. Jack is already asking to meet with us again. He particularly wants to talk with you about this. I'll give him your cell number so you can consult with him while you are away. But you take care of whatever it is that your grandmother needs taking care of and get right back here. Keep in mind you can always hire someone to take care of a lot of things. And let me know when you will be back."

Her voice was still firm and demanding, but she seemed to be softening a bit. Maybe she was beginning to realize how unreasonable she was being. There was no need to be so bent out of shape and to treat her like this. No wonder she had trouble keeping staff. Elizabeth wondered why she put up with her. She hung up and rubbed her forehead with her hand. Her head was throbbing. She threw her phone onto the flowered coverlet that was bunched up on the bed and shook her head.

The bright spot of the morning was the brilliant sunshine spilling in through the windows. The sun always lifted her spirits; she couldn't wait to get outside. Perhaps she would take her sketch pad on a walk down to the lighthouse. Then she remembered the inn's famous brunch and Amelia's French toast. The lighthouse would have to wait.

A knock at the door startled Elizabeth, but was followed by a familiar voice. She smiled and let Rashelle in. She was carrying a tray laden with covered dishes and a vase with a long stemmed yellow rose from Amelia's garden.

"Breakfast, sleepy head!"

"Oh, Rashelle. Thanks. You didn't have—"

"Well, of course I did. Brunch only runs for twenty more minutes and I knew you wouldn't want to miss the French toast."

Rashelle carried the tray over to the windows and placed it on the small table with a floral tablecloth on it that did not match the floral bedspread. Elizabeth glanced at the clock next to the bed and noticed it was later than she realized. "Ten-forty! How did it get to be that late?"

"Yeah, Amelia has been asking for you. I think she wants to see you as soon as you can get downstairs." Rashelle offered no details, but scurried out the door under the guise of returning to work.

Breakfast tasted even better than she had remembered. She savored every bite, while watching the sea gulls circling outside the window. They were mesmerizing. She had a front row seat to the ocean. After finishing the very last morsel of her scrumptious meal, Elizabeth pulled herself away from nature's performance and made her way to the bathroom. She showered quickly, left her bed looking like she had just rolled out of it and went in search of her grandmother.

On her way out the front door of the inn, Elizabeth noticed there were two squad cars parked on the circular driveway. Chief Austin must be back to continue the search for the girl. She headed in the direction of the garden, a half-acre plot located twenty-five yards behind the main building of the inn and surrounded by a white picket fence. An oversized gate on the side facing the inn enabled the roto-tiller to pass through the opening for the spring tilling. Elizabeth was pleased to find her grandmother puttering busily in her garden. Amelia looked up as her granddaughter reached the gate and smiled warmly. She took off her gardening gloves and placed them next to the basket she was using to collect herbs and squash, but left her wide-brimmed rattan hat on her head, meeting Elizabeth at the gate.

"Well, hello, Elizabeth. You're finally up and about." She glanced at her watch. "I'm afraid you missed brunch, through."

"Oh, Rashelle made sure I didn't. She brought a tray to my room."

Amelia chuckled. "What a good friend. She really looks out for you."

"Yes, she does. It's great to see her—to see everyone."

"It's wonderful for us to see you, too. It's been a long time. We've missed you." Amelia paused. She sensed she might be making Elizabeth feel a little guilty so she quickly changed the subject. "Let's take a walk down to the light," she urged as she closed the gate behind her. Elizabeth was always up for a walk, but this time she had a feeling that the conversation would not be pleasant. They started across the side yard toward the path to the lighthouse. The breeze off the ocean tugged at the brim of Amelia's hat. She reached up and held it down with the palm of her hand until they reached the path where the trees protected them from the wind off the water.

"Elizabeth, thank you so much for coming up on such short notice like this."

"Nana, I would do anything for you. You know that."

"And I really appreciate that. Things are somehow always better when you're around." They shared a smile between them. Amelia had a tired twinkle in her eye. "Elizabeth, I don't know how much Rashelle told you last evening, but there are some things that are going on that I think you should know about." She glanced over to see if there was a nod of acknowledgement from her granddaughter.

"Shelle did tell me about the missing guest and, of course, the real estate attorney…"

"Yeah, he's been a bit annoying…rather persistent, that one. If I didn't know better, I would wonder if the disappearance has anything to do with him. I have a feeling he won't stop until he gets what he wants."

"Nana!" Elizabeth scolded. Her feet stopped abruptly on the path.

Amelia stopped a few feet away. She turned back to see her granddaughter's look of disbelief and disappointment. "Oh, I'm not entirely serious. He has just worn me to a frazzle. I don't know where to turn at this point. He calls, writes letters. He won't let up." She grabbed Elizabeth by the arm and started her moving back down the path. "That's why I asked you to come. I just need a little help with this one. It's getting to be too much for me. I'm not as young as I used to be."

Elizabeth hated to hear those words. She knew they were true. She couldn't imagine the inn without Nana. She couldn't imagine life without Nana. She took a deep breath and pushed those thoughts out of her mind for the moment.

"I'm a little concerned about this girl's disappearance. With these woods and the rocks at the lighthouse…well, it just doesn't seem like there could be a happy ending in all of this. It has already been since Thursday afternoon since anyone has seen her. What if one of the other guests did something to her? I can't even bear that thought. I haven't let Chief Austin near the guests yet. I really don't want to involve them…upset them until we absolutely have to. Of course, he thinks I'm jeopardizing the entire investigation."

"I hate to say it, Nana, but he may have a point. If one of the guests did do something, he's not going to stick around long enough to be interrogated the next day." Amelia shot her a look of concern.

Elizabeth suddenly wished she hadn't gone so far. "But really, that probably isn't the situation anyway. It may just be a matter of the girl wandering off, not knowing the area, and finding herself somewhere that she is not familiar. Thank goodness it's summer so the nights aren't terribly cold. It could be a lot worse. The Chief and his men will find her this morning. You'll see," she reassured her grandmother. She only wished she could believe her own words. She didn't have a good feeling about any of this.

A snap of a twig in the woods a few yards in startled the two so they stopped and listened. They couldn't see anything. The woods got thick just a few steps off of the path so whatever made the sound was out of sight. They both dismissed the sound as a couple of scampering squirrels and started back down the path.

Elizabeth was anxious to keep the conversation going so she continued even though they were walking single file down a narrow section of the path. "So, now what about Girard?" she asked speaking loudly to send her voice over her grandmother's shoulder.

"Oh, I spoke to his brother, Renard, this morning and he told me Girard had returned. He said his errand to find the right parts for the riding lawn mower took longer than expected. He had to travel quite a distance and try a few places before he was successful."

Elizabeth shuddered to herself. The mere mention of Renard's name gave her the creeps. She just wished he would leave her alone. She wished he didn't work at the inn. She would have to try to avoid him while she was there. "So you haven't actually seen him. But Renard says he's back."

"Yes. I have no reason not to believe him." She turned and looked back with a puzzled expression on her face. "Besides, I think I have more important things to worry about right now."

Elizabeth had to agree.

Amelia stopped at the bluff overlooking the lighthouse. The two Penningtons leaned against the railing looking out to sea. "You know. I hate to admit it, but this guy has me thinking about what it would be like if I did sell the place."

"Oh, Nana, you don't mean it!"

She paused to gather her thoughts. "Elizabeth…I have been doing this my whole life. Believe it or not, I'm getting tired." She took her granddaughter by the shoulders and looked squarely into her eyes. She spoke softly. "There is no one to take over. It takes an awful lot to run a place like this. I'm not sure I have what it takes anymore. Maybe it's time for a change…for all of us. You have your career in the city and there is nothing wrong with that. No one is asking or expecting you to give up everything you've worked so hard for."

Elizabeth felt herself reeling, "Well, Rashelle is working out well. You could give her more responsibility and I could check in from time to time." She was desperate to change her grandmother's mind. She was giving in too easily.

"Lizzi, you can't do a good job of running a place this size by checking in once in a while. You would spread yourself too thin and do neither job well. Besides, it's not like I haven't had a long time to think about this. It's not exactly a snap decision."

"But the inn has been in the Pennington family for generations," she choked on her words. A tremendous wave of guilt flooded over her. She had left home and gone off to the big city in search of a place to establish herself as a designer, leaving everyone behind to carry on with the inn. Now her grandmother was considering the wild suggestion of a greedy attorney whose only intentions were personal gain. "I could make it work," she continued to plead. Her world was slipping out from underneath her. She grew up here. How could she possibly say goodbye to all of this? Her heart was breaking wide open. She was fighting back the tears.

"Elizabeth, things would be different if your parents were alive. Unfortunately things turned out differently than we all expected. Life works that way sometimes." She felt as though she was throwing far too much at her granddaughter. So much of this was falling on Elizabeth's shoulders even though she had no control over it.

This was probably not the best time to broach the subject, but Elizabeth really wanted to know what had happened to her mother and father so many years ago when she was too young to remember or understand. She needed to know now. "Nana, could you tell me what happened to my parents? I know we never speak of it…but I really would like to know."

"Oh, I know we never really talked about it over the years. And you deserve to know. Unfortunately, no one really knows *exactly* what happened. Do you remember them at all?" She was changing the subject slightly. Elizabeth shrugged her shoulders. "Your parents loved you so very much. Either one would have given their life for you."

Elizabeth stared intently at her grandmother as Amelia paused to gather her thoughts. Voices from below caused them both to turn. They saw the police chief and the inn's tennis pro making their way up the path from the lighthouse toward them. Chief Austin was a man of insignificant stature and a little extra weight around his middle. He had a large round head with a receding hairline of stringy, almost oily, short, white hair. He was carrying a clear plastic bag at his side that he held close to his leg as if he were trying to be as discreet as possible about it. There was something light purple in the bag, some sort of fabric. Perhaps an article of clothing. Evidence? The two seemed like an odd couple of people to hook up. She wondered if the chief was questioning Kurt. There was something about Kurt that Elizabeth found intriguing. She was trying very hard to push away the feeling, but it surfaced involuntarily. Her stomach felt like a couple of Monarchs had just emerged from their cocoons. She willed herself to get a hold of herself. She had a nagging feeling that he could be a suspect. Something was making her feel very uncomfortable. The two men stopped at the bluff to join them.

"Well, good morning, gentlemen," Amelia offered.

"Good morning, ladies," the chief responded.

"Ladies," Kurt nodded and remained slightly behind the chief. Elizabeth averted her eyes from his.

"Amelia, I wonder if I might have a moment of your time." The chief kept to the business at hand.

"Certainly." Amelia turned to Elizabeth and took her hands in hers. "Lizzi, I'm sorry. Why don't we have dinner this evening on the veranda? Anthony is doing a clambake on the beach so it should be rather quiet there. We can continue our conversation then."

"Sure, Nana. You go ahead," trying desperately to hide her disappointment. She watched the trio head back up the path toward the inn, wondering why Kurt was tagging along.

It was such a beautiful day, Elizabeth decided to continue her walk to the lighthouse. She only wished she had brought along some drawing supplies. She really needed to get started getting some design ideas down on paper. Her conversation with Vera was weighing heavy on her mind.

―――――――

The path Elizabeth had been following brought her down the steep hill, out of the woods, to a small clearing. Just off the end of the path to the right was a small shed that had been used to store kerosene, back in the days when a full-time lighthouse keeper tended to the light before it was automated. Kerosene was deliberately stored far enough away from the lighthouse so that a fire in the shed wouldn't take the lighthouse with it. In those days, lighthouses were essential to ships passing near the shore. They were not equipped with sophisticated navigational equipment like they have in present day to warn of impending danger.

Directly in front of her was the lighthouse at the end of a breakwater that jutted two hundred yards out into the water. It stood majestically before her like an old friend. A fortress of sorts. A form of refuge to a young girl escaping a bit of her childhood. A fortress to a young woman who needed some time to herself to get her head on straight. The tower was not open to the public, but she knew where the key was kept and proceeded to push open the door to the shed. The inside of the little shed was quite dark but her eyes were adjusting quickly. She could just make out some tools hanging on the walls, boxes of who knows what stacked up against the far wall. It wasn't a large space by any stretch of the imagination, approximately fifteen feet by twenty feet. After groping in the semi-darkness for a few seconds, Elizabeth's hand touched the familiar key hanging from the nail to the left of the door. It was still kept where it had been for years. The door to the lighthouse was kept locked at all times. Guests were given tours upon request by a member of the staff. It was a favorite spot for painters and photographers as well.

She lifted the key off the nail hook and stepped back out into the bright sunshine. Her eyes took a moment to readjust to the light. She pulled the shed door closed and headed out to the breakwater toward the lighthouse. It was a treacherous walk across large boulders with blunt edges lying at precarious angles. She would have to keep her eyes focused on her feet and where she was placing them. Many times as a teenager, she was in a hurry to get out to the lighthouse and caught a foot between two rocks, falling in her haste to escape the inn, scraping knees and hands in the process. She had the scars to prove it.

Elizabeth headed out across the rocks, starting slowly, but picking up the pace after she got rhythm in her step. It was like hopscotch with consequences. One wrong move and she would be suffering a scrape on her knee or a twisted ankle. She chose her steps carefully, looking up briefly from time to time to check her progress. The closer she got, the tinglier her body became. After a few minutes of total concentration and careful placement of her feet, she found herself at the door of the lighthouse. She inserted the key into the lock of the huge wooden door and turned. There was an audible click and she pulled with all her might to open the door. The bright sunshine penetrated the entryway as she opened the door slowly. There was a cold, musty, but familiar smell that hit her in the face upon entering. Again, her eyes took a few seconds to adjust to the darkness of the tower. She turned and pulled the door closed. It made a familiar, loud thud. She locked it from the inside and tucked the key securely inside the pocket of her capris. She'd rather not have any company; she wanted to enjoy the solitude of the lighthouse—just like years ago when her grandmother would come looking for her for dinner. At first, the lighthouse was the last place she looked. Maybe it was because of the rocky hike to get out there. Eventually, Amelia caught on and the lighthouse became the first place she looked for her granddaughter. Elizabeth headed toward the narrow wooden steps that spiraled to the top of the light. Her footsteps echoed in the base of the tower.

Elizabeth was a little winded when she reached the top of the stairs, but it felt good to be back at the light. She could see the world from way up there. She pushed open the door and stepped out onto the outside balcony, a narrow walkway with a railing around the top of the light, sixty feet above the rocks below. The sheer height of the balcony from the rocks could make almost anyone feel lightheaded. Elizabeth immediately felt right at home. She headed around to the side facing the open ocean, passing an apparent work area complete with yellow tape across a section of the missing railing. She made a mental note to avoid that section on the way back. Reaching the far side of the light, she backed up against the outer wall, bent her knees, and eased herself down into a seated position with her legs crossed. She took a deep breath. With everything that was going on at the inn, she had some things to think about and this was a great place to do it.

Her grandmother needed her help. She was about to throw in the towel and give up the inn. She is focusing more energy and time on locating the missing teen than getting the attorney big wig off her back. It's time to figure out what's going on. Chief Austin doesn't have a lot of experience solving a missing person's case, much less a murder...murder at Pennington Point Inn? Could it be possible? It was important to consider and evaluate each piece of evidence objectively.

Her gut was telling her that the Renard/Girard situation may not really be resolved. She needed to follow through on that. She couldn't just take her grandmother's word who took Renard's word. Also, she wondered what the deal was with Mitchell. Is he legitimate? Is he really a tennis pro? One way to find out. She could take a lesson...What about the previous pro? What was his name? Aaron something or other. What happened to him? Who are the parents whose daughter is missing? Who is the daughter? Who are the other guests? Who is the attorney that is harassing her grandmother? These questions needed answers.

Elizabeth was feeling overwhelmed. She gazed out to sea and enjoyed the breeze off the water caressing her face. She was completely secluded on the far side of the light in her own little refuge. She stretched out her legs toward the water with her back still against the outer wall. It was early afternoon so the sun was still high in the sky, but on its way back down to the horizon. The warmth felt good to her. She soaked it up and started to drift off to sleep.

Chapter 5

The loud thud of the lighthouse door startled Elizabeth. Her eyes flew open. At first it brought her back in time and she thought it was her grandmother. Then she gasped, realizing she had locked the door on the way in and she had the key! Her eyes grew wide. She jumped to her feet and tiptoed to the balcony doorway and quietly stepped to the top of the stairwell inside the lighthouse. She held her breath and listened. She couldn't see anything in the dark and there were no audible footsteps. Was someone waiting at the bottom of the stairs for her? Who had another key? Did someone break in? Her mind was racing. She wanted to hear a sound, any sound. *What am I going to do?* There was nowhere for her to go. She was trapped. Trapped on a walkway that was high above the rocks below and entirely unsafe with the railing under repair. She wondered what had she been thinking when she decided to ascend the stairs.

She waited and listened. Still nothing. She reached for her pants pocket. No cell phone! *So much for calling a knight in shining armor.* She was on her own...The silence was deafening. She was nearly paralyzed with fear. Did she just imagine the door slamming? Had she been dreaming? It was taking everything she had to convince herself to head down the lighthouse stairs but she knew she had work to do, for her grandmother and her boss.

She cursed under her breath and started to slowly make her way down the dozens of steps on the inside of the lighthouse, stopping and listening periodically. There seemed to be many more steps than there were when she had headed up earlier. The occasional small windows that punctuated the sides of the lighthouse let in enough sunshine to negotiate the stairs safely but she could not see if there was anyone waiting for her at the bottom. It was quite dark there, darker than she imagined. As she reached the last step the shadows overwhelmed her. She jammed her right hand down into the pocket of her pants, groping for the key to the lighthouse door and her freedom. Quickly retrieving it, she took a few more steps toward the exit in the shadows, guessing where the door was, and fumbled with both hands to grasp the key and guide it into the lock. She squinted in the dim light to help her aim. In her haste, the key kept missing its mark. She sensed someone lurking behind her. She tried the key again. Suddenly she felt a large hand on her right shoulder. Letting out a shriek, she whirled around, slamming her back against the door, eyes wide in fright. The sound of the key hitting the floor took a second to sink in.

"Need help with the key, miss?" It was a low, almost sinister male voice.

Suddenly, there was a click. Elizabeth was staring into the eyes of Renard, his face illuminated by his flashlight. He was a large man. Not really that tall, but what he didn't have in height, he made up for in bulk. She didn't remember him looking so threatening before. She tried to conceal the fact that he had startled her. The sound of her heart racing was loud in her ears. Could he hear it? Was she breathing? *Keep breathing!* Her body had an annoying habit of shutting down the breathing function in extreme situations or even during periods of intense focus. But she couldn't afford to pass out right now.

Renard bent down to retrieve the key, never taking his eyes from hers. Elizabeth froze, not knowing what he was going to do. He stood up with the key resting in the palm of his hand. She started to reach for it and he quickly closed his fingers into a fist, still looking deeply into her eyes. She pulled her hand back slowly, returning his gaze. *What was he up to?* She was completely trapped. She wondered why she hadn't pulled the key out of her pocket sooner, as she was descending the stairs. Of course, taking her eyes off of where she was placing her feet on the narrow stairs could have caused her to misstep and go tumbling—certainly not a better scenario...*What is this guy going to do?* She searched his eyes looking for a clue.

Elizabeth watched in amazement as he started tossing the key into the air, just a few inches at first, and then higher and higher until it reached a height of twelve to eighteen inches. Her nostrils flared as she caught a whiff of his sweaty body odor mixed with the mustiness of the old building. Should she try to grab the key in mid-air? Even if she successfully snagged it, she still would have to get it into the lock, turn it, push the door, and get out. He didn't look like he would allow her to do that. Maybe she should try reasoning with him.

Before she could speak, he opened his mouth and barked, "What were you doing here?" His eyes narrowed, demanding an answer.

She gasped quietly, taken aback by his question. Who was he to question her about why she was there? She could ask him the same thing. She decided to just play along and not get him riled up. He literally held the key to her release from the lighthouse. And no one really knew she was there. Could this guy be connected to the disappearance of the girl?

"Well?" He was getting impatient. She needed to choose her words carefully.

"Oh...I used to come here all the time as a kid. My grand-mother, Amelia, would come find me here when it was time for dinner," she desperately threw that out as thinly veiled justification.

He furrowed his brow slightly, looking a bit puzzled. Just as quickly, though, his face brightened, acknowledging his under-standing. "Oh, Miss Elizabeth. It's you." His voice softened slight-ly. His words were slow and deliberate. "I didn't realize you were back," stopping short of an apology for scaring her half to death. "I was just concerned about just anyone, ya know, one of the guests, finding their way up here and getting hurt, what with the railing being repaired and all."

"Well that's certainly understandable…and very responsible of you," she added, trying to give him a verbal pat on the back. Lord knows she wouldn't want to touch him. *Please let me out of here.* She felt panic starting to rise inside of her and she was doing everything in her power to repress it. "Thank you for doing that. I'm sure my grandmother would be very pleased to hear that. I should go and catch up with her now…thanks for your help." Did she dare ask a question? "But if the door is kept locked, how would any of the guests be able to get in?"

He carefully considered her question before answering. "Because one of the keys came up missing recently." He let that hang in the air for a while.

Great! It could be in just about anyone's hands. This was not good. She needed to get out of there. "Well, I should really be going." She looked at him expectantly and stepped to the side so he could open the door for her.

"Yes. Well, let me help you with the door. It can be a bit stubborn, especially after we had it re-keyed not too long ago. Gives me a bit of trouble now and again, too." He skillfully slipped the metal key into the lock in the door, turned it, put his hand on the handle, but stopped short of actually opening the door. He paused. Elizabeth held her breath. *Please let me out.* He turned and met her eyes. "You need to be careful that you don't get hurt while you're here, Miss Elizabeth. I'm sure your grandmother would not like anything to happen to you." He turned back toward the door, leaving Elizabeth to wonder what that meant. She didn't have long to ponder. He gave the door a solid push, allowing the bright sunshine to flood the small, dark room.

Before he had time to stop her, Elizabeth pushed past him, brushing against his body, into the warmth of the day and the freedom of being on the outside of the lighthouse. She took a deep breath. The brisk sea air never smelled so good. Then she considered the key that was still in his possession. She turned back toward the door and boldly put her hand out for the key. Renard was standing, straddling the doorway with the door pulled close to him, as if trying to prevent her from seeing what was inside. It made her curious what she wasn't able to see in the dim light but her desire to flee was much stronger than her curiosity at the moment. She would have to return another time to find out. "I should return the key to the shed," she ventured.

He didn't move. It was as if his feet were cemented in place like a sentry at his post. He held his gaze into her eyes and calmly answered, "I'll take care of it when I head back up the hill."

Realizing she really had no choice, she turned back toward the rocky breakwater and headed away from the light. She pushed an outstretched arm into the air and offered, "Okay, thanks. See you later." She hoped that sounded as casual and nonchalant as she needed it to be. She then scampered deftly across the rocks, not taking the time to look back.

Elizabeth reached the clearing in front of the inn, after racing up the hill and through the woods from the lighthouse, a little winded again and still trying to shake off her encounter with Renard. She made a mental note to get to the gym more often. Arriving with a sense of determination to help her grandmother get to the bottom of whatever was going on, she needed to find Chief Austin to find out as much as she could. She wasn't sure what just transpired at the lighthouse and was feeling very uncomfortable about it. *What is Renard's deal, anyway?* Elizabeth also had a nagging feeling about those tunnels. She shuddered at the thought, but her gut was telling her she should take a look just to be sure there was nothing amiss below. First, she would find the chief and start with him.

Just as she reached the front door to the inn, she had to step back because Kurt pushed the screen door from the inside. She was face to face with him again, a little too close for her comfort. She stepped backwards, bumping into one of the bikes parked near the porch railing. Elizabeth whirled around just in time to watch it fall over, knocking over the bike next to it. She cringed. Thankfully it was just the first two and not the entire fleet lined up on the porch waiting for guests to take them for a ride. Kurt rushed to her aid to right the bikes. "Here, let me give you a hand with these."

Elizabeth felt her face turning red in embarrassment. *Way to make an entrance!* "Thanks…not one of my more coordinated moments," trying to make light of the moment. She took a double take at the entire offering of bikes, noting that there were a couple more available than she remembered seeing last night. Of course, it had been late and it is possible she just didn't notice all of them.

"So, how about a little tennis?" he offered.

"Oh, I don't know…I didn't bring my racquet," she blurted out, as if that was going to make a difference.

"Not a problem. I've got several demos that the sales reps have been pressing me to try. Besides, I actually just had a cancellation so I'm free for the next hour."

"Well, I don't know about a lesson…" She was trying hard not to blush.

"It doesn't have to be a lesson. We could just hit the ball around a bit."

Elizabeth recognized this as an opportunity to get to know him a little better and, perhaps, find out what he knew. She wondered what she was afraid of.

"C'mon. What are you afraid of?"

She tried not to look startled at his question. "Alright. Give me a minute to get changed." The chief would have to wait. So would the tunnels.

Chapter 6

Elizabeth re-emerged through the inn's front door onto the porch to find Kurt leaning up against the railing, his right arm extended upward with a flip phone pressed to his ear, his left hand on his hip. He quickly ended the conversation and dismissed the unknown person at the other end. In one swift motion, he flipped the phone closed, slid it into the right pocket of his white Adidas warm up pants and crossed his arms as a warm smile spread across his face, a twinkle in his eye. She felt herself being drawn in and she was fighting hard to push away. There was something about him she wasn't sure about. She wasn't prepared to trust him just yet, if ever. "All set?" he finally spoke.

"Well, I guess I'm as ready as I'll ever be." She was sporting an outfit pulled together quickly with Rashelle's help. When she had gathered her essentials for the weekend as she was leaving the city, she hadn't planned on playing tennis while she was in Maine. Fortunately, she and Shelle were close enough in size to borrow clothes.

They headed down the path to the left of Amelia's garden through the pines to the tennis courts, engaged in small talk as they walked. She was careful what she revealed to him, but also tried to learn a little something from him. He did tell her that he had gone to school at Colby, where he played varsity tennis. *Okay, so maybe he could play the sport and might be qualified to teach.*

Arriving at the courts, Elizabeth noticed there was another couple on the far court of the two courts who were standing together at the baseline closest to the entrance gate. A chain-link fence wrapped completely around the two courts. The couple in tennis whites were sipping water and conversing softly. She couldn't tell if they were finishing up or just taking a water break, but tried not to show her disappointment that she and Kurt were not alone. This encounter with Kurt might not turn out to be productive after all. She was beginning to wonder why she had let herself get talked into doing this.

Kurt stopped at the small tennis shop, located just in front of the courts, and was fondly referred to as "the shack." "I'll just grab a couple racquets for you to try." Elizabeth nodded and waited outside the door. Kurt re-emerged holding out three racquets for her to choose from. She was starting to feel a little out of her league. She couldn't tell one from the other. "Why don't you hold each one so you can see which feels right." She took the racquet closest to her.

"Kurt, look. I'm not really going to know which is right... maybe this wasn't such a good idea."

"Nonsense. Let me see what your grip looks like." He placed the other two racquets on the ground so he could use both hands. "Here, place your hand on the grip like so." He held the racquet head with one hand, placed his free hand on top of hers and rotated her hand slightly around the grip. One quick look at the distance between her thumb and index finger and he could tell that the grip was too large for her. He picked up the other two and read the side of each to see the size of the grips. One was the same size and the other was even larger so he gathered all three racquets and headed back into the shack for another lot.

"You know, Kurt, this is turning into a lot of trouble for you," speaking into the doorway of the shack, but not setting foot onto its threshold. Kurt popped his head out with three more racquets in hand.

"Don't be silly. It's my pleasure. Besides it's about time these demos got some use. They're brand new racquets that are just sitting idle, gathering dust. Sorry it's taking a couple go 'rounds. I didn't realize you had such feminine hands."

Elizabeth took that as a compliment, but didn't acknowledge it. Instead she busied herself with comparing the feel of the three new racquets. "This one feels okay." She held out her right hand that was wrapped around a black and green Yonex. He examined the placement of her fingers and adjusted them slightly with his hand. It made her uncomfortable with his hand on hers, but she tried to ignore it.

"Looks perfect. Right grip size. Not too heavy, not too light for you. Good choice." He turned and dropped the other two racquets just inside the door. "Okay, let's go hit a few." Elizabeth's stomach was in knots at the prospect of setting foot onto a tennis court with a guy she had just met. She couldn't remember the last time she had held a racquet in her hand. She really didn't want to make a fool out of herself. To her relief, the other couple was heading off the court. They would at least have the courts to themselves.

After exchanging pleasantries with the departing twosome, they turned their focus to the tasks at hand, his to give a lesson to a reluctant student and hers, to find out more about him and what he knows about what was going on at the inn. After all, he had spent some time with the chief. *Was that because he knew something or because he was a suspect?*

"Uh…it actually has been a while since I played tennis—quite a while. I probably could use a lesson," she grudgingly admitted.

"No problem. Why don't we warm up first at the net with some gentle volleys and then we can back up and work on your ground strokes." He picked up a racquet leaning up against the ball basket that was parked next to the gate into the court. The basket looked a lot like a grocery cart and was full of bright yellow, fuzzy balls. He pulled the cart by the front of the basket as he walked to the other side of the net on court one. "Start out a couple of steps in front of the service line. Just take it slowly. Nice and easy. Just block the ball. Don't swing." He started by feeding her a slow ball that she managed to return, but was way out of his reach so he calmly took another and kept the warm-up drill going. "Just squeeze the racquet right before the ball makes contact. You don't have to squeeze hard all the time. In fact, try to relax your hand in between." She took his advice and the volley improved dramatically, at least it appeared to be. *Who knows what he's thinking.* They plowed through two to three dozen balls.

"Okay, let's back it up to the base line and try some ground strokes. Why don't you show me what your forehand looks like without a ball coming at you?"

Oh, this ought to be good. I was nervous enough with *a ball and you want me to do it without one? Great!* Elizabeth took a feeble attempt at a forehand.

"Pretty good, now try to step forward and then swing. And follow all the way through so your elbow points toward the net when you're finished with your swing." Considering his advice, she ventured two more swings. "Very good! Much better, Elizabeth! Now let's try backhand. Show me your swing."

Oh, the infernal backhand. Why did it have to be part of tennis? Elizabeth felt so uncomfortable playing tennis and even more uncomfortable attempting any kind of backhand. She took the obligatory couple of backhand ground strokes so he could critique her again, feeling herself blushing with embarrassment. She hadn't learned tennis as a child so this was rather awkward. *At least he's trying to be gentle. And he's not laughing. Maybe he* is *a pro.* "Not bad. Think about what I mentioned for the forehand. Step and then swing, following through so that you complete a half circle with your elbow pointing at me. The only difference is that you have both hands on the racquet for the backhand. Try a couple more." Elizabeth obliged and he nodded in approval. "Good. Now let's add balls."

The groundstroke drill turned out to be less embarrassing than expected. He certainly knew what he was talking about. This was not enabling her to speak to him one on one, though. She was learning a lot about tennis, but not what she came for. After several minutes of forehands and backhands, she was relieved to see he had stopped feeding the balls to her. "Well, that wasn't so bad. How about a little help with my serve?" She was feeling a bit braver—but it would also get him over onto the same side of the court as her.

"Sure thing." He pulled the ball cart around to join her on the other side of the net. Elizabeth was surprised at how few balls were left in the basket. It was completely full when they started. No wonder she felt like she'd already had a work-out.

After showing him her version of a tennis serve, he gave her a few pointers to refine it. "Bend your knees. Toss the ball up over your head, but a little in front of you, because you want to be moving forward when you make contact with the ball." At first she felt awkward trying to apply his suggestions to her technique, but slowly she felt more comfortable as she served her way through the rest of the balls in the basket. She needed to get him talking.

"Terrific. You certainly are a quick study. Alright, let's get these balls picked up and we'll play a bit so you can apply everything you just learned." A sideways grin spread across his face as he walked toward the outer fence near the gate. He retrieved two ball tubes hanging from the chain-link fence surrounding the courts and handed one to her. They headed for the net to gather the balls that had collected there. Elizabeth was going to ignore the sheer number of them and the fact that they were clear evidence of her inconsistent effort to clear the net, whether volleying, ground stroking or serving.

"So, Kurt, what do you make of what's been going on around here?" trying to leave the question as open as possible.

Kurt very calmly stopped trapping balls with his tube and shot her a sideways glance as if trying to determine her intentions. She hoped she didn't sound as obvious as she felt. He resumed gathering balls. "Do you mean the situation with the lost girl?"

"Yes…and everything else that might be going on." *Ugh! That sounded lame.* She was not very good at this game.

"Well, I'm not really privy to a lot of what goes on around here."

Are you serious? Do you really expect me to believe that?

"Last time I spoke to Chief Austin, which was this morning when we saw you on the path to the lighthouse, he had few leads to go on. He did find a zippered sweatshirt down on the rocks that actually turned out to be the missing girl's.

"Really?"

"Yes. Her family thinks she wandered off and fell prey to foul play. Chief is not so sure about that. He did share with me that the parents admitted their daughter had really fought with them about accompanying them on this trip. It was supposed to be one last weekend away before she started school. But she's fourteen or fifteen and you remember how it can be at that age. The last place you want to be is with your parents, especially on a vacation."

"But he *is* gathering evidence and seriously considering other, more serious possibilities, isn't he?"

"Oh, I'm sure he is. He seems to have a handle on this."

Elizabeth tended not to agree, but she kept her opinion to herself for the time being.

"So, is there anything else I should know about?" It was worth another shot at eliciting more information from him.

Kurt chuckled as he emptied his tube of yellow tennis balls into the basket. "What else could be going on? Isn't that enough for this quiet little inn?"

She had to agree that it was. Unfortunately it wasn't all. Was he really oblivious to everything else or did he know more than he was sharing?

"Of course," she answered, at bit disappointed.

"Alright, let's play a little." He grabbed three balls from the cart, handed her two, jogged over to the other side of the net. "Okay, you serve first." And so began a set that went on for twenty-five minutes and ended with a score of 6-1. Elizabeth was convinced the single game she won was a token of sportsmanship. He couldn't beat a lady in a shut-out. At least it seemed like the guy was a gentleman.

She approached the net with her arm extended. They shook hands, but he looked surprised. "You don't want to play another set?"

"No. I think I've had enough of a workout." She wiped the perspiration from her forehead with the back of her hand. "I need to save enough energy to be able to function during the rest of the day." Kurt chuckled. "But thank you, though. That was a lot of fun. I learned a lot, too." She handed her racquet back to him.

"Elizabeth, you were being too modest. You were great! We'll have to play again before you leave." He had that little twinkle in his eyes again. She turned away to break the connection between their eyes. She couldn't think of a comeback that wouldn't sound like she was getting sucked in. Suddenly, she felt his hand firmly grasping her upper right arm. Her left foot froze in mid-air and mid-step, a couple inches off the surface of the tennis court. Slowly she turned back toward him. He stepped closer and looked deeply into her eyes. "Be careful, Elizabeth. You don't know what you will be sticking your nose into around here...just be careful."

He slowly released his grip and she resisted the urged to rub her arm to restart the circulation. Taking one step backwards away from him, she didn't take her eyes off of his, "I'll see what I can do," she said in an even, unemotional tone, that took everything she had to keep it under control. She turned away again and walked briskly toward the gate, this time unencumbered.

What was that supposed to mean? Was that a warning or a threat? She really couldn't tell, so she would consider it the latter until she could be sure. He made her feel so uncomfortable. A shiver ran down her spine.

As she headed back to the inn, hunger pangs gradually replaced the nerves affecting her stomach during tennis. After a quick shower, she would have to stop in the kitchen to see if Tony had anything for her to eat. It was already the middle of the afternoon, so he would be working on dinner, but she should be able to grab a quick bite.

Chapter 7

Elizabeth emerged from the small bathroom, after a refreshing shower, with a fluffy white towel wrapped around her torso. Holding it all together with her left hand at the base of her neck, she reached with her other hand for the clothes she had selected to wear and tossed onto the bed. She froze. Out of the corner of her eye she noticed someone was standing by the door. Elizabeth gasped and retreated back toward the bathroom. She looked at the woman and thought she was the elderly lady she had observed in the lobby when she first arrived. She opened her mouth to speak, and then closed it again. Suddenly, it dawned on her that it was her great aunt. *What is she doing here, in my room…in her room? I knew I shouldn't stay in this room. What was Nana thinking?* Elizabeth opened her mouth again but before she could make a sound, Cecelia was already talking. "Elizabeth, you have to save the inn," her voice barely a whisper.

"I'll…I'll do everything I can," scarcely believing they were having a civil conversation. During Elizabeth's formative years, Cecelia only yelled at her.

"You must. Amelia has all but given in and walked away. This place has been in the family for too long to let it go like this." Her tone was one of desperation. She was imploring Elizabeth to do everything in her power to rescue the inn from the hands of… God only knew. The two women stood facing each other from across the room. No more words were spoken. They seemed to be reconnecting what time had pulled apart. The moment was shattered by the piercing ring of her cell phone. The sound brought Elizabeth's thoughts back to the present. She could guess who was calling. She turned and took a step forward toward the bed, bending slightly to rummage through the clothes to find her phone buried beneath them. One glance at the caller ID on the cover confirmed her apprehension. She felt a sinking feeling creep into her stomach. Absentmindedly, she placed her hand on her abdomen. The number was none other than Vera's. Leaving the phone on the bed where she had uncovered it, she didn't bother to flip it open to answer the call. Better to let her leave a message and Elizabeth would call back later when she had something for her. After a heavy sigh, she turned her attention back to Cecelia, but she was gone. In all the anxiety over Vera's call, she didn't even notice her slip out.

Elizabeth quickly dressed in a pair of light khaki twill capris and a white polo with feminine capped sleeves. She put the sneakers she had used for tennis back on. They were not hers, but they were much more practical for…well, just more practical.

After tossing Rashelle's tennis clothes into the bathroom sink to soak, Elizabeth headed out the door with drawing supplies in hand and a rumbling in her stomach. She was practically skipping down the carpeted hall. Had she looked back, she would have seen her great aunt at the other end of the hall, watching her scamper.

At the bottom of the stairs that led to the lobby, one of the regular guests of the inn spotted Elizabeth and made a point of connecting with her. Mrs. Leibowitz was a feisty little old lady who had been staying at the inn every summer for many years. What she lacked in stature, she more than made up in spunk. The frosty, white hair framing her face was soft and wavy on good days and puffed out and frizzy on bad days. Her nose was large for her face, rather angular—resembling a hawk's beak. Her dark eyes penetrated through black, rectangular framed glasses that may have been in style twenty years earlier. She was known for enjoying her wine. She preferred a nice dry red, but would drink a glass of cognac if someone handed it to her. The funny thing was that the alcohol didn't seem to take the edge off of her cross disposition. Being a long-standing, regular guest at the Pennington Point Inn, she tended to throw her weight around, making demands of Amelia and her staff. Elizabeth rued the day that Mrs. L figured out she was Amelia's granddaughter. There was no slipping past her without getting an earful about something. To top it off, she had a grating voice to match her personality.

Mrs. Leibowitz' lips were pursed and her arms were swinging alternately at her side, hands clenched into fists as she strode up to the first Pennington she could find. "ELIZABETH!" The sound of her name spoken by Mrs. L. was like fingernails on a chalkboard. It sent a chill down her spine. "Elizabeth! What the hell is going on around here?!" Elizabeth wondered if she kissed her grandchildren with that mouth. *Was she always this abrasive?* "There are cops everywhere! Crawling all over the place, sticking their noses into everybody's business, asking a lot of questions." She was indignant. "You know how many years I've been coming here?" Elizabeth didn't know exactly and really didn't care. She just wished she would stop talking and go away. "I didn't come back again this summer to be interrogated like some common criminal. This is absolutely ridiculous! Why would I ever come back again?" Her voice was getting louder with each sentence. "What are you going to do about this?" She was wagging her crooked old index finger in Elizabeth's face, a little too close for comfort.

Mrs. L. paused long enough for Elizabeth to jump in. She tried to make her voice sound compassionate. This was going to take some serious acting, but she had to be careful not to be patronizing. "Mrs. Leibowitz, I realize how much of an inconvenience this is for you, and everyone at the Pennington Point Inn empathizes with your situation. We really do. And we are confident that if everyone cooperates with the officers conducting the investigation, they will be able to wrap up very quickly and we can all go back to what we would rather be doing. Please be patient. I'm sure this will all be over very soon. Thank you for being so understanding." She was running out of breath, but she didn't slow down until she started walking away from her. "Why don't I have someone from our wait staff bring up a nice bottle of Chianti to ease your discomfort? Would that be alright?" Mrs. L. opened her mouth to speak, but Elizabeth beat her to it. "Let me go take care of that right now." She turned and walked briskly, with a purpose, toward the kitchen, leaving Mrs. L. standing alone in the middle of the lobby with her mouth half open. She looked like she wasn't quite sure what had just happened. A quiet "thank you" was all she could muster in Elizabeth's direction. Elizabeth shivered ever so slightly, trying to shake off their encounter.

Chapter 8

As expected, Tony and all of his staff were bustling about the kitchen in preparation for the evening's dinner, a clambake on the beach. She watched for a while as Tony skillfully chopped several vegetables as quickly as she had ever seen a hand, with a knife in it, move. The movement was mesmerizing. He looked up to see her watching him. He paused and chuckled. "Elizabeth, check out my new knife." Tony held out his latest gadget for her to see more closely. "Believe it or not, the blade is made of ceramic, but it is incredibly sharp. I don't think I've ever worked with anything sharper." Quite a testimonial considering how long Tony had been a chef. He demonstrated its sharpness on a nearby tomato. He sliced it in half with very little effort, using only one hand. Elizabeth was impressed. Of course, she wasn't much of a cook, but she had tried to slice tomatoes before and usually struggled to get consistently sized slices. She usually ended up with a mushy mess when she finished. She probably could use a decent knife to do a better job. Elizabeth looked up from Tony's neat line of tomato slices to look directly into his face. She blinked when she saw his expression. He was enjoying his new gadget far too much. His eyes had a strange, sinister look. Tony put down his tool. "What can I do for you, Lizzi?" He always had a moment for Elizabeth. Upon hearing that she needed a little something for a late lunch, he skillfully pulled together a lobster wrap, to Elizabeth's delight, accompanied by a fresh fruit salad, including some of Maine's wild blueberries, and a sparkling water. She was thrilled. Tony's lobster roll was the best she had ever tasted. Of course, it should not be confused with lobster *salad* roll that has mayonnaise in it, possibly even small pieces of diced celery. True New England lobster roll was simply generously sized chunks of lobster slathered in butter and nestled in a soft, fresh hot dog roll, slit along the top. Tony probably added a special ingredient or two. She could travel up and down the rocky coast of Maine and not find better lobster roll. Elizabeth preferred hers in a wrap.

With her boxed lunch in hand, she headed out through the lobby, giving a nod to Rashelle, who was busy with guests at the front desk. They appeared to be husband and wife with two little girls in tow. The man was not very tall, a bit dumpy with drooping shoulders, brown, curly hair. The wife seemed like a church mouse, with straight, shoulder-length, brown hair, parted in the middle. The girls looked to be less than five years old and very close in age with brown curly hair, like their father's, that bounced softly on their shoulders with just the slightest movement. The younger one turned to see who was crossing the lobby. Elizabeth looked back as she reached the door, catching her eye. Elizabeth smiled gently. In a strange way, the younger girl reminded her of herself.

Picking up a folding chair from the front porch and tucking it under her arm, Elizabeth headed down the broad front steps, across the circular drive in front of the inn. She noted that her car was still parked at the top of the curve, and she would have to try to remember to move it later. It was time to get some ideas down on paper and get Vera off her back.

As Elizabeth set off across the front lawn toward the path in the woods toward the lighthouse, Tony was sending a staff person to deliver a bottle of red to Mrs. Leibowitz. Elizabeth noticed a couple of guys from the kitchen staff were headed across the front lawn to the left of her, toward the stairs to the beach. The beach side of the peninsula was accessed via a set of wooden stairs that were installed years ago. The steps washed out from time to time, usually during the occasional hurricane, and required constant maintenance. They were configured so that you descend about a dozen or so steps, reach a landing, turn and descend another dozen steps in the opposite direction, and repeat this pattern several times before you reach the sandy beach below. As long as you didn't look down in the process, it wasn't too scary.

On nights of a barbecue or a clambake on the beach, Tony and his staff went the extra effort to transport everything necessary for dinner from the kitchen down to the beach. Sometime during the summer, someone rigged a primitive pulley system to send down as much as possible, everything that will fit in a wooden box measuring three feet by four feet. The rest was carried by hand down the stairs. Since it is so labor intensive, only a couple of beach barbecues were planned per month. The guests really seemed to enjoy them, though. Tony and his staff dug a pit in the sand and roasted corn on the cob still in the husks and steamed native Maine lobsters over coals. He rounded out the meal with coleslaw, homemade rolls, and scrumptious pies made with Maine raspberries or blueberries depending upon which berry was in season at the time. Tonight's pie would be raspberry. Some of the raspberries were from Nana's garden and the rest were from a local farmer who delivered to the inn on a regular basis. Elizabeth loved raspberry pie. It reminded her of when she was little and her grandmother would send her out to the garden to pick some berries. Little Lizzi usually ate more than she brought back to the inn, but her grandmother never seemed to mind.

Grown-up Elizabeth needed to get focused and head for a quiet place to get some work done. She reached the path that led to the lighthouse and headed down it, as she had done so many times before. On the way through the woods she could hear rustling sounds. She kept her eyes forward trying desperately to ignore what was happening deeper in the woods. She kept telling herself it was just squirrels playing. Nothing more. She covered the half mile distance to the bluff very quickly. Once there, she plunked down her drawing supplies and her lunch, freeing up her hands to unfold the old fashioned lawn chair that was woven with faded yellow and white fraying strips of vinyl. A throwback to the seventies when yellow was the happy color. She situated herself facing the railing, looking out to sea. She was anxious to get some ideas down on paper so she let her lunch lay untouched in favor of the drawing pad. Vera often scoffed at her use of paper and pencil, calling it an archaic practice in the modern world of technology. Elizabeth, however, felt a certain sense of control with a pencil in her hand and found her creative juices flowed more easily. So she often plodded right along using her old fashioned equipment, in spite of her boss's objection. It was hard for Vera to criticize too loudly when she saw the design creations Elizabeth produced.

Elizabeth had already envisioned the lobby of Drescher's newly renovated luxury hotel with magnificent panels of rich fabric draped from the ceiling and from random points high up on the walls. She quickly decided the panels should be loosely woven to allow air flow and be constructed of a heavy duty faux silk that could be removed periodically to be cleaned. Always the practical one, Elizabeth was. The fabric would look luxurious, but would also help to absorb sound which was important in a public space like this three-story lobby. She sketched what she was picturing in her mind's eye onto the pad of paper on her lap. Before long, she slid down in her chair, pulling her knees toward her body, bracing her heels on the edge of the chair, converting her legs into a make-shift easel on which to rest her paper. After several quick sketches of the fabric panels from different perspectives, she turned her attention toward the front desk, the concierge station, the bell hop's stand, skillfully drawing each one with rich Italian marble counters, dark mahogany wood walls with antiqued brass fixtures and soft lighting. Next she focused on the furniture. She was picturing upholstered chairs and loveseats with clean, contemporary lines arranged in conversation clusters throughout the lobby. No particular color palette had crossed her mind yet, but she would just put that question in the back of her mind to work on while she kept going with this. Nice thing about the subconscious. If she was ever on overload or really didn't have time to work out a problem at the moment, she tucked it back in and checked back later to see what she had come up with. It was amazing how well it worked. Obviously her subconscious had been putting time in on this lobby because she was surprised at how easily the plan was coming to her.

Now, to turn her attention to individual guest rooms. In a hotel of this stature, they would all be suites and each floor would have a different design style, perhaps with an international flair. She was on a roll and didn't want to stop sketching before she had put down on paper, everything that was spilling out of her imagination. Her late lunch would have to wait a little longer. Her stomach growled a noisy protest, but she pressed on. As her grandmother always said, "strike while the iron is hot." As a youngster it took her a while to figure out what she meant by that, but as an adult, Elizabeth not only understood the cliché, she lived by it.

After about an hour of fluid arm movements, Elizabeth had produced a couple dozen detailed drawings. A few discarded pages lay at the base of her chair, scrunched up into balls. She took a deep breath and exhaled a long, loud sigh. It was time for a break. Her body was starting to send a more desperate signal for food, the beginnings of a headache. Good thing she had eaten a late breakfast or else she never would have lasted this long before eating. She began with the sparkling water to quench the thirst in her parched throat, and then she eagerly opened the sandwich and fruit salad. What a treat. While her taste buds delighted in the succulent lobster and the sweet crunch of the fruit salad, she breathed in the fragrances of nature by the sea, closing her eyes and enjoying the sounds of the seagulls, playfully floating on the air currents above her. After a few minutes of nature's serenade, she slowly opened her eyes and her gaze fell on the railing in front of her. Beyond the railing, she noticed a figure standing on the breakwater, near the lighthouse on the right side. It looked like Chief Austin. His hands were on his hips and he seemed to be gazing out to sea. Perhaps in a reflective mood. He had a lot to ponder. A lot to sort out. She watched him start to pace back and forth as if waiting for something. Elizabeth slowly stood from her lawn chair, a squeak reminding her of its age. Reaching her left hand forward to grasp the railing, she furrowed her brow. What was he up to? She watched for a while longer, with a feeling she shouldn't take her eyes off the scene. Suddenly, the chief started to make his way down toward the water. Elizabeth shifted her gaze slightly and noticed a figure emerging from the water. Someone in a wet suit, complete with an oxygen tank, mask and flippers. In the frigid waters of coastal Maine, such an outfit was necessary in order to spend any time underwater.

Elizabeth was holding her breath, waiting to see if the diver had found anything. The black rubber skinned individual was speaking to the chief, gesturing with his or her hands. From the distance, she was observing from on the bluff, it was hard to tell if the diver was a man or a woman. Suddenly, she took in a quick breath and started breathing again.

It was time for a closer look. She couldn't tell what was going on from way up there. But she couldn't very well lug all of her paraphernalia with her so she shoved the drawing pad and pencils in the portfolio and folded up the gaudy yellow and white striped lawn chair. Grabbing one in each hand, she glanced down and noticed the remnants of her lunch; the parchment paper from her sandwich, the clear plastic take-out box from the fruit salad, the green water bottle and the white cardboard picnic box in which they all had traveled. Absentmindedly, she shook her head. There was no way she was going to leave that mess behind. That would violate what was, in her mind, the eleventh commandment; thou shalt not litter in the pristine state of Maine. She put down her load and quickly gathered her litter, placing all the loose items inside the box. Tucking the box under her left arm, she picked up the chair and portfolio again and looked around, assessing the area near her to see where she could stash her stuff for the time being. A large tree on the far side of the clearing, just a few feet into the woods, would suffice. She quickly stepped behind the towering conifer and leaned her things up against it, freeing her to move quickly and quietly, down the trail to the lighthouse.

Elizabeth headed back onto the path. She wished she could break into a light jog to get there more quickly. Unfortunately the trail did not lend itself to that. You had to be careful where you stepped. After the bluff, the path became narrower and was riddled with tree roots that could easily catch a toe and send you airborne, landing you on your face. There were also branches that protruded into the path to grab onto when navigating down the steep slope that descended to the breakwater.

Elizabeth paused for a moment to peer through the pines toward the lighthouse. The diver was no longer talking to the chief. He was not even in sight. For that matter, the chief wasn't there either. Suddenly, she heard voices below her on the path. They were heading up the hill! Elizabeth quickly slipped off the path to the left into the trees growing on the side of the hill. She grabbed onto the trunks of small pine trees as she went. Each step put her further away from the path. She could hear the voices getting closer. They were both male. Maybe she could glean something from their conversation as they passed. She squatted to try to stay out of sight and took hold of the trunk nearest her to steady herself. She looked down to find herself on a steep incline huddled up to a small pine tree. There were footsteps on the dirt path. They were close. She held her breath and listened, hoping she was successfully concealed. It would be embarrassing if she wasn't. Then it got quiet; no footsteps and no voices. Even the gulls overhead were quiet. *What was going on?* The idea to hide in the trees was starting to seem foolish. Then the conversation began again. The feet weren't moving, though. The Chief must have needed a breather. Only the extremely fit can make it up the hill from the light without getting winded.

"Look, Chief. This is getting us nowhere. Precious time is slipping away from us. We need to close down the entrance to the inn. No one gets out until we figure this out." Elizabeth stifled a gasp.

"We have no concrete evidence that this is anything other than a teenager who has run away from her parents for a while. Amelia will never go for closing down the—"

"It's not her choice!" The other man insisted. His voice was loud and demanding. "We have a very serious situation and could be losing vital evidence or allowing key witnesses or even the perpetrators the opportunity to walk away, Scot free."

Elizabeth was starting to feel uncomfortable eavesdropping on their conversation. If they could see her, she would look rather guilty. She was starting to shift her focus from keeping her balance, crouched behind the tree, to what they were saying. Her left foot, which was further down the hill than the other, started to slide. Her body weight must have been balanced predominantly on that foot because her whole body started to slide down the steep hill toward the water. The trunk slipped from her grasp and she felt her whole body heading downward. She could hear the surf crashing against the rocks below. Panic set in. The edge of this part of the cliff wasn't very far away, but she didn't know exactly how far. Desperately she snatched at low branches as she tried to stop herself from sliding further. The first branch pulled right off the tree. The second slipped from her hand, but slowed her down a bit. The third branch was the charm. She felt her whole body jolt to a stop. She quickly grabbed the trunk of the tree and held her breath. She wondered how much noise had she made slipping down the side of the hill. Had they noticed? She listened. The air was silent. She couldn't see their faces to tell if they were just pausing in their conversation or listening for her. She prayed it wasn't the latter. She would have a hard time explaining herself if they found her. She slowly exhaled and glanced down the hill, beyond her left foot. Her eyes grew wide. She was mere inches away from an abrupt drop off. She was on the edge of the cliff. She stifled another gasp. Her head suddenly felt dizzy. This was where the trail took a right turn and zigzagged the rest of the way down the cliff. They would have been investigating another situation at the inn if she had kept going over the edge. Elizabeth decided to put that out of her head and concentrate on holding on and keeping quiet. She listened for what seemed to be a very long time, longing to hear their voices again. Hopefully, they thought she was just a squirrel. She listened. Finally the voices came back to life again.

"Lieutenant Perkins, look. We don't know that it's a serious situation. It could just be –"

"Not a serious situation! Check with the girl's parents and see what they think! It most certainly is. The evidence we've collected so far certainly indicates it is and speaking of checking, I'd like to check with Mitchell and see what he's been up to."

The voices started to trail off so the chief must have caught his breath while he was getting yelled at and they started heading back up to the top of the hill again. The squelch from a two-way radio confirmed they were further up the path.

Poor Nana. She will absolutely flip. This will be terrible for business. And Kurt. What did the Lieutenant mean by that? Do they suspect him? If he really is a suspect, what would his motive be? And are others in danger? And what evidence...what have they collected?

Elizabeth waited several minutes to make sure the men were really gone. She wondered what her next move was going to be. She didn't know where to start. *Were they investigating a murder or a disappearance? Or two disappearances; the girl and Girard. Are they connected?* As she was struggling with these questions she started to slowly make her way out of the woods, carefully placing each step on the hill so she wouldn't slip again. Finally, she emerged from the pines, relieved that the body sliding was over. She looked up the hill to see someone coming down the path through the trees. The chief? The state trooper? It was too late to dive back into the woods so she stayed put and tried to think of something intelligent to say. Whoever was coming was going to wonder *what she was doing there and why they hadn't seen her on their way up the path?* In a rash decision, she decided, instead, to continue down the cliff. Chances are she could get down to the bottom faster than whoever was behind her and buy herself more time before she came face to face with him or them. Being out in the open at the bottom of the trail was a safer place to be than cornered in the woods on a trail that was treacherous to descend.

Elizabeth quickly negotiated her way down the steep decline, grabbing protruding pine boughs as she went, skillfully stepping around exposed roots. Footsteps thudded behind her. She felt her pace quickening which made her descent that much more challenging. If she remembered correctly, there were two more hairpin turns in the trail before she was safely at the bottom. She was curious who was behind her but was afraid to sneak a look. Finally she couldn't resist. She took her eyes off her feet, and where she was placing them, long enough to turn her head and look. Just as she did, she felt her right foot catch on a root or a rock so her head spun back around in time to see herself diving head first toward the trunk of an evergreen. She instinctively put her hands out to break her fall. She landed with a thud on her chest and stomach, knocking the wind out of her, her forehead making contact with the base of the tree trunk. The impact stunned her for a moment. Then she realized the person behind her was approaching. Gasping for air, she tried to scramble to her feet, but was a bit dazed. A firm hand grabbed her from behind.

"Lizzi, are you alright?" Elizabeth's relief in hearing a familiar voice was palpable. "What happened? You look terrible. Are you all right? I'm so glad I found you! I should have looked at the lighthouse first. That's where your grandmother suggested but it's such a long walk down—"

"Shelle, I've got my cell phone. Try that next time." Elizabeth was still trying to catch her breath. She was sure she looked quite awful. She had just cleaned off a five foot section of the path with the front of her clothes. Rashelle helped her sit up. Her cell phone. Had she remembered to put it on silent? Could that have given her away in the woods if it had rung? She decided that she really needed to get better at being in stealth mode or she wasn't going to find out anything. Worse yet, she could put herself in danger.

"What were you doing?"

"Oh, just poking around." She brushed off her clothes and Rashelle started to pull pine needles out of Elizabeth's hair. "Listen; let's head back up the hill." She was struggling to get to her feet. "I overheard part of a conversation. I need to let Nana know Chief Austin is going to start making things miserable for everyone—"

"Starting! He has already put the inn in lockdown. No one in or out. He is determined to get to the bottom of this mess."

"Wow, he moves quickly. He must have radioed ahead on his way up the hill." *Great. Vera is never going to believe this!*

"Yeah. Basically everyone is a suspect until proven otherwise."

"What? A suspect? For what crime?" She wondered what the diver could have found.

"Poor Amelia. She's not taking this well."

Elizabeth grabbed Rashelle firmly at the shoulders with both hands and looked deeply into her eyes. "You and I are going to find out what is going on!"

Rashelle looked bewildered. "W-we are?" she stammered.

Elizabeth released her grip. "We have to!" She turned away from her and started heading to the top. Rashelle quickly fell in behind her. "My grandmother is on the verge of giving up the inn which has been in our family for…for Lord knows how many years. But several generations anyway. And just because some aggressive attorney is harassing her. Do we know anything about this guy?" She turned to look at Rashelle behind her to make sure she was getting her point. She could feel her voice getting louder. Rashelle opened her mouth to answer, but Elizabeth pressed on. "A female guest is missing and everyone fears the worst at this point. This inn is in lockdown—not good for business! On top of it all, the chief is way out of his league here. He's never had any experience with missing persons, extortion, or worse. He wasn't around when that student disappeared years ago, but that was never really resolved and a shadow has hung over the place ever since. We don't need another scandal." The pace of her words was quickening with each sentence. She stopped on a turn to catch her breath.

Silence hung in the air as they both pondered the situation. Elizabeth wondered how loudly she had been speaking and if the woods around them had ears. She nervously glanced around them in a three hundred sixty degree swath. One thing she knew for sure, they needed to rally behind Amelia.

They continued up the hill in silence until they reached the bluff. Elizabeth nearly walked right past the bluff in her determination to get to the top as quickly as possible. Suddenly, she realized she had to make a little detour. "Oh! I almost forgot. I left my drawing supplies and chair behind a tree."

Rashelle gave her a look of confusion.

"Oh, don't give it another thought. I just needed to travel lightly. It will just take a second." She stepped into the trees heading for her belongings. "I put them right here behind this…" Her voice trailed off as she walked a few feet into the woods as she had done earlier. She looked from tree to tree and she didn't find her things. "They were right here," a tone of panic rising in her voice. *Where could they be?* She retraced her steps from the bluff back to the trees. She was sure of the area. She had played there as a child. She kept looking, certain she was not mistaken. Even if they had fallen over, she should still be able to see them. The underbrush was not thick here. She walked in a circle around the area where she thought she had left them. Rashelle searched the fringes of what Elizabeth was covering. Elizabeth started crisscrossing the small area above the bluff. She was becoming very anxious. Her drawings… They were gone She had nothing to fax to her boss. Vera was definitely not going to be happy about this. She turned to Rashelle with a look of shock and disbelief. "They're gone." Her words were barely audible. She was absolutely devastated.

"Where could they have disappeared? Do you think the Chief would have picked them up and kept them thinking they might be evidence?"

"Oh, why would he do that?!" She was completely exasperated. "Let's go see."

Rashelle and Elizabeth reached the top of the trail winded. Elizabeth was looking worse for the wear, but resolute. They walked out into the clearing toward the inn and things looked amiss. Three police cars lined the circular drive. Then it dawned on her.

"Shelle, my car is gone!"

Chapter 9

There was quite a commotion going on between state troopers milling about and their squawking radios. Reinforcements had been called in. It was beginning to look like they were being occupied by a foreign police state. Elizabeth searched frantically for her friendly local chief. She finally found him in a sea of navy blue shirts with navy blue wide brimmed state trooper hats. She got as close as she could to the chief and rose up onto her tiptoes.

"Excuse me, Chief Austin….." He didn't hear her with the din around him so she reached in and grabbed his forearm and repeated more loudly, "Chief Austin!" He spun around quickly to face her, pulling his arm out of her firm grasp.

"Yes!" a bit short tempered. The chief was starting to wear the stress from the situation on his shirtsleeve. "Oh, Miss Pennington." He tried to lighten up his tone.

"Do you know where my car is?" She was trying to keep her voice from sounding desperate.

"Well, you may want to speak with Lt. Perkins of the Maine State Police. From what I understand, they had reasonable suspicion to search the car and upon inspection, ordered it impounded and towed to the evidence collection center at the Portland barracks."

"WHAT!? THEY TOWED MY CAR?" Several officers' heads turned toward her raised voice. She lowered her volume a couple of notches. "What could they have possibly found that they thought was suspicious?" *What did I leave in it? Did someone put something in it?*

"And Elizabeth…," he leaned over and put his hand firmly on her left shoulder like a father reprimanding his delinquent daughter, "I wouldn't be making any plans to go anywhere in the near future. I'm sure the lieutenant will want to have a little chat with you."

The chief removed his hand from her shoulder but held his gaze for effect, then he was quickly swallowed by the sea of state police as the troopers jockeyed for position to hear instructions from Lieutenant Perkins. Elizabeth took a step back to avoid being bumped by the entourage. She couldn't believe it. They took her little Z4. How was she going to get back to the city? She spun around to reconnect with Rashelle. Then she remembered her portfolio and turned back. "Hey, Chief, did they take my portfolio, too?" She doubted that he had heard the complete question. He looked in her direction from inside the crowd with a look on his face like he was wondering if someone had spoken to him. He was quickly brought back to the task at hand by a man in blue. They had a lot of questions for him. If Elizabeth could have seen through the crowd to the edge of the woods, she might have noticed Kurt lurking just out of sight, keeping his eye on the activity. In particular, he had his eye on her.

Elizabeth took a deep breath. Everything was happening too quickly and was making her feel like she was getting sucked in by the whirlpool of activity. Her head was spinning. She wanted to be in control again. She turned back away from the crowd to search for Rashelle who was right where Elizabeth had left her. Her good friend was standing off to the left side of the driveway with her arms folded and a look of trepidation on her face. Their little Camelot known as The Pennington Point Inn was in a veritable state of turmoil. *Where was a knight in shining armor when you needed him?...or her?*

Rashelle looked at Elizabeth for direction. "I have *got* to get back that portfolio. I don't know who has it but my job, my career, depend on it. My boss is going to be on my back to get design ideas to her. I already got an earful this morning." Her voice was starting to quiver and Rashelle could tell her friend was starting to lose it. The best thing she could do was to keep her moving. They needed to be productive.

"One step at a time," she advised. Extending her arm around her friend's shoulder, she guided her toward the inn. It was time to find Amelia and check in with her. Elizabeth and Rashelle headed up the front steps to the inn and were greeted by Tony on the porch. He wore a furrowed brow and stood at the top of the stairs with his hands on his hips, the cool sea breeze tossing his wavy brown hair about his head.

"Tony, this whole thing is unbelievable!" She was relieved to have someone else to commiserate with.

"Oui, incroyable!," he agreed, with his French Canadian background showing through.

"What's going on?" she pressed. It's always good to get a fresh perspective on a particularly stressful situation.

"What's going on? I'll tell you. I stand here and wait while the police are trying to decide if it's okay for me to go ahead with the clambake on the beach. The majority of the food is prepared and the guests are going to start complaining any minute."

"Where is my grandmother?"

"Amelia was not feeling so well so she went upstairs to lie down for a while."

Elizabeth suppressed a gasp and asked softly, "Is she alright?"

"She's fine, Lizzi. She was just overtired. I think this whole thing is starting to get to her."

Elizabeth knew her grandmother was having a hard time dealing with this, which made her very concerned about her. *Dear Lord, please allow me to help her through this difficult time with her health intact.*

Rashelle knew they needed to act quickly and any time spent chit-chatting was not going to help their cause. She grabbed Lizzi's arm again and directed her toward the front door.

Elizabeth bid Tony adieu and followed Rashelle through the inn's door like a sheep in tow. The tennis instructor watched them from a distance as they disappeared into the inn.

Once inside, Rashelle turned to Elizabeth with her usual spunk and enthusiasm. "I've got some more info on the missing girl." She led Elizabeth through the lobby to the door leading to the front desk. No one was at the desk. Elizabeth casually wondered if that was where her friend was supposed to be. Once behind the desk, Rashelle closed the door behind them and began speaking in hushed tones. "I was at the front desk earlier when the chief came into the lobby with a state trooper and the parents of the girl. They didn't notice me because I was seated at the computer down below the counter, updating some reservations that had just come in. Well, anyway, they said that this girl is fourteen years old, is about five feet, six inches tall, dirty blond hair, usually pulled back into a pony tail. She was last seen about 3:00 on Thursday afternoon when she headed out to get some fresh air. She wearing a pink t-shirt and jeans, with a light purple, zippered GAP sweatshirt—like the one they found at the lighthouse today."

She let her last comment hang in the air for a moment. Elizabeth considered all the info, and then asked, "Did the parents confirm it was their daughter's?"

"Yes."

"To get some fresh air…," Elizabeth repeated. "Is that another way of saying they were having words and she needed her space?" Rashelle looked at her expectantly, looking for an explanation. "You know, it's tough to be fourteen. It's even tougher to be fourteen and on a weekend away with your parents. What were they thinking? This was supposed to be a last fling before she went back to school. For who? Did they really think—what is her name?"

"Uh, Kelsey…Kelsey Hutchins."

"Did they really think this would be fun for her?"

"Supposedly."

"Did anyone hear them arguing?"

"There was no one in the room next to them. They requested the end room in the Acadia building, the one closest to the woods."

"Where are they from and when did they check in?"

"Let's see. I remember I was on duty when they checked in. It was Thursday, around noon. They had arrived before check-in time. I wasn't sure that their room was ready so I sent Marion from Housekeeping to check."

"What did the Hutchins do while Marion was gone?"

"Mr. Hutchins—Bill—just did a lot of pacing in the lobby and his wife, Sara, wandered into the sitting room and sat down to wait."

"What about their daughter?"

"Kelsey? Well, I never really saw her. She must have been outside or still in the car."

"So, you wouldn't know what she looks like if you saw her?"

"No."

"Did Bill and Sara at least have a picture to show the police?"

"I don't believe so. I know they apologized for not being more helpful."

"So, just the three of them registered at the inn."

"Right."

"They didn't have any other children?"

"...not that I know of. I guess I don't really know..."

"How old would you say the parents are?"

Rashelle looked a little surprised by this question. "Well, I would say around the mid to late thirties."

"That's all?"

"Yeah, they seemed kind of young."

"Elizabeth shook her head slightly and pressed on, "How long were they staying?"

"They were to check out on Sunday morning...tomorrow. Although, they asked if it would be possible to stay longer, if necessary."

"Really?"

"What does that mean?"

"I don't know. It just seems odd. It's Labor Day Weekend. Wasn't this the last weekend before their daughter started school? Wouldn't they know how long they could stay when they arrived? Who knows what it means, if anything."

Silence occupied the small space behind the front desk for a moment. Elizabeth continued, "Wait a minute. You didn't tell me where they were from."

"Oh! Let me just double check." Rashelle leaned over the ergonomically correct chair parked in front of the computer monitor. Her long slender fingers danced skillfully across the keys until she accessed the screen she needed. "West Hartford, Connecticut."

"And how did he pay for the room?"

"Well, usually we just have the guests give us a credit card number up front and we settle up when they check out. He insisted on paying in cash up front."

"Cash."

"Yup."

"Who does that?!"

Rashelle assumed that was a rhetorical question so she let it go. Elizabeth continued, "Okay, so one theory may be that she went out for a walk and got lost in unfamiliar woods and darkness fell before she could find her way back."

"But the woods have been searched and they found nothing."

"It doesn't mean there isn't anything yet to find." The friends exchanged looks of understanding. "Another theory is that she went for a walk on the beach and went too far beyond the beach break water and the tide came in. It got dark before she could make her way back. She fell asleep and missed the first low tide so now she's waiting for the next low tide. Or perhaps she simply left; she'd had enough of the 'rents and wanted out. She wanted to do something for the last few days of her summer freedom. She may show up tomorrow morning in time to go home. Won't she be surprised to find such a large welcoming party waiting to greet her?"

"Yeah!" The friends shared a chuckle. Rashelle got serious again. "She could also have gone down to the lighthouse and gotten too close to the water. She wasn't with her parents when I passed along the standard warning that we give to all of our guests about rogue waves."

Elizabeth realized she had to consider that as a possibility as well. It wasn't just the possibility of getting swept off the rocks; the temperature of the ocean in Maine, even in the summer, made it impossible to survive in the water for any length of time.

"I know the diver didn't find anything—"

"You do?"

"Yeah, but like you say, that doesn't mean there wasn't anything to find."

"True…I don't know if the current would take away a body from there or wash it back up on shore."

The voice from behind them took them by surprise. "It would carry it away and no one would ever see it again."

The girls whipped around. "Nana! I didn't know you…What are you doing here?" Elizabeth couldn't help but notice how tired she looked. The dark circles under her eyes told of trials and tribulations that had spanned a lifetime. The latest may well be the last for her grandmother. She needed to help her get through this.

Then Elizabeth remembered what Amelia had said when she had interrupted their brainstorming session. "It would wash it away? H-how do you know?" She asked with trepidation.

"Oh, Lizzi, it happened a very long time ago, but unfortunately it did happen." Her grandmother sounded exhausted, spent physically and emotionally. "Different circumstances, but perhaps the same result. Someday I'll tell you about it."

"Amelia, do you think that's what happened this time?"

"Oh, I don't know. Anything is possible. She could have gone too far down the beach and around the stone outcroppings where the tide comes in and cuts off the passage back." Elizabeth glanced at Rashelle. They had already covered that possibility. "For all we know she could have found her way into the tunnels and is lost down there somewhere."

"The tunnels!" Elizabeth shuddered to herself. Her voice was not much more than a whisper. "I thought they had been all sealed off years ago."

"Well, they were. But every once in a while one of the staff catches a kid nosing around one of the old entrances and shoos them away. A couple of weeks ago, Kurt mentioned he found two brothers trying to open the back door on the tennis shack. That door leads to the tunnel that goes between the main inn and Acadia House. Acadia was one of two buildings used as dormitories back when Pennington was a school. The other dormitory burned down and was never rebuilt. So the tunnel leads out from the inn and forks part way out, one tine of the fork ends up under the guest rooms in Acadia and the other eventually arrives at an abrupt dead end. Moosehead Lodge was built years later, not far from the footprint of the other dorm, after the main building was operating as an inn. Acadia was converted to guest rooms first and then Moosehead was built further behind it after some of the woods were cleared."

The girls were listening intently. Amelia always seemed to have something she could teach them about this old inn, yet never seemed to reveal the whole story.

"Well, I just came back down to find my reading glasses." She glanced at the desk behind the girls that held the computer. "Oh! There they are. I really should tie them around my neck so I won't lose them all of the time." Reaching past the girls, she chuckled to herself. Stepping back to face them, she offered a simple explanation, "I just need to lie down and rest for a while. I find if I read first, it relaxes me. I'll see you girls later."

They watched her go back through the door. She closed it behind her. The friends turned and looked at each other. It was as if Amelia had tried to steer them in a direction to look.

"Okay. Lizzi. We've got to check out those tunnels."

"Shelle, you don't know what it's like down there."

"You heard your grandmother. She practically spelled it out for us."

"What?" She didn't like where this was going.

"Look. The police haven't extended their search to beneath the property. They're having a hard enough time covering the grounds. Here, let's grab a couple of flashlights." She yanked open the bottom drawer in the desk under the computer and fumbled around in the back of it. She came out with two old, banged up metal flashlights that she proudly held up like two rainbow trout from a fishing expedition.

Elizabeth still couldn't get her mind around the idea of the two of them descending into the depths below the inn. She had never been down there before. She was strictly forbidden from doing so as a child and she had no desire to enter the dark, dank tunnels as an adult.

"How are we going to get down there without being seen? They don't want anyone down there."

"You heard Tony. He's out on the front porch waiting to get the okay to do the clambake. There's probably no one in the kitchen right now. We'll just go through the wine cellar."

Elizabeth couldn't think of a good comeback. She really didn't want to go, but at least she would have someone to go with. *What if the girl was lost down there? What if the two of them could put the whole matter to rest?* "It could be so easy...alright, let's do it!" Rashelle handed Elizabeth one of the two clunky flashlights. They each instinctively turned them on in tandem, as if on cue, to check the batteries. Both lights sprung to life.

"Wow. They actually work. Who knows the last time these artifacts were used."

That did not help Elizabeth feel any more at ease about their expedition.

Chapter 10

After slipping quietly through the empty kitchen, past the wine cooler, down the creaky wooden steps into the wine cellar, the girls found themselves standing on the other side of the racks of wine staring into an unknown black void. A narrow separation between two racks in one corner had allowed enough room for two thin young ladies to slip through. Rashelle switched on her flashlight and headed into the dark, dank tunnel slowly placing one foot in front of the other, sensing the tunnel floor was slippery. "Let's meet back here if we get separated." Elizabeth was behind her, having trouble getting her flashlight to stay lit. She shook it and the large D batteries rattled inside. Finally, the dim light brightened and seemed to be staying on. She started walking toward Rashelle's light. She was surprised how far her city slicker friend had reached during the time she was struggling with her light.

The tunnels were constructed of field stones just like all the stone walls which were found throughout New England. The walls measured approximately seven feet high by ten feet wide at the largest sections but there were smaller areas of the passageways that were constricted by underground rock ledges. Construction had been long and arduous, but critical to the continued success of the school. Coastal Maine winters could be absolutely brutal so the tunnels were essential for the continued day-to-day operations. Rudimentary lighting that had been installed to facilitate the students' passage through the tunnels had long since stopped functioning, however. Without flashlights, the darkness was darker than dark. An abyss for all light.

A rather nasty smell hung in the damp air and the floor was quite wet from water seeping in through the stones. An occasional drip from the ceiling gave the impression of being in a cave. Over the years, the walls had turned into a patchwork quilt as sections gave way to frost heave and were replaced with brick and, more recently, with cement. From the initial observation, it didn't look like anyone had done much repair work beyond the wine racks at the bottom of the stairs from the kitchen. Errant stones could be seen littering the floor of the tunnel for as far as the eye could see with a weak flashlight.

Elizabeth started down the tunnel toward Rachel when something brushed softly against her forehead and she jumped back. She aimed her light toward the ceiling and noticed an elaborate spider web, replete with a large black spider that was scurrying away from the giant human intruder. Closing her eyes, she shuddered and rubbed her forehead with the extended fingers of her right hand, trying to remove the sensation that the web was still touching her. Opening her eyes again, she noticed how beautiful the web really was, glittering in her beam of light, and wondered how long it must have taken the spider to construct it. It was truly a work of art.

Elizabeth looked past the web and noticed Rashelle's light was no longer bobbing in front of her. She was no longer moving. Maybe she was waiting for her to catch up. Elizabeth navigated carefully past the spider and its beautiful home, being careful not to touch the sticky strands again. She resumed her trek down the tunnel toward Rashelle, keeping the light moving back and forth, up and down, not really knowing what she was going to find. Coming up behind Rashelle, she noticed an opening to the right with dining room chairs stacked in columns like a wall, partially closing off the access to a tunnel. This could either be a route that led to another building on the campus or a dead end. *Only one way to find out.* She couldn't resist the urge.

Rashelle was standing perfectly still with her back to her, staring straight ahead when Elizabeth came up behind her. Rachel spoke first.

"I can't."

"What?"

"I can't."

"You can't what?"

"I can't do this."

"What?! Why the sudden change of heart?" An otherwise outgoing, gregarious New Yorker just turned into the Cowardly Lion and they were a long way from Oz.

"I don't know what it is, but I just can't do this all of a sudden. It's like the place has a personality and it doesn't want us intruding. It just doesn't feel right."

"None of this feels right. Since when has that stopped us before?"

"Maybe I just need time to get used to all of this."

Elizabeth silently wondered if she would ever get used to this. It gave her the creeps, too. "Alright, you stay put. I'll go for a ways and come back. Okay? Will you be alright?"

Rashelle seemed frozen to her spot on the dirt floor, staring straight ahead.

"Shelle...SHELLE!"

She jumped and turned toward Elizabeth. "Y-Yes. You go ahead. I'll be fine. I'll just catch my breath."

"Okay. Focus on breathing."

"Okay," she muttered without really focusing on the words.

Elizabeth turned right to explore the first offshoot from the main tunnel. She turned back to take another look at Rashelle. Hopefully she would be all right. Elizabeth wasn't very comfortable leaving her behind but she needed to cover some ground. Besides, she had left her near the entrance to the tunnel so she could find her way out if she needed to. She could only be a few yards away from the steps back up to the kitchen. Elizabeth just wished it wasn't so dark down there.

She headed down the dark passageway, her light projecting a narrow swath. She slowly made her way through the darkness, not sure what she would find with each step. After about twenty feet she could sense the tunnel was starting to take a turn toward the right. She proceeded cautiously. *I can't get lost. All I have to do is turn around and follow the tunnel back the way I came.* After several minutes of baby steps forward, she noticed she was slowing down. Her flashlight was getting dimmer and that caused her to walk more slowly. She banged the bulb end of the flashlight on the palm of her hand, trying to coax it brighter. It flickered on and off until finally it went off completely. Elizabeth shook it some more. It was still pitch black. It was so dark in the tunnel; she couldn't see her hands in front of her face. She banged the lifeless battery holder against her palm again. Nothing. Not even a flicker. "Great!" *Time to head back and find Rashelle.* She groped to find the wall and kept her hand on it as she crept back toward the main tunnel, keeping her fingers splayed against the cold, damp, sometimes wet stones. She was beginning to think she knew what a bat felt like. *One foot in front of the other.* It was darker than dark in front of her yet she pressed on, fighting the sensation that she was going to run into something. She didn't want to think about what might be behind her. Her feet started to head down a slight decline. With the light on earlier, she hadn't noticed that she had been making her way up a slight hill. Now that she was headed back down without the use of her sight, her remaining senses were heightened. She quickened her pace. Suddenly her left foot slipped on a wet, slippery spot, and it shot out from underneath her. Her upper torso snapped backwards, but she desperately tried to compensate with the rest of her body. Her arms flailing, she managed to snap her body forward again. Unfortunately, she overcompensated and her right foot landed hard on the dirt below. The force of the impact caused her ankle to roll. She gasped when she realized she was going down. She released the flashlight just in time for her hands to break her fall. She landed on the cold, damp ground with very little sound. A soft thud. "Great!" There she was, sprawled out in the dark with a throbbing ankle. Groping around, she located the useless flashlight. Forcefully rubbing her ankle, she hobbled to her feet and continued to make her way in the dark. *It can't be much farther.* Then she remembered Rashelle. Suddenly it didn't seem like such a good idea to have gone off and left her friend on her own. She persevered through the ache in her ankle and kept walking, more like hobbling, with one hand on the right wall. She walked for what seemed like five minutes. She wondered if she should be able to see Rashelle's light by now. Then she stopped for a moment in the dark to think. It seemed like she had been walking longer to get back than the original trip down the passageway. Was she just taking longer because of her ankle and the lack of light or did she get up from her tumble facing the wrong direction?! Panic was welling up inside of her and she tried desperately to remain calm so she could think.

She could hear herself breathing. She held her breath to see if she could hear anything else. Slow, but steady drops of water were audible. She took a deep breath and made the decision to keep going in the same direction for a while longer. If she didn't reach the main tunnel after a certain number of steps—a hundred steps, she would turn around and head the other way. She couldn't panic; she just had to be methodical about this…"one, two, three." She continued the rest in her head. *19, 20, 21.* Elizabeth wondered where Rashelle was and if she would see her light if she got close. *34, 35, 36. I never should have left her. I didn't like the idea in the first place. She had found the old flashlights…51, 52, 53. This had better be working. I need to reconnect with Rashelle, especially since she has the only working flashlight. Or does she? What if hers died too? Oh, Elizabeth, what have you gotten yourself into? 68, 69, 70. Is this working?*

Then the smell hit her right in the face as if someone had taken the back of their hand to her nose. She stopped dead in her tracks. *What is that?* She obviously had not been this far before and she was certainly not walking in the right direction. Her curiosity would not let her turn the other way, though. Now that she knew which direction was the correct one, she really should be heading in that direction. Something kept her from turning away from the smell. A few more steps? Did she dare? What would she find? Not much in the absolute darkness. Without a window in the tunnels or an operating flashlight in her hand, there was no chance of seeing anything. Still she was held fast, not changing direction. The smell that had caught her by surprise was still very strong. It was a sour smell, like the early stages of something decaying. What was the source? She started walking forward again, completely blind. Two more steps. Then one more and she brought her foot up alongside the other. This was insanity. Even if she found something, she wouldn't be able to see it. It was time to turn around.

Very carefully she pivoted in place, groping for the wall to stabilize her. Just to be sure, in a somewhat irrational moment, she decided to count her steps again, this time backwards. She was fairly sure this was finally the right direction but she wasn't going to take any chances. Where had she left off before? Somewhere around 70 or 80? She decided to go with 73…72, 71, 70…She just wanted out of this tunnel…66, 65, 64…Hopefully Rashelle was okay… and was not getting lost. She was probably smart enough to stay put…53, 52, 51…Counting her steps was turning into a nonsensical exercise, but it gave her something to do besides panicking. She had reached the decline in the floor again. She slowed her feet to baby steps to keep herself from slipping all over again. Where had she left off counting? She couldn't remember. *Just keep walking. This has to be the right way.* Keeping her hand running along the wall, she pressed on. *Just one foot in front of the other. Not too fast. But keep moving.* The darkness was really starting to get to her. *Just keep going.* Suddenly the wall felt as if it was turning slightly to the left. Elizabeth felt a wave of relief pour over her. She had to be close to the beginning. She remembered it turning slightly to the right not long after she started. She kept her feet moving but she held them back from going too fast. Just a few more steps. It had to be twenty more? 30? *Just keep moving. One foot in front of the other.* Then it seemed as though it was getting brighter. Was she just imagining it or was it real? *A few more steps.* The darkness in the tunnel was starting to get lighter. She could just make out her hand holding the dead flashlight. She pressed on a few more steps.

What she saw next made her stop. She had finally reached the end of the curve in the side tunnel so she could see where it met up with the main tunnel. She stifled a gasp. In front of her was Kurt, walking in the main tunnel toward the direction she had left Rashelle. He was far enough away so he didn't notice Elizabeth. He was creeping along slowly. As Elizabeth crept closer she could see Rashelle just to the right in the main tunnel. Kurt was moving closer to her. Just a few steps separated them. She didn't like the looks of this. She quickened her pace, risking slipping again, but she had to catch up to him. A few more steps and he would no longer be in her line of sight. He was getting closer to Rashelle. Elizabeth kept walking briskly. She needed to catch up to them.

She reached the end of her tunnel, pivoted right toward Mitchell, and saw Rashelle just a few feet beyond him. Elizabeth had the element of surprise on her side and she was going to prevent him from hurting her friend. She switched the clunky flashlight to her right hand, raised it above her head as she crept up close behind him. She drove it down onto his head with everything she had. She watched him fall as his legs buckled beneath him. Rashelle spun around and looked into Elizabeth's eyes, a look of shock on her face.

Chapter 11

"I'm sorry." Elizabeth didn't know what else to say. She looked helplessly at Kurt holding an ice pack to the back of his head. He appeared crumpled and disheveled, slouched at the far end of the faded plaid couch. Chief Austin hovered nearby like a doting nanny. "I'm really sorry. How was I supposed to know you're on our side? I'm sorry I hurt you. I thought you were about to hurt Rashelle." Rashelle shot her a troubled glance. Confusion and fatigue were competing for front row in Elizabeth's head.

Kurt perked up. "What were you doing down there in the tunnels anyway?" His voice was half whining, half demanding.

"Oh, they're my old stomping ground," she fibbed, not daring to look at Rashelle. "I did grow up here, ya know." Elizabeth was trying hard to convince him of her confidence. She had a nagging feeling he wasn't buying any of it. He wouldn't have if he had caught the look on Rashelle's face. "I could ask you the same thing," she tossed back his way; a tone of indignation permeated the air. Things were starting to feel a bit adversarial. The chief mumbled something and headed outside. Now that he had straightened out this mess, he had other, more important, things to attend to.

Mitchell, in his wrinkled and soiled tennis whites, removed the ice pack from his head and cradled it in the palm of his right hand, which was hovering over his lap. He sat forward on the couch, a look of sheer annoyance spread across his face. "Look, we really need to work together here."

"…We do?" Elizabeth wasn't sure she liked this idea. She still wasn't sure she trusted him. She was feeling very angry toward him. What exactly had his intentions been in the tunnel? What would have happened if she hadn't stopped him? Just because Chief Austin said Kurt was a good guy didn't mean much in her book. What did the chief really know anyway?

"Yes. I've been doing some digging around on my own and I could use your help—both of you." He glanced from Elizabeth to Rashelle and back again. "You in particular, Elizabeth. As you mentioned, you grew up here. You know the place inside and out."

Elizabeth was beginning to think she shouldn't have led him to believe she was quite so comfortable in the tunnels. What was he planning? She needed to try to get more info out of him. She needed to know what his agenda was.

At that moment, a state trooper stepped inside the front door of the inn. The sound of the screen door banging closed caused everyone in the sitting room to turn their attention to him. He paused on the threshold of the sitting room. Elizabeth recognized his voice when he spoke, "Miss Elizabeth Pennington?" It was the same voice she heard talking with Chief Austin while she was clinging to the side of the cliff earlier. His name tag read "Lt. Perkins." He was a tall slender man with short cropped hair and dark, piercing eyes that exuded maturity and experience beyond his years. Perhaps he had been in the military before he wore the proud, blue uniform of the Maine State Police. Elizabeth figured he was in his mid to late thirties. She imagined he didn't have much of a sense of humor.

"Yes?" she spoke softly. She blushed, wondering if he knew she had been hiding in the woods when he had walked by earlier.

"Ma'am, I need to have a word with you…in private. Would you mind stepping outside with me, please?" His voice was calm, but firm. He was someone in authority here, to be sure.

Once again she was going to fall short of her objective to extract more info out of Mitchell. That would have to wait. "Sure," trying to sound more cooperative than she felt. She turned back to Rashelle and Kurt. "Carry on without me, guys. I'll be back." She hoped this little chat wouldn't take long. Maybe she could find out about her car while she was at it. She couldn't believe they would just take it like that. She stood and walked toward the front door leading to the porch, with the trooper a few feet behind her.

Once outside, Lt. Perkins took the lead and seemed to be heading toward a police car, complete with the rack of lights on top. He walked up to the passenger side and opened the front door. Elizabeth's eyes grew wide. "Are...are we going somewhere?" She could feel herself putting on the brakes. Where was he taking her?

A brief but detectible smile crossed his face. "No ma'am. We just need a quiet place to talk. I figured this was as good as any." His voice was low and rough. With a bit of levity, he added, "Step into my office," while motioning with his free hand.

She still didn't feel completely comfortable. She had never sat in a squad car before. She guessed that was a good thing. Reluctantly, she slipped into the front seat without a sound. Once her legs were clear, the officer closed the door firmly behind her. The sound made her jump slightly. The silence that followed was deafening. She was beginning to feel guilty without having done anything. It was as if she was sitting in the principal's office waiting to be scolded. She braved a glance into the backseat, which was empty, but she started to imagine what it must feel like to be back there with your hands in cuffs. She shuddered. Finally the lieutenant reached for the handle of the driver's side door, opened it with a quick jerking motion, and dropped down into his seat. A strange aroma entered the car with him. She couldn't place it. She continued to feel uncomfortable. She instinctively glanced toward her door to ascertain where the handle was. She needed an escape route.

"Miss Pennington, during our initial sweep of the premises we entered and searched any and all vehicles parked at the inn.

One such vehicle was parked out front of the inn on the circular drive."

My car! Elizabeth did not like where this was heading.

"It turned out to be your car. Upon searching your vehicle, we located an item that placed you on our list of persons we are interested in."

"What! I can't imagine what you could have found. What is it? What does it have to do with? I'm sure I can explain it." Panic was clear in her voice. Were they going to take her somewhere for questioning, lock her up? She wouldn't be able to help her grandmother if she was behind bars. She started to feel trapped. Her breathing quickened.

"All I can tell you is that it is related to the missing girl."

"It is?" She was incredulous. *How can that be?*

"So you need to stay put at the inn until we can figure this all out."

She held her breath and struggled not to sigh out loud. She was so relieved that they weren't detaining her or transporting her anywhere. They were obviously going to be keeping an eye on her.

Lt. Perkins let his last words hang in the air for a moment before reaching for the door handle and exiting the squad car. The door closed with a loud thud. Elizabeth jumped again. He left her sitting in the vacuum of the four door sedan. As the seconds ticked silently away, she felt anger rising up inside of her. She was getting hot under the collar. Why was this happening? They were practically accusing her of being involved with the girl's disappearance. Her anger was turning to fury. She needed to get out of that car. She grabbed the handle and forced the heavy door open, slamming it behind her. As she stepped onto the uneven lawn in front of the inn, her right ankle, which was already weakened by her earlier spill, turned slightly so her knee gave way. She caught herself, just in time, before hitting the ground. Then she reached down and rubbed the ankle. She reminded herself to keep breathing. She headed straight for the front steps, deliberate in her stride, arms swinging alternately with each step. She ran up the steps and headed in.

Elizabeth burst into the foyer, immediately turning right toward the sitting room to rejoin Rashelle and Kurt. She stopped short of entering. The room was empty. Where had they gone? She felt herself turning her anger toward them. Where did they go without her? She told them she would be right back. She decided it was time to head to her room and splash some cold water on her face before trying to find them.

Chapter 12

With the face towel still in her hand, Elizabeth headed for the table and chairs by the window. She dropped into one of the creaky antique chairs. She was fighting exhaustion. Somehow she was becoming involved in this mess, whether she liked it or not. She decided it was best to lay low and stay under the radar while the police were nosing around. She would need to buy herself some time, though. Her grandmother was expecting to have dinner with her that evening. A quick look at her watch told her it was nearly 6:00 p.m. She would have to leave her a note to beg off that commitment. She would need to locate some paper. Looking around the room, she suddenly remembered the table she was sitting at was really an old desk that had been transformed into a table. It was topped with a circle of plywood, a tablecloth, and a circle of glass, the same size as the wood, to complete the makeshift table. She lifted the tablecloth and peeked underneath. Fortunately the drawers were situated facing her so she crawled under and began opening drawers. One by one she pulled the wooden knobs. The drawers were rather sluggish, wood dragging across wood. They all seemed to be empty. They must have been cleaned out before the desk was converted to a table. She decided to extend her arm down into each one just to be sure. It was pretty dark under the tablecloth, so it was hard to see. When her fingers explored the depths of the drawer on the bottom right side, she felt some sort of paper wedged way down in the back. Whatever it was, it would have to do. She would have had plenty of paper to use if someone hadn't taken her portfolio with all her supplies in it. The police must have picked it up during one of their searches. She started mentally kicking herself for not remembering to ask Lt. Perkins during their chat in the squad car earlier. At least they were in good hands, she hoped. She didn't want to think about Vera at the moment. She pulled out the paper from the back of the drawer. It turned out to be several pieces of yellowed paper that were of different sizes and were folded over. She gently unfolded them and realized she was holding very old newspaper clippings. Her eyes grew wide as she began to read the headlines.

August 5, 1984 Portland Herald
THREE SWEPT OFF ROCKS AT PENNINGTON POINT
– Search Continues

August 7, 1984 Lewiston Sentinel
ROGUE WAVE CLAIMS TWO LIVES

There were a half a dozen articles, all with similar headlines and presumably similar story lines. Elizabeth wondered briefly why there seemed to be a discrepancy in the number of victims and then let it go. This was the event she had only heard people mention from time to time. It made sense that she didn't remember it because she was only four years old in 1984. She decided to fold up the articles and put them back where she found them for safekeeping. She would sneak another look at them later.

Quietly, she closed the drawer on the old desk and adjusted the tablecloth to look like it had when she sat down. She pushed the chair back in place and headed for the door. She stopped abruptly in her tracks; she could hear water running. It sounded like it was coming from the bathroom. She turned and listened. She could have sworn she had turn off the faucet. Wouldn't she have heard it before now if she hadn't? She crept slowly toward the sound, holding her breath as she went. The hair on the back of her neck was standing straight up. She reached the door to the bathroom and peeked in. All she saw was the water falling from the faucet. No one else was there. Keeping most of her body safely in the doorway, she very slowly leaned in and reached for the handle, carefully turning off the water. She stood there for a moment once it was off, half expecting it to turn back on again. She backed out of the doorway of the little bathroom and just shook her head. That was strange. She knew she had done that once already. She didn't want to consider how it got turned on again. There was no time to dwell on that. She needed to catch up with Rashelle and Kurt. She would grab paper to write a note to her grandmother from the front desk. Heading for the door to her room, at last, she put a spring in her step. She reached for the doorknob only to freeze again. There was something on the floor just in front of the door. Elizabeth stared at it. It appeared to be a folded piece of paper. She bent down and retrieved it. Slowly she unfolded the paper to reveal a hand scrawled note. It merely said:

I knoW wHere the Girl Is

It appeared to be written in black grease pencil. Elizabeth gasped. Someone had slipped the note under the door. But who? She refolded the note and slipped it into her pants pocket. It was time to get back in the game. Things were about to get interesting, it seemed.

Elizabeth hurried down the carpeted main stairway, turning right at the bottom toward the dining room and kitchen. She nearly ran head on with Rashelle as she burst through the doorway with a tray in her hands. "Shelle! Whatcha doin'?" The tray contained two covered dishes, two glasses with ice, and a couple cans of ice tea. A basket of rolls, pats of butter on a plate, napkins and silverware rounded out the presentation. A single rose from Amelia's garden was displayed in a tall, slender, crystal, cut-glass vase. It looked out of place, considering the circumstances.

"Tony asked me to drop this off at the Hutchins' room. They didn't request it, but Amelia figured they would need it. Wanna come?"

"Would I!" Elizabeth was thrilled with her fortuitous timing. "Oh, thank you. I really didn't want to go alone."

Elizabeth reached over and snatched the vase from the tray with one hand and took hold of Rashelle's upper arm as if to escort her to the door. Rashelle examined her friend's face, as if searching for an explanation.

"I'll carry this so you don't have to worry about it falling off." They headed off toward the back of the inn, through the back porch, to make their delivery.

The path from the inn was part brick, part stone, part dirt, and it meandered through the shady pine trees on its way to Acadia House. Elizabeth followed Rashelle's lead since she knew where the Hutchins' room was. Before long, they arrived at Acadia House, which was much more modest than the grand, main building of the inn. The one-story building was sided with simple, white, clapboard siding; large windows dotted the front and back in a neat row. A narrow wooden porch, painted white to match the rest of the building, ran the length of the front. The Hutchins' room was an end unit furthest from the path, furthest from the ocean, but closest to the woods. Steps on either end of the porch led up to the building. Rashelle headed for the farthest set of steps with Elizabeth right behind her, vase in hand. When they got to the top of the steps, the door to the Hutchins' room lay in front of them. Curtains were drawn on the windows to the left side of the door. They paused on the welcome mat. The two friends turned to look at each other. Rashelle took a breath and firmly knocked on the door. As an afterthought, Elizabeth returned the vase to the tray. Several seconds lapsed. The girls looked at each other again, both listening for movement inside the room. Elizabeth raised her fist to knock again when she heard someone fumbling with the knob.

A very tired looking man quietly opened the door a few inches and peered with little emotion through the narrow opening at the duo standing outside. Elizabeth presumed this was Mr. Hutchins. He looked too worn out to have emotion. He looked numb. They couldn't really see past him but the room looked rather dark. Rashelle was the first to speak.

"Mr. Hutchins, we thought that you and Mrs. Hutchins might be hungry…that you could use some food…you really should eat." She was struggling to find the right words. "Anthony, our chef, prepared a couple of dishes for you. Just let us know if there is something else you would like instead." His face lit up slightly with that idea, and then he seemed to think better of himself and became more subdued. He reached out to take the tray.

"Thank you for thinking of us. I'm sure this will be fine." His voice was soft and his head was bowed toward the tray, not making eye contact with the girls. "We really appreciate this—everything you are doing, we really appreciate it. Thank you." He backed into the room and closed the door quietly in their faces.

The girls exchanged glances again, not quite sure what to make of their encounter. They turned and headed back down the stairs to retrace their steps to the inn. Rashelle found her voice first. "He looked so sad."

"Yeah."

"Hope they find her."

"Me, too…alive." Elizabeth thought of the note scrunched up in her pocket but decided to keep it to herself for the time being.

Katydids were starting to chirp in the long grasses along the edge of the woods. Elizabeth breathed in a long cleansing breath of briny sea air. She never tired of how that made her feel.

In the waning daylight, their surroundings were becoming bathed in shadows. Elizabeth much preferred the inn and the extensive grounds around it in the bright sunshine when everything was sharp and clear. Yet, even in the limited light, something caught her eye as the two walked along the path next to the woods. "Shelle!" She half-whispered, half-yelled. Rashelle stopped her feet abruptly and spun around in one swift movement. "Look at this!" Elizabeth was already off the path and headed toward the edge of the woods, just a few feet away. She was pointing to a couple of branches of a low bush that were broken but still dangling. "And look at this!" She was staring at the ground next to the bush. It appeared to be soft and sandy with a couple of small, narrow footprints embedded in it.

"What do you think it means?"

"Well, I'm not sure it means anything. But this is directly across from the stairs up to the Hutchins' room. What if Kelsey headed out their door after an argument and headed straight into the woods? This could be the lead that the troopers need to find the girl."

"Maybe we should go in. See if we see anything." Rashelle was far bolder than Elizabeth.

"We will just let them know what we found!" She grabbed Rashelle's arm and headed for the inn. She was not about to head into the woods at dusk. That was not her idea of fun.

Chapter 13

T he two close friends were sharing a late dinner on the back porch, what Amelia liked to refer to as the veranda. Rashelle was adept at slipping into the kitchen even at the height of activity to gather food. Tonight, all of the kitchen staff were busy with the clambake down on the beach so there was no one around to notice. She had scavenged enough food to make a full sit-down dinner for the two of them, including a lobster and a few clams for them to share. They were trying to enjoy the meal on the porch, but they were both a little distracted. It was certainly a pleasant setting. The jalousie windows were cranked out to their fullest setting, allowing the cool evening sea breeze to penetrate the screened-in porch.

Suddenly Elizabeth's phone rang in her pocket and she jumped slightly. She cringed as she pulled it out and flipped it open, fully expecting it to be Vera. To her surprise it was an unfamiliar number with an area code of 917. Elizabeth was fairly sure that it was one of the codes for Brooklyn and then it dawned on her. Drescher. Hers eyes widened and she looked up to Rashelle.

"I'm sorry. I really should answer this."

Rashelle shrugged to reassure her it wasn't a problem.

She stood up and turned away from the table, pressed the "talk" button and tried to sound professional, "Hello, this is Elizabeth." She held her breath in anticipation.

"Elizabeth. How are you?" His voice was smooth and lilting.

"Fine, Mr. Drescher. And you?"

"Elizabeth, please…Jack. Please call me Jack. We've known each other for too long to keep up such formalities."

A shiver coursed through her torso. "Alright, J-Jack. If you insist." She started to pace as she spoke.

"Of course I do. That's much better. Thank you…so what are you up to? You mentioned you were going away for the weekend. Any place good?" He waited for her to respond.

Her mind was racing. Her boss thinks she should be back in New York City working on a project for him and, if she's not careful, it could appear that she has cast her responsibilities and priorities aside for a mini-vacation. "I'm actually visiting my grandmother in Maine…"

"Maine. Well that's quite a hike from the city, isn't it?" His voice was calm and almost soothing, one that could talk anyone into almost anything.

"Yes, well I came up to give her a hand with some things. It was kind of last minute but I have also been working on your new project," she tried to reassure him.

"Well I hope you find the time to fit in some relaxation while you're there. You work so hard. You need to reward yourself once in a while."

She was a bit taken back by his words. He wasn't angry at all that she had taken some time off. She started to let down her guard.

"And I hear the lobster there is like no other. Make sure you get one of those red crustaceans before you leave."

She smiled. "As a matter of fact, I am having one for dinner right now."

"Nice! Where are you dining? A favorite restaurant of yours?"

She smiled again. She found herself slightly amused. "Not exactly. My grandmother runs an inn up here and a friend of mine and I are having a quiet dinner on the back porch." Then she thought she should clarify so he wouldn't get the wrong idea. "A girlfriend and I. There is a clambake down on the beach for the guests so the veranda was available for us to enjoy." Suddenly she felt a little silly, like she was giving him unimportant details that an important man, such as himself, wouldn't be interested in.

He feigned interest, however. "Sounds absolutely wonderful."

There was an awkward pause while Elizabeth scrambled to think about how to turn the conversation around so it was no longer about her.

He came to her rescue. "Well, I didn't intend to interrupt your dinner. We'll talk again, Elizabeth. I would like to talk in more detail about my project."

"Absolutely, Mr. Drescher...Jack. I would be happy to go over the concept of my designs with you, if you would like." She hoped that was sufficient to keep him happy for a while.

"That sounds great, Elizabeth. I'll call again." His voice was uncharacteristically gentle. It crossed her mind that he probably didn't speak to everyone in that tone.

"Good-bye." She spoke softly, finding it hard to believe that she had just had a conversation with Jack Drescher on her cell phone, outside of work and not really about work. And all she could come up with to talk about was what she was doing on a Saturday evening, or really, what she wasn't doing. "Wow that was lame." She turned back to her friend.

Rashelle looked up.

"I just talked to one of the most powerful business men in the city, perhaps on the East Coast, and all I could talk about was eating dinner on the back porch...clearly I don't have much of a life."

She returned to her seat and looked up to see her friend frowning. Elizabeth feared she had taken offense at her comment.

"Oh Shelle! This has nothing to do with you. I just get so nervous when I talk to him. He is such a huge client of Loran Design. Extremely successful with his real estate empire. If his name is associated with a project, it seems as though it is an instant success, or at least a guaranteed success. He has a way of making things happen..."

Elizabeth recalled a phone conversation that she inadvertently overheard, not long after she had first met him, during which Drescher yelled quite loudly at the person on the other end of the line. She didn't intend to eavesdrop but she just happened to be walking near an office in Loran Design that he was using while he was there. He tended to move in and make himself at home. The volume of his voice made her stop in her tracks and pause for a moment. Clearly he was not someone you wanted to be in disagreement with and certainly not someone you wanted to cross.

Returning her focus to Rashelle, "Probably travels to exotic places and has vacation homes all over. He lives a life that you and I probably can't imagine and certainly can't relate to. Nothing I say could possibly sound very interesting to him. All I do is work. I don't have much of a life outside of it."

A smirk spread across Rashelle's face. "Maybe you should do something about that."

Lizzi opened her mouth to respond but closed it again.

"Interesting that he wants to speak to you about his project, not Vera."

Elizabeth studied her face to see if she could decipher what she meant.

"I just mean that speaks well for you. Obviously, you are a very talented designer and he recognizes that." She could tell that Elizabeth was shrugging off her compliment. "You are, Lizzi. Think about it. You have seven years of incredible experience at one of the top design firms in the city. This major client wants to discuss his project directly with you. I wouldn't be surprised if Vera feels a little inadequate around you. At this point in her career, she probably finds it more difficult to come up with fresh, new design ideas and to stay on top of the latest trends in the industry than she did when she was your age. Her energy is waning and she has to try to keep up with the likes of you."

"Oh, Shelle. You exaggerate so!"

"Don't believe that for a minute! I'm serious. Don't sell yourself short. And if this guy is so influential, he could be a big help to you when you decide to break out on your own, leave Vera behind and start your own design firm. I bet he would jump ship and give his business to you."

Elizabeth's eyes widened. "Vera would have my head if that happened. Oh my God." She cringed at the thought. "Besides, he scares me a little bit. I'm not sure I want to be alone in the same room with him when the day comes that he doesn't get his way."

"Doesn't sound like that should be a problem for you." Rashelle had a twinkle in her eye.

Elizabeth sighed. Her friend had no idea what the man was like and she really wanted to put him out of her thoughts for the time being. She would deal with him when she returned to the city. That would have to be soon enough. "Well at the moment, we've got more important issues to worry—"

From their left, the screen door squeaked on its hinges. Someone entered the porch and quietly passed next to their table. It was a young man in his twenties who appeared to have a bit of a Latino background. Elizabeth and Rashelle didn't pay much attention to him until he reached down and picked up Elizabeth's napkin off the floor. He placed it quietly onto the table, to the right of her dish, between the two of them. "Excuse me, ladies." He looked directly at Elizabeth. "You dropped this." His interruption startled her. She had been completely engrossed in her thoughts and their discussion of Drescher.

"Oh! Oh, thank you," she stammered, slightly embarrassed. He turned and headed for the door into the lobby. Once he had cleared the porch, she leaned over to Rashelle, "Who is that?" She hadn't recognized him and she thought she knew everyone on the staff.

"…That must be the new guy—" Rashelle looked as though she was trying to recall the details surrounding this new character.

"Another new guy? I thought Kurt was the only one."

"Oh, well, this guy—I think his name is Armand—is a kind of an all-around guy. He goes where he is needed. He is a friend of Slater's. Tony must have needed his help with the clambake tonight."

Rashelle didn't seem to know Armand that well. Elizabeth thought that was a bit odd.

Slater was a local fisherman who would take guests of the inn out on his lobster boat, teaching them about lobstering, while pulling up traps on an abbreviated version of his regular route. Although only in his thirties, he was a seasoned fisherman. He was the son of a retired fisherman who now captained a very successful tour boat company further north in Boothbay Harbor. Slater kept to the lobstering. It wasn't as seasonal as the tour boat business and he was comfortable with it; he had grown up around it. Around the bend from the Pennington Point Beach, further to the east, was a quiet little cove that boasted a small dock where Slater kept his boat. He would take out small groups from the inn on Wednesdays and Saturdays.

Elizabeth picked up the ivory cotton napkin Armand, or whatever his name was, had placed next to her plate. She slid it across her lap. Something fell to the floor that caught Rashelle's eye. "Liz, you dropped something." She leaned over and picked up a folded piece of paper and handed it to her friend.

Elizabeth had a puzzled expression on her face and slowly opened it, holding it so that Rashelle could see, too. There was a brief note scrawled in grease pencil. It wasn't directed specifically to any one person. It was very blunt.

wHerE's tHe glrl? do you wANt tO knOW?

The handwriting was fairly neat with random capitalization throughout. Elizabeth's heart skipped a beat. She looked at her friend. "Who could have written this?" she whispered. "This is the second one I have seen today." They were so absorbed by the note that they didn't notice Amelia approaching from behind.

"Hey, girls. I see you found something to eat."

They jumped and spun around to face her. Elizabeth scrunched the note into the palm of her hand.

"Oh! Nana, hi! Uh...I'm sorry. I know we were supposed to have dinner together tonight—"

"Don't give it another thought, Hun. I'm the one who should apologize. I totally forgot, what with all that is going on around here. I'm glad you were resourceful and got some food for yourselves."

"Well, what about you Nana? Have you eaten?" A twinge of guilt pinched her stomach. She had never checked up on her grandmother to see if she had taken time for food. She really should be keeping a better eye on her.

"Oh, I grabbed a bite already. I was with the police officers when Tony brought them dinner earlier."

Elizabeth really wanted to believe her grandmother, but something told her she was covering up so that her little Lizzi wouldn't worry and wouldn't feel guilty about standing her up for dinner.

"Girls...I'm afraid I have more bad news." She moved right on to the business at hand. "Lt. Perkins just told me that things are going to be going from bad to worse. There is a hurricane that they've been watching down the coast and it looks like it is heading our way. At first, it looked like it was going out to sea, but it hasn't taken the right turn that they expected it to take. It's barreling right up the eastern seaboard on its way here."

The girls' mouths hung open. Elizabeth was the first to regain her voice. "That's awful, Nana! Now what do we do?"

"Well, there's not much we *can* do." She looked like she was struggling to keep her composure. "They will keep monitoring the storm while they continue their investigation which they hope to complete by the time the hurricane arrives. All the guests will have to evacuate by then."

"When do they expect it to hit?" Rashelle had found her voice.

"Well, it's hard to say exactly, seems to change by the hour. It's a rather volatile storm. Could be sometime Labor Day or Tuesday morning or as early as Sunday evening."

The girls gasped at the thought.

"In the meantime, we need to assist in any way we can with the investigation. Hopefully we will find the girl safe and sound somewhere. Maybe she's just playing a teenage prank on her parents and it will all be over soon.

"Wouldn't that be nice?" Elizabeth joined her grandmother's daydream.

Rashelle decided to play devil's advocate again. "Of course, if she has caught wind of the commotion she has caused here, she may not surface for quite some time."

Amelia looked at Rashelle and seemed to be considering her point. "Well, I just hope it all turns out alright. We just have to keep believing it will…praying it will. It's so unproductive to think otherwise." The tone of Amelia's voice seemed to reprimand Rashelle for not being optimistic.

Elizabeth knew her grandmother believed in the power of positive thinking, but she thought this situation was going to take a lot more than the three of them sitting around saying "everything will be alright…" And she didn't dare tell Amelia about the note she held crumpled up in the palm of her hand or the one shoved deep into her pants pocket.

"Nana, do you happen to know where Kurt is? We haven't seen him around in a quite a while."

"Oh, I don't know." She sounded disgusted. "He may be helping the chief with something. I know he has his hands full. Slater didn't return from his lobstering trip this afternoon when he was supposed to. Chief was looking into it."

"He didn't come back yet?!" Rashelle quickly glanced at her watch and slid to the edge of her chair, anxious to hear more.

Lt. Perkins appeared in the doorway. "Ladies." His voice was firm. He was the man in command. "I need to have a word with you."

"All of us?" Amelia queried.

"That would be fine." Steady as he goes. He paused for effect or just to gather his thoughts and then continued. "Miss Pennington, first of all, we analyzed the contents of your car. We found a necklace that we have determined to belong to the missing girl."

"What!" There was a collective gasp among the three women.

"Yes, ma'am." He was looking right at Elizabeth.

What is he talking about? How is this possible? Elizabeth felt herself scarcely able to breathe. Nana jumped in to her rescue.

"Officer, there must be some mistake. That can't be possible."

"Well, ma'am. I'm afraid it is." His voice was deep and firm.

"She didn't even know the girl. None of us met her." Amelia's mind was racing.

"Is that so?" He was just as calm and collected as at the start of the conversation. This guy definitely did not have much of a sense of humor.

"As a matter of fact, it is. And Elizabeth didn't arrive here until late Friday evening because I called and asked her to come. She wouldn't have had the opportunity to even meet the guest who is missing. She couldn't possibly have any connection."

"Well, ma'am, I understand what you're saying, but it does appear there is a connection."

There was no swaying him. He turned to leave the back porch and stopped just short of the doorway. He turned and looked right at Elizabeth again. "I don't think I need to remind you what that means…stay in sight." He spun back around and left the ladies alone with their mouths hanging open.

Rashelle turned to Elizabeth. "What the hell is that supposed to mean! He can't be serious, Lizzi!" Her voice was loud and demanding.

Amelia jumped in. "Alright, Rashelle. Calm down. This whole thing will get sorted out and everything will be alright." She seemed to be trying to convince herself as she spoke. "I'm sure this is just one big misunderstanding." Without another word from any of them, she turned and exited the porch for an unknown destination. The two friends were left alone with their dinners.

They ate in silence. The food didn't taste quite as good as it had when they first sat down. It was getting late into the evening and it had been a very long day. Both of their heads were spinning. Lt. Perkins' comments didn't make any sense. Elizabeth felt anger rising up inside of her. She wasn't going to take this sitting down. She needed to do something. The trained professionals had to be missing a key piece of information. She knew these grounds and the people that worked here better than they did. "C'mon, Shelle. Let's get rid of these dishes." It was time to make themselves scarce. As an afterthought, she added, "Want to grab a glass of wine? I think better with one." The girls shared a nervous giggle, gathered their dirty plates, and headed toward the door to the kitchen that led from the porch. It was a hinged door without a window and tended to be more stubborn than the swinging door from the main dining room into the kitchen. Elizabeth turned sideways to use her shoulder to get better leverage. She gave the door a firm jolt with her entire body behind it. The door flew open so unexpectedly that she lurched into the kitchen nearly tripping over her own two feet. She struggled to hold onto her plate and keep her feet on the floor. The door thudded against something behind it and then swung back out toward Rashelle, who was standing in the doorway watching the whole thing unfold. Just as she reached out to stop the door from swinging any further toward her, Elizabeth let out a blood curdling scream.

Chapter 14

Rashelle couldn't get through the kitchen door fast enough. "What, Lizzi? What!" With her dirty dishes in her right hand, she pulled the swinging door back with her left to see what Elizabeth was looking at behind the door. Her eyes grew wide. "What happened?" Rashelle's mouth gaped open and her eyes were open wide.

There, in a heap on the floor, was the body of a middle-aged man wearing a crisp, white chef's jacket with black and white hounds tooth check pants. His jacket was stained with blood oozing from the wound caused by the chef's knife sticking out of his chest. Rashelle looked from the body to her friend and back again. She couldn't believe what she was seeing. Elizabeth had the same look of shock on her face.

Rashelle tried again. "What the hell happened?"

"I just opened the door!"

"Was he standing behind the door?" her voice had quieted to a whisper.

"I have no idea! I just pushed the door open and it hit something!"

Rashelle cupped her full hand across her mouth as if stifling a shriek. She was trying hard to comprehend the bloody mess on the kitchen floor.

"I don't think I did anything but this looks terrible!" Anger was rising inside of her. Her voice was getting louder and starting to sound desperate. She wasn't sure what to think. Her first instinct, as irrational as it was, was to run and get out of there. The lieutenant just accused her of having a connection with the missing girl and now she was standing over the body of a dead cook. She didn't even recognize him. This was not good. Could he be a guest? She took a closer look at the knife sticking out of the body and thought it looked at lot like Tony's new knife.

"Liz, let's get out of here!" Shelle yelled in a whisper. Fortunately no one was in the kitchen, but at any moment, someone could come bursting through the door and find them in a very incriminating situation.

"Shelle, we can't just walk out of here. We need to let someone know—"

"NO, WE DON'T! The next person through the doors will just have to handle it. It doesn't have to be you. He is obviously dead. He can wait. You can't do anything for him." She gestured toward the bloody man on the floor behind the door. "If Lt. Perkins sees us here, he won't waste any more time. He'll just cuff you and take you away. One way or another, you'll end up being charged. They will probably charge you with the disappearance of the Hutchins' girl, too. You have got to get outta here!" She grabbed Elizabeth with her free hand, still holding her plate and silverware, and led her back out onto the porch. They put their plates back on the table where they were sitting, exactly as they had been arranged before, as if they had just got up and walked out, never entering the kitchen. Both girls felt an awful twisting sensation in their stomachs. They knew what they had just done was not right, but neither could come up with a better idea. Stepping into the foyer they watched in horror just as Lt. Perkins was entering the dining room from the foyer. They hurried to the doorway of the dining room to see him heading straight for the kitchen door. They both gasped. "Oh, no!" one of them murmured softly. *This can't be happening.* What they did next was a split second decision, but one that they both made simultaneously.

"Lieutenant!" they shrieked in unison as he lifted his hand to push open the kitchen door. He stopped in mid-stride and turned his head to respond to the girls. The look on his face told him they had startled him.

Not trusting what Rashelle was going to blurt out next, Elizabeth did the talking. "Lt. Perkins, if you are looking for Tony, he is down at the beach." She tried to make her voice sound calmer than she felt. Hopefully her face did not have a look of terror on it.

Rashelle couldn't resist chiming in as well, "And if you are looking for coffee, Tony set up a beverage station in the sitting room." She motioned across the foyer.

Perkins paused for a moment and examined the girls' faces for a hint of ulterior motive. His hand was still poised near the door. He considered their suggestions, turned the rest of his body toward them, and lowered his hand. "Thank you, ladies." His voice was low and steady. He headed back across the dining room, the sound of his firm footsteps on the old wooden floor echoed in the empty room.

The girls stood back while he passed them, and then breathed a huge sigh of relief. They followed behind him, making their exit to the left up the carpeted stairs. Out of their line of sight, the kitchen staff were returning to the inn through the back porch, each one loaded down with the essentials necessary for the clambake on the beach. Once the girls reached the landing and they thought they were out of Perkins' earshot, they stopped long enough to strategize. Elizabeth turned toward Rashelle, grabbing onto both forearms. Her voice was barely a whisper. "Now what!" She was scared.

"Let's go to my room. I've got a stash there."

Elizabeth was puzzled. "A what?! A stash? What stash? What do you have—" She was getting the wrong idea.

"Wine…I've got a little fridge with a few bottles of wine—." Rashelle set her straight.

"I don't care about the wine!" She was losing her patience. "If you haven't noticed, I have a couple other things to worry about right now." Her voice was rising with her frustration and fear.

Rashelle slowed the tempo and lowered the volume. "Oh, I know you do. But I know you could use a glass of wine, too." She practically winked.

Lizzi almost smiled. She would have, under different circumstances. She thought about Rashelle's suggestion for a moment but changed her mind. "No, not now. I'm going to go down to the beach and take a look around."

"The beach. A look around?! It's dark out!"

"I know. The moon is out, though. I just need to take a look down there. Satisfy my curiosity."

"Satisfy your curiosity." Rashelle did not like the idea at all. "And I suppose you want me to go with you."

"That would be great, but you don't have to." Elizabeth was sounding braver than she felt.

"Alright, let's go." Rashelle reluctantly reached out to take her friend's arm. Together, the two did an about face and started heading back down the stairs. "Hold it!" They both stopped abruptly on the second step. Elizabeth had to reach out and grab onto the railing to keep herself from falling forward from their momentum. Rashelle reached into her pants pocket and retrieved her vibrating cell phone. "Hello?" Elizabeth listened to the one sided conversation. "Uh-huh…Yes, of course…Yes…I'll take care of it right away." She flipped her phone closed and turned to look at Elizabeth. Awkwardness hung in the air. "I'm sorry. There are some things I need to take care of…I…I can't go with you."

"What kind of things? They can't wait?"

Shelle shook her head, but remained tight-lipped about what she needed to do specifically.

Elizabeth looked at her puzzled for a moment and finally decided she wouldn't pursue it. She let it go. She didn't need to stick her nose in her friend's business when it pertained to her job. She needed to be a good friend and just trust her. Of course, that was the tough part, knowing who to trust around there, even her friend. Rashelle didn't seem as forthcoming with information as Elizabeth would like. "Okay. I understand. You do what you need to do. I'll go alone."

Rashelle gasped. "Are you serious? I'm so sorry. I would go with you if I could—"

"Don't sweat it. I'll just meet you back here…in your room. Okay? We'll have that glass of wine."

"That sounds great. See you then." Rashelle was obviously very uncomfortable with her going alone. "Ya know, Liz. I'll try to finish up quickly and meet you down there…on the beach. Okay?"

"Great." She tried to make it sound as noncommittal as possible. She really didn't expect to see Rashelle on the beach.

They continued down to the bottom of the stairs to the lobby. Rashelle took a left into the office and Elizabeth headed toward the front door. Rashelle watched from behind the reception desk as her friend exited the inn.

Elizabeth reached the bottom of the stairs of the porch and set off across the front lawn at a steady gate, determined in her purpose. She noticed that the grass was getting a little long. It tickled her ankles as she trekked through it. Her feet crunched on the gravel in the circular driveway and then she was back onto the grass heading for the top of the stairway leading down to the beach. The hedges along the edge of the cliff were getting scraggly and unshaped. Renard and Girard had been slacking off a bit.

A brisk breeze off the water caressed her face. She slowed her pace and took a deep breath as she neared the stairs. The salty sea air was invigorating to her. It was dark and the fog hung in the air, but the half-moon provided some illumination as she started to descend the wooden stairs. She held onto the railing, trying not to look down, and focused on where she was placing her feet. This wasn't her favorite set of stairs to walk on. She moved at a steady pace, not too fast to risk tripping or slipping, but fast enough so she could cover ground in a reasonable amount of time. Elizabeth just wanted to take a look at the beach, to see for herself that everything was as it should be. She could hear the waves crashing against the beach and she could just make them out. The impending storm had stirred up the ocean ahead of it.

Suddenly she heard the whir of a car engine nearby. It sounded like it was approaching the circular drive. Elizabeth headed back up the stairs far enough to peak around the bushes. She watched the lights of a car drive toward her before it rounded the circular drive and came to a stop near the front door of the inn. It looked like a small car, perhaps a sports car. It was hard to tell in the limited light of the grounds and the glare of the inn's porch lights. Who had been allowed in? Wasn't the inn in lockdown? She watched to see who got out. Instead, the car remained idling at the base of the porch stairs. The front door opened and a female headed down the stairs—Rashelle!—opened the door to the passenger side of the car and slipped in quickly. What was she doing?! Who was she going with?! The small car sped off leaving a cloud of dust from the gravel it had stirred up in its wake. Elizabeth was left to wonder if that was the same sports car that had passed her on the way in on Friday evening. Then it dawned on her. The man driving that car… was Aaron, the tennis pro who had been fired last spring. She wondered how Rashelle knew who he was. Elizabeth's mind was racing. She needed more answers from her friend. In the meantime, she was going to go back to her task of surveying the beach. She turned toward the stairway and slowly headed back down.

She reached the bottom step and took her first step onto the sandy beach. She hesitated before setting off down the beach. She felt very alone. Suddenly her idea of heading down by herself didn't seem so smart. Her eyes were adjusting to the dim light. The fog was limiting visibility. She took a deep breath and started off down the beach. There didn't seem to be anything amiss so far but she couldn't see very far in front of her. The fog was getting thicker. She could hear the waves crashing on the beach to her right. A few more steps and Elizabeth's foot landed on something hard that was embedded in the sand. She reached down and picked up an object that looked cylindrical. "Corn cob." She sounded disgusted, even though there was no one there to hear. A leftover from the clambake on the beach. "No one knows how to pick up after themselves." She tossed the cob to the side, shook her head, and pressed on.

After a few minutes of shuffling through the sand, she could just make out the outline of the rocky outcroppings on the east end of the beach. Elizabeth kept walking, feeling very vulnerable in the darkness on the beach. Suddenly Elizabeth stopped in her tracks. There was something ahead, partially obscured by the fog. It looked like a person standing several yards ahead of her. Was someone on the beach with her? It looked like a young girl. Elizabeth kept squinting her eyes, trying to see more clearly through the fog. Her feet were frozen in place. The figure seemed to be looking at her. Who could it be? Was it the fog playing tricks on her? Slowly she started to move her feet toward the girl. The fog was suddenly thicker where the girl was standing, making it more difficult for her to see. "Who's there?!" Elizabeth called to her. Would she be able to hear her over the roar of the surf? No response. She could no longer make out a figure. The fog had completely obliterated her view. She kept walking in the direction she had seen the girl. It seemed like she would have caught up to her by now. She kept walking. "Hello!" Where could she have gone? Had she really been there at all? Elizabeth stood still, paralyzed with fear. She was barely breathing. The fog swirled around her. She could feel the moisture caressing her face. She listened to the waves crashing against the shore. Her thoughts turned to Slater and his boat, *The Seward Lady*.

It was a modest-sized boat, probably forty feet in length with a main deck and a lower level that only Slater and his crew frequented. The main deck was set up with bench seating along the sides at the bow and stern so the passengers could observe Slater pulling in lobster traps. About a third of the way back from the bow was a very primitive captain's deck with a wheel, a two way radio, and the throttle behind a simple windshield that protected the captain on three sides from inclement weather. On the right side of the boat was a rig with a pulley system that he used to pull up the lobster traps. He would steer the boat close to one of his buoys that was bobbing on top of the water. There was a rope attached to the buoy, the other end of which was attached to the lobster trap that was sitting on the ocean floor. Each lobster fisherman had one or two specific color patterns that he or she had the exclusive right to use on their buoys so that there would be no mistaking which buoys belonged to which fisherman. Most could tell you who owned each one. Slater would use a long handled tool with a hook on the end of it to snag the buoy and pull it up onto the side of the boat. He would then raise it up over the rig, threading the rope onto the pulley, and use the crank to wind in the rope and pull the trap to the surface. Fingers were always crossed so that, after all the cranking, there would be a lobster in the trap and it would be large enough to keep. There were very strict guidelines as to which lobsters were large enough to keep and each lobsterman had a measuring tool handy to verify his catch. In addition, any female lobsters that were carrying eggs must be returned to the sea, even if they were otherwise large enough to keep, so the eggs would have the chance to hatch. These rules were in place so that the lobsters were not over fished and the industry could sustain itself. Sometimes the lobsters were just large enough. Other times the lobsters were too small or there was no lobster in the trap at all. Lobstering could be a very frustrating industry, one that required long days of back breaking work. Those who lasted any length of time usually had lobstering in their blood and came from a long line of lobstermen.

She wondered with a sad heart what had become of Slater and his passengers. This was absolutely awful. Poor Slater.

Elizabeth suddenly felt very vulnerable out on the beach alone, shrouded in fog. She had seen enough. She suddenly needed to get out of there. Little did she know, if she had taken just a few more steps, she would have kicked something very hard that was lying in the sand. A life preserver with a name printed on it: *The Seward Lady*.

She turned to start heading back across the beach toward the wooden stairs. Elizabeth stopped in her tracks. In the time she had been standing there remembering Slater and his vessel, the fog rolled in and completely swallowed the beach. She could only see a few yards in front of her. Elizabeth was fighting panic rising up inside of her. She needed to remain calm. The ocean was on her left and she could hear the waves crashing onto the beach. She just needed to keep that sound on her left as she headed back across the beach. Without anything to look at besides the white fog all around her, she started her feet moving again and reminisced about the times she and her grandmother would walk the beach after a storm when the waves were still crashing in. The sound was like a roar. The large shells she harvested from the beach faintly mimicked the sound if you held them up to your ear. Right after a storm was the best time to find wonderful shells and sand dollars that had been washed onto the beach by the powerful waves. You had to get to the beach before everyone else found the treasures that the sea had left behind.

Elizabeth had covered a few yards across the sand when she realized the texture of the sand had changed beneath her feet. What had been soft and transient was now flat and firm. She was on wet sand! She was veering toward the ocean! She stopped in her tracks again. She resumed her trekking at a snail's pace, a little further to the right. Soon she was back on the soft sand. She kept walking slowly with her arms out in front of her, hoping to feel the railing of the stairs. Suddenly a rational thought entered her mind. She decided to try sidestepping. If she was heading in the right direction, then if she sidestepped to the right, eventually she would run into the cliff. Then she could just run her right hand along the cliff wall and walk forward until she found the stairway. Slowly she stepped to the right. Methodically moving her right foot, and then bringing her left up next to it. Over and over she did this. Was it working? Or was she veering too far to the right and heading back toward the rocky outcroppings? She listened for the waves. She thought they were still directly to her left so she resumed her sidestepping with her right arm extended, hoping to feel the side of the cliff. Step one, two. One, two. One, two. After several minutes, her right hand pushed against a cold, hard, wet surface. The cliff! Now she picked up her pace and headed toward the stairway with her right hand running along the cliff, brushing across the occasional tuft of grasses or cliff roses along the way. She held her left hand out in front of her. *One foot in front of the other. Keep going. Steady pace. Keep breathing.* Suddenly the palm of her hand bumped against something hard. "Ow!" *The stairway railing!* She breathed a sigh of relief and headed up the stairs, with one hand firmly on the railing.

When she reached the top, the fog was not quite as thick as it had been down on the beach, but it was rolling in off the water quite rapidly and starting to obscure the inn and its outbuildings. The roar of a car engine caught her attention again. A car was already heading back down the inn's access road. Between the fog and the distance between the car and herself, she couldn't really tell what it looked like. If anyone had gotten out of the car, they were already safely inside the inn. She retraced her steps across the front lawn in the hopes of hooking up with Rashelle again—if she was back yet.

To Elizabeth's surprise, Rashelle met her at the front door of the inn. She imagined that her face showed what she was thinking. She was dying to ask her where she had been and whom she had been with, but she kept her mouth shut. It was probably none of her business. "Alright, let's go get that wine now."

Rashelle nodded.

Chapter 15

The two friends headed up the stairs, down the hall and turned into the third room on the right, right across from Elizabeth's room. It was a mirror image of Elizabeth's room. Rashelle pulled the chilled bottle of chardonnay out of a mini fridge that she was apparently using as a table, on the side of the bed closest to the door. She had the bottle opened in no time and was quick to apologize that it was not Lizzi's favorite, as she poured two large glasses.

"Oh, at this point, I'll take anything." Elizabeth eagerly put the glass to her lips and took a sip. The friends looked deeply into each other's eyes. The event in the kitchen earlier in the evening came rushing back to both of them. They were in territory they had never visited before and never dreamed they would ever be near. They both stood there and sipped the dry white wine, lost in their quiet thoughts for a while.

Finally the designer from the city spoke, "Rashelle, what the hell is going on here? And how did I get so involved?" She was shaking her head in disbelief. "It seems like things only got worse after I got here—like I've made it all worse."

"Lizzi, don't be ridiculous. This whole thing has nothing to do with you. Unfortunately you've gotten all wrapped up in it just by being here. Your intentions were good. You came to help."

"And I made it worse by leaving the scene of a crime earlier! What was I thinking?" She turned and headed for the chair on the other side of the bed.

"Liz, you had to!" She suddenly realized their voices were escalating. Her Brooklyn accent was coming through loud and clear. She tried to bring it down a notch or two. "You know how that would have looked if someone had seen us." With the heel of her hand she jammed the cork back down into the neck of the wine bottle and placed it back in the small refrigerator and flopped down on the bed.

Elizabeth whipped around and looked right at Rashelle. "Thank God no one did! I thought sure someone was going to walk in on us. And that was a close call with the lieutenant." She dropped into the comfortable floral armchair.

"That's for sure."

"I wonder how long it will take them to find the body." She kicked off her shoes and propped her feet up on Rashelle's bed.

"I don't even want to think about it." Unbeknownst to them, the body had already been discovered. The lieutenant was reviewing a CD that had mysteriously shown up in his squad car that was related to the corpse in the kitchen.

The two friends polished off the bottle of wine, opened a second, and got about halfway through that one when they fell asleep, Lizzi in the chair and Shelle on top of the covers on her bed. Neither one heard the officer knocking on the door across the hall in the middle of the night.

Seconds later the two friends were awakened by a hard knock on Rashelle's door. It startled them. They both struggled to get to their feet, still half asleep, trying to grasp what was going on. Rashelle was chilled from lying on top of the covers most of the night. She wrapped her arms around herself. Elizabeth immediately grabbed her neck that was screaming from being in an awkward position while she slept in the chair. She groaned and rubbed the side of her neck hoping for some relief. The firm knocking began again, this time even louder. Rashelle rubbed both eyes with her hands, trying desperately to wake up, as she headed for the door. They both were afraid of who it was going to be. Rashelle glanced back to Elizabeth as she grabbed the doorknob, her forehead wrinkled with concern. Slowly she turned the knob and pulled the door open.

There stood Kurt. Behind him was Lieutenant Perkins. Kurt was holding a computer disc. Perkins had a laptop computer tucked under one arm. "Ladies…" Perkins spoke sharply. "You have a little explaining to do." Kurt pushed his way into the room with the lieutenant right behind him. Rashelle's lack of sleep left her in no mood for their intrusion.

"What are you doing?!" She was already shouting. "What time is it? How dare you barge in here!" She was furious. "What the hell are you doing?"

"SILENCE! Miss Harper, Miss Pennington, you both need to take a look at this." The lieutenant wasn't taking questions.

The girls' eyes grew wide. They ventured a glance at each other while the lieutenant made his way toward the table by the window. He and Mitchell got busy setting up the computer. Elizabeth noticed through the window that the sky was getting slightly brighter, but the sun was nowhere to be seen. It was still very early morning. She wondered what kind of a day it was going to be. It couldn't be good if it was starting out with a state police lieutenant barging into your room, looking for a chat.

The lieutenant seemed to be all set to share his discovery with them. He turned around and looked from Elizabeth to Rashelle and back again. "Alright ladies, see if you can explain this." He pushed a button that set the screen in motion. The girls stepped closer, tentatively, not sure what they were going to see.

They stood there watching carefully as the video advanced and they started to recognize the setting. It was the kitchen in the inn. Suddenly they recognized themselves. They both gasped. How could it be? They were suddenly reliving the nightmare from which they had fled hours earlier. How could they possibly be watching what they had been replaying in their minds over and over again?

There they were, standing over the body in a heap on the floor in the kitchen. Elizabeth chanced a look at Kurt but his eyes weren't sympathetic. *What is going on? Who could possibly have filmed what happened earlier? No one was around!* Lizzi's head was spinning. She looked to Lt. Perkins who returned an expectant gaze. She realized she had some explaining to do, but she wondered if she needed a lawyer before she opened her mouth.

To Elizabeth's surprise and horror, Rashelle spoke first. "It was all my fault. I told her to run."

"We can see that." Kurt was unusually quiet. Rashelle realized the video did not leave anything to the imagination, except who shot the footage. "What we would like to know is what happened before the video starts." It dawned on them that the video started after they burst through the kitchen door and found the body. The video implied they were caught on the CD after they committed a heinous act.

It was Elizabeth's turn. "Look, I know this looks bad—"

"Yeah, it looks bad!" The lieutenant's voice was booming. "Looks like you guys have been caught red-handed!" He was not amused.

"Red-handed!! We didn't do anything! We walked in on this!"

"So why did you run? That makes you look a little guilty when you run."

"I know. It wasn't the smartest idea." She turned toward Rashelle and glared. "We were scared with everything that was going on at the inn. But you have to believe me that we just stumbled into the kitchen and found this body. I don't even know who it is. Besides, you had just accused me of having some sort of connection with the missing girl. I was scared!"

"Well, lucky for you we are more interested with who shot the video, than in what you were doing. It is entirely possible that the person filming the event set it all up. Who do you think it is? What can you tell me about the scenario? Is there anything unusual that you noticed?"

Elizabeth realized she didn't have a lot of information to help the lieutenant. "I wish I knew..."

Perkins slammed the laptop shut. "Great!" He snatched up the computer, turned and stormed out of the room leaving the tennis pro, or whoever he was, behind. The three just stood there and looked at each other. The silence was deafening. Finally, Kurt threw out a suggestion to break the ice.

"Why don't we go get some coffee? Looks like it will be a long day."

"Yeah, great idea. We'll catch up with you." She still wondered whose side he was on.

Kurt turned to connect with Lizzi. He looked into her eyes.

"...we, uh...," she realized they were fully clothed in yesterday's outfits, never having taken the time to change into pajamas earlier. "We just need to freshen up a bit." That sounded plausible to her. He shook his head slightly.

"Yeah, okay. See you downstairs." He headed for the door. His dirty blond hair was looking tired and limp, probably the way the rest of his body felt. Who knows how much sleep he had gotten since the girl's disappearance. For some reason, he seemed to be very involved in the investigation. Maybe the police were just keeping him where they could keep track of him.

Once he had cleared the doorway, Rashelle and Elizabeth's eyes locked. Lizzi followed his footsteps to the door and watched him head down the hallway. Gently she closed the door and turned to Shelle. "We need to find out who filmed us in the kitchen!" She restrained herself from saying 'I told you we shouldn't have run!' She needed to focus on being more productive than that. "Let's go grab some caffeine. We need to wake up and get in the game."

Rashelle mumbled something unintelligible, but followed along behind her friend as she headed downstairs.

Chapter 16

After an unsettling awakening, Elizabeth and Rashelle found themselves in the sitting room in search of coffee. They drained the coffee carafe leftover from last night that had been set up in the corner, into two Styrofoam cups. Rashelle sipped hers black while Elizabeth stirred in a little sugar and then pressed the cup to her lips. The liquid morning was luke-warm, but welcome under the circumstances. Kurt was already sipping his early morning java, standing over by the windows on the front of the inn, looking out to the tempestuous ocean. Elizabeth and Rashelle didn't dare look at each other or at Kurt. They busied themselves with their coffee at the little table in the corner, feigning sleepiness.

The lieutenant burst through the front door with two people in tow. Elizabeth looked up and was puzzled to see Mr. and Mrs. Hutchins. They were swiftly escorted into the dining room where a sleepy Chief Austin and other police officers were milling about, and were no doubt dealing with the body discovered in the kitchen. Perkins was obviously interested in what connection the Hutchins might have with the victim.

Elizabeth glanced to Rashelle. She had to work at keeping her facial expression under control. Kurt appeared from behind them and exited the sitting room heading for the dining room. It was as if he had a silent pager and had been beckoned. Once he was lost in the crowd Elizabeth felt comfortable to speak.

"Shelle, we need to get out of here!"

"What are you talking about?" Her face showed particular confusion.

"Trust me." She grabbed her friend by the arm and headed through the lobby toward the back porch, keeping her feet as quiet as possible. They passed through the porch. Lizzi tried to put out of her head the scene they had witnessed and become part of a few hours earlier as they neared the door to the kitchen. Quietly they slipped out the back door of the porch leading to the backyard. Lizzi let go of Shelle's arm long enough to turn around and catch the screen door so it wouldn't slam shut. She re-established her grip on Rashelle's arm and led her toward the path to Acadia House. Rashelle was starting to catch on. Their feet moved swiftly and quietly down the path. It was still quite dark out.

Before long they were heading up the steps to the porch in front of the Hutchins' room. Rashelle knew what was on Lizzi's mind. She watched as her friend reached for the door knob. It turned slightly, but soon met with resistance. They must have locked it behind them when Perkins retrieved them.

"Who locks their door in Maine?" Elizabeth threw her hands up in the air.

Rashelle decided that was a rhetorical question. She watched as Elizabeth tried the windows on the left side of the door, grunting with each attempt. Both stubbornly wouldn't budge. She headed down the steps of the porch with Rashelle right behind her and turned at the bottom to go around the side of the building. The grass sloped downward, dropping to an elevation several feet below the windows that ran along the side of the Hutchins' room. She was grateful that theirs was an end unit. There were three double hung windows of equal size that were spaced evenly along the wall. She reached up to the nearest one and grabbed onto the window sill but couldn't get enough leverage to push it open. Rashelle quickly laced her fingers together with her palms facing upward and formed a stirrup for Elizabeth to step into. "Here, Lizzi! I can give you a boost!"

Without hesitation, she stepped into her friend's hands and found herself sliding up the clapboards on the side of the building, clawing with her hands. She was waist high with the sill, but she knew she was working on borrowed time so she very quickly gave the bottom half of the window a push upwards. To her surprise it moved! They had forgotten to lock their windows, as least this one. "Shelle, we did it!" In their excitement, they both jiggled a little too far in opposite directions and Elizabeth toppled out of Rashelle's hands. Head first, she plummeted toward the ground. She reached out with her hands in time to break her fall, landing in a heap on the grass, a little stunned. Under different circumstances, this would have been hilarious, but neither was laughing.

"Liz, I am so sorry!" Rashelle rushed to her side.

"Shhhhhh!" She struggled to her feet and brushed off her pants. She didn't have time for apologies. They were speaking in hushed tones, "Don't worry about it. Just get me up there again. It's our way in."

They repeated the successful steps leading up to Elizabeth's fall, this time being careful not to get too exuberant in their success. Elizabeth pushed upward on the window and it slowly moved in the right direction a little further. She could feel her foot slipping in Rashelle's grip. She gave the window one more push and it opened to a full twelve inches. Hopefully it would be enough to squeeze through. She grabbed onto the sill with both hands and hoisted herself up with a grunt. For one crazy moment she was balanced on the sill on her stomach, half-in and half-out, with her head aiming toward the floor and her feet dangling outside. She felt stuck! It was almost comical. It reminded her of a time when she was little and she tried on an old ring that was in her grandmother's jewelry box. It must have been a ring that was meant for an infant or at least someone smaller than her at the time. It really didn't fit little Lizzi but she really liked the little pearl ring. She kept pushing until it was all the way on her finger, so she could admire it. When it came time to remove the ring, it was even more stubborn than when she struggled to get it on. The more she pulled, the more her finger swelled. Elizabeth was stuck with her grandmother's ring on her finger. A ring that she didn't have permission to be wearing. Finally, in tears, she had to go find her grandmother and tell her what she had done. The pain in her finger was nothing compared with her fear of her Nana's reaction. Remarkably, Amelia quietly helped Elizabeth remove the antique ring with soap and hot water, with few words spoken. Little Lizzi's lasting feeling about the event was one of tremendous guilt. She would have felt better if her grandmother had at least raised her voice. She often wondered what the story was behind that ring, but never dared to ask.

There was no turning back. She was practically in. Obviously there was no comfy couch below this window. Her dangling arms could feel nothing soft to land on upon entry. She would have to try to land as gracefully as possible. A couple more wiggles and her rear end just cleared the bottom of the open window. She could feel the floor with her hands. She pulled her legs in and spilled into the Hutchins' room with a quiet thump and a groan.

Rashelle watched in silence as Elizabeth disappeared into the window. She stood alone in the quiet before the dawn, with the dark woods behind her. The cool ocean air gently played with her hair.

"Pssst!" Rashelle was startled. There was Elizabeth standing at the end of the porch in front of the Hutchins' room motioning for her to move. "Come on!" She was beckoning her to slip in the front door. Rashelle quickly headed to the porch and followed her friend inside. They closed and locked the door behind them to leave it exactly the way they had found it.

Once inside they turned and looked at each other. "What are we doing?" Rashelle didn't seem so sure about this. She probably didn't want to get fired.

"We just need to have a closer peek. It could be nothing, but something about these guys…well, I don't know. We have the opportunity because Perkins has them tied up for a while."

"Hopefully it's long enough." The assistant day manager at the Pennington Point Inn was looking a little uncomfortable that they had just broken into a guest's room.

The room was set up in an open floor plan divided into three areas, each with its own purpose. Once inside the door, there was a sitting area with a solid blue, denim loveseat positioned under the front window and two tulip chairs, upholstered in a complimentary floral, located across from the love seat. A floor lamp in the corner to the left was the only light on and was set on low, providing a soft glow on the room. The focal point of the seating arrangement was a distressed pine armoire positioned on the outside wall to the right of the lamp. The doors were closed but, presumably, they concealed a television. The window Elizabeth had entered through was to the right of the armoire. The girls glanced at the coffee table in the center of the seating area. There were magazines tossed haphazardly across the top of it, as well as a couple of soda cans and wrappers from snack food bags.

They started moving away from the front door, further into the room, away from the only light source. They didn't dare turn on any other lights so as not to draw attention to activity in the room. Elizabeth led the way with Rashelle right behind her. Their feet were moving slowly but methodically. Lizzi saw something out of the corner of her eye toward her left. She stopped her feet and Rashelle nearly ran into her from behind. Elizabeth glanced back at the windows on the left. Softly she gasped. The face of a young girl was at the window that she had shimmied into earlier. Elizabeth's eyes grew wide.

"What?!" Rashelle whispered but was desperate to know what her friend was looking at.

"Look at the window...the window I came in before!"

"What?!" Rashelle obviously wasn't seeing what she was seeing, even though she was looking right at it.

Elizabeth shuddered as she watched the girl slowly fade away. "Don't worry about it. It was nothing. Must have been my imagination. Let's keep going." She tried to shake off the image of the young girl.

The next area contained a small dining table that was cluttered with papers. There were also what looked like a fax machine, a color printer, and a laptop computer taking up the center of the table. This area made the Hutchins' room look more like an office than a vacation destination. There were some other items on a credenza against the outside wall, but it was hard to tell exactly what they were in the limited light. Elizabeth furrowed her brow and kept walking. She didn't know how much time they had before the Hutchins were going to come strolling back through the front door. This would not look good. They had to get out of there quickly. Beyond the dining area was a small kitchenette with a microwave, mini-fridge, sink, and some cupboards. Straight ahead was a doorway into the bedroom area, which was pitch black, but they didn't have the luxury of turning on any other lights. Just inside the door, they stood still for a moment to allow their eyes to adjust to the dark room. To the right was a small bathroom and the bed was to the left. It was so dark in the corners of the room that they couldn't tell what was really there. Hopefully nothing was hiding in the shadows. Straight ahead was the back door. They started to move again very slowly. The girls had just slipped past the queen-sized bed when they heard the distinctive sound of breaking glass behind them, near the front of the unit. They froze in place and looked at each other. Hopefully they were concealed in the shadows of the rear of the room. Elizabeth whispered, "Let's go!" She grabbed Rashelle and pulled her toward the back door that opened to stairs leading down to the grass below. Quietly they exited, holding their breaths, closing the door softly behind them. They prayed their presence would not be detected. Once clear of the stairs, they ran along the back of the Acadia House trying to clear the area as quickly as possible. When they got to the end of the building they turned right to head back toward the main building. They weren't expecting company.

"Good morning, ladies." Elizabeth and Rashelle looked like two of The Three Stooges, trying to stop without bumping into Mitchell. "Funny time of the day to be out for a stroll. What brings you out here?"

Elizabeth and Rashelle hesitated and didn't dare look at each other. They knew this looked rather suspicious, but Elizabeth was getting tired of Kurt's questions. She decided to act belligerent.

"Oh, for God sake, would you get out of our way. I could ask you the same question." She moved toward him intending to push her way through, but he reached out and grabbed her arm so firmly that it hurt. What had she been thinking, that she could really muscle her way past him? Reality check.

"You listen to me and you listen good." He pulled her toward him. His face was inches away from hers. His tone was almost scolding. Rashelle stood there helplessly watching the scene unfold. "This is not the time for being a smart ass. I don't have to tell you what this looks like after the video we watched earlier. There is a murder investigation in progress and your cooperation is imperative." He loosened his grip and let her pull back slightly but still had her in his control.

"Okay, okay. We just needed a little fresh air…and thought it wouldn't hurt to see if there was anything unusual going on outside since it seemed like everyone else was inside." Elizabeth held her breath, hoping her off the cuff explanation would fly. He glared into her eyes for a few seconds longer as if he was considering her excuse, and then slowly released his grip. She fell backwards, but caught herself after taking a couple steps in reverse. She was indignant that he had treated her that way.

"Kurt!" Rashelle didn't like the way their encounter was deteriorating.

He shot her a look of annoyance. "Oh, give it a rest! We are all under a lot of pressure right now. We don't need anyone fooling around, sticking their noses where they don't belong." He looked from Rashelle to Elizabeth and back again. "Follow me." His tone was gruff. He sounded tired and angry.

The girls looked at each other and decided to play along and follow Kurt as he headed back to the inn. They were both heaving a sigh of relief. Perhaps they had been able to slip out of the Hutchins' room without being detected. They got in a single file behind the frustrated tennis pro, like they were back in elementary school heading for gym class. The horizon was getting a little lighter. It was almost daybreak. It was an overcast, Sunday morning with an ominous gray sky; a harbinger of worse weather to come. The dark clouds were…like a blanket of sadness that enrobed the inn.

Chapter 17

The threesome re-entered the inn through the front door where the aroma of fresh brewed coffee greeted them. In the time they were gone, Anthony had put out food for everyone. Instead of the usual elaborate weekend brunch that he and his staff usually prepared, there was a simple breakfast buffet spread out on long narrow tables just inside the entrance to the dining room. It was less a celebration of food and more a basic meal to keep everyone going, nothing fancy, just the basics; scrambled eggs, waffles, buttermilk pancakes, fruit salad, bacon, and sausage. There were urns with coffee and hot water for other beverages. The plates were even sturdy disposables to help keep things simple. A toaster stood by, plugged in, ready to make toast or to crisp a bagel or English muffin. The two friends grabbed fresh coffee from the dining room and headed into the sitting area as directed by Kurt. They felt as though they were being babysat as Mitchell entered the room and took his place in a worn leather chair near the doorway. Elizabeth was starting to feel trapped.

With few words exchanged, they sat in silence and watched as a couple of state troopers entered the lobby of the inn through the front door, disappeared into the dining room, reappeared into the lobby with coffee and food to go, and exited through the front door. At least the troopers were being well fed.

Before long, Amelia appeared at the guest reception window. She appeared to be keeping busy with matters behind the desk. She looked up to see the quiet occupants of the drawing room. "Well, good morning, everyone!" She tried to sound as cheerful as she could manage, looking particularly tired this morning.

"Morning, Nana."

"Morning."

"Morning, Amelia."

"Did you help yourself to breakfast?"

"No, not yet. We'll get it in a minute, Nana. We thought we would start with coffee."

Voices at the dining room doorway announced the re-emergence into the lobby of Lt. Perkins, of the distinguished Maine State Police, with Chief Austin right behind him.

"Good morning, Lieutenant. Good morning, Chief." Amelia decided to come out from behind the reception desk. They mumbled something in response. Instead of lingering with them, she joined the threesome in the sitting room. The two officers remained in the lobby area, talking quietly between themselves for a few minutes before entering the sitting room behind Amelia. Elizabeth started to feel uncomfortable, boxed in. It looked as though they were going to be in for a briefing or an interrogation.

No one heard Renard quietly slink up behind them. His head was heavy, shoulders slumped, arms down at each side, a pistol in his right hand. He looked disheveled; his clothes were wrinkled and dirty. His brown, shoulder-length hair was tossed about his head. You could almost detect a foul odor emanating from him, Pig Pen straight out of the Peanuts comic strip, just sixty years older. When he spoke, everyone spun around in sync toward him. There was an air of precision in the movement as in a military maneuver. Everyone was on edge when they saw who was speaking. Perkins and Austin backed further away from him to give him some space. They looked apprehensive.

"I've held the secret in for too long...It's time I confessed."

There was a muffled gasp from someone. He had everyone's undivided attention. He spoke as though he was talking to himself, gesturing with the gun from time to time. He looked anxious, desperate.

"It was an accident. I was only trying to help. I didn't mean for her to get hurt..." His voice was cracking. He was starting to break down. The lieutenant, who was positioned to Renard's right, was keeping a close eye on him, on his gun. Renard was becoming distraught as he unfolded the story. He had a captive audience. Suddenly he looked directly at Elizabeth and he became very uncomfortable, shuffling his feet.

"I'm so sorry, Miss Pennington...to your grandmother, too. I wish I could change it all. But I can't. I've ruined everything..." He burst into sobs, which the trooper took as a sign to move in. Renard detected movement and recoiled, pointing his gun at him. "NO! DON'T MOVE! DON'T COME NEAR ME!" he lashed out at the officer, his eyes possessed with terror. The situation was deteriorating quickly. He was a desperate man, seemingly with nothing to lose. They all had to proceed cautiously. Elizabeth tried to look around the room discretely without making much movement. This guy was a ticking time bomb and there had to be a way to calm him down. The trooper wasn't much help. Now, he was undoubtedly gun shy. She decided to take action.

"Renard," she spoke as softly and gently as she could, like a mother speaking to a small child, hoping to diffuse his anger. "Renard no one is going to hurt you." She spoke slowly and deliberately. "Just talk to us. Go on with your story. What happened?"

"Miss Pennington, I'm so sorry."

"I know you are. You didn't mean for things to happen the way they did. It was an accident." Her voice was very calming.

"Yes!" He looked right at her, spoke directly to her. She understood. His face showed recognition. As far as he was concerned, no one else was in the room. He was talking with Elizabeth. Sweet, adorable, little Lizzi who had grown into a beautiful woman. She had always been so kind to him. He had had a wonderful fantasy that someday she would care deeply for him. She would see what a good job he did taking care of her Pennington Point Inn and re-alize how much he cared for it, how much he cared for her.

"So keep going, Renard. Tell us how it went."

The room got very quiet. Renard averted his eyes from hers. He seemed to be trying to recall the details, gathering his thoughts. Perhaps he was embarrassed to be confessing to her. He raised his left arm, extended his fingertips to his forehead, and rubbed away the tension. His right arm was limp at his side, the gun dangling from his pudgy hand. He regained his composure. He picked up his head and looked directly at the far wall across the room, avoid-ing all eye contact. He continued.

"The door to her room was open and I saw she needed help. I don't remember exactly what she was doing…hanging something at a window or something. She was up on a chair. The window was open. I didn't mean for anything to happen. I know I'm not sup-posed to go in a girl's room, but I was just trying to help. Girard always told me that. I knew that…he knew I knew….well, lately he kept saying he was going to tell if I didn't, so I made him be quiet." He broke down in sobs again.

"Renard, it's okay." She glanced at Perkins and Mitchell to confirm that they were holding steady. She—they—needed to hear his story. "What happened?" she implored.

"I must have scared her—I didn't mean to! I guess she didn't know I was there. When I asked her if she needed help she spun around quickly on the chair and lost her balance." His eyes were glossing over as if he were relieving the horror. "She fell backwards through the open window. It was awful. I tried to grab her before she fell but it happened so quickly. I couldn't get to her in time. I ran outside and she was lying there on the ground all contorted, not moving. I knew she was dead. I'm so sorry…" The weight of his confession was too much for him. He dropped to one knee and his head drooped. As if on cue, Mitchell and Perkins lunged for him from either side and tackled him to the ground. The tennis pro skillfully kicked Renard's gun well out of his reach while the trooper cuffed him. A well-orchestrated team maneuver. The rest of the room heaved a collective sigh of relief. The two muscle men hoisted Renard to his feet. His shoulders slumped. His hands were shackled behind his back.

Elizabeth felt anger rising up inside of her. *How could Renard have let this happen?* She decided she wasn't finished with him yet. She jumped up and lunged toward the trio. She grabbed Kurt's forearm to impede his progress toward the door. "So, Renard, where is she now?" She spoke directly at him and the tone of her voice was a loosely veiled attempt to hide her anger. She needed the rest of the story. She thought they all deserved to hear it. She got as close to him as she dared to be sure she heard every word.

"I buried her in the woods," he mumbled, seemingly to himself. Elizabeth could smell his rancid breath. Wrinkling her nose, she turned her head away from him and released her grip on Kurt's arm. The daring duo escorted the beast out the front door of the inn—a door he had walked through many times over the years, but this may very well be his last. He had changed everything in a horrible split second decision.

His final comment hit everyone hard. How devastating. There had been such hope that this situation would turn out positive, that the girl would be found alive, just in a lot of trouble with her parents for wandering off. One thing was certain. If he had misinterpreted her unconsciousness as absence of life, she was dead now. He had buried her in the woods. Elizabeth was still trying to get her head around Renard's bombshell. This was just terrible. Terrible for the girl's parents. Terrible for her grandmother and terrible for the inn. This could very well spell the end for a wonderful seaside inn that had been in the family for generations. No one was going to want to stay here anytime soon. Looks like the real estate attorney was going to get his way after all. Elizabeth was livid, but not yet ready to give up the fight.

Elizabeth glanced at Rashelle, and then at her grandmother. "Nana, I'm so sorry. This couldn't have turned out worse." For a passing moment, she wondered who was going to have to tell the girl's parents.

"Oh, Lizzi, it *is* awful. These poor parents. That poor little girl…at least it's over. I hate to say it. I know it sounds terrible. But I don't know how much more of this I could have taken." Her voice was barely audible. "It's so agonizing not knowing…I never even had a chance to meet her. I usually meet all of my guests, at least before they leave…" Her eyes were brimming with tears. The situation was heartbreaking.

Chapter 18

The ceiling fan on the porch was rotating lazily above Elizabeth. She was staring downward at its reflection in the bowl of her spoon. It was hypnotizing. The two friends were sharing a few minutes together trying to eat some breakfast and sort through the surprise confession they had just witnessed. Finally Elizabeth broke the silence. "It just doesn't make sense …" She was deep in thought, almost not aware she was speaking out loud. "Something that Renard told us in his confession doesn't jive…" She wrinkled her forehead, rubbing it with the outstretched fingers of her right hand, still gazing at the flickering reflection in the spoon. Suddenly she looked up at Rashelle and came alive. She scooted to the edge of her seat toward her friend. "Rashelle, think about it. He said she fell out the window backwards. The Hutchins' room is on the first floor."

Playing along for the sake of argument, Rashelle bantered back, "Well, what if she hit her head the wrong way or snapped her neck?"

"…I suppose that's possible, but from the first floor window?"

"He did say she was standing on a chair and the side windows are higher up because of the grassy slope next to the building."

"That's true…" Elizabeth considered Rashelle's retort. "But he also said he knows he is not supposed to go in the girl's room. Did he mean girl apostrophe 's' or girls apostrophe?"

Rashelle gave her a puzzled look.

Elizabeth explained, "In other words, did he mean one girl, like the guest Kelsey Hutchins or many girls—like the girls who were students at the school many years ago?"

Rashelle gasped. "Do you think he was talking about the death of that student years ago?"

"I don't know. He was certainly around back then. Besides it was a student's disappearance and *presumed death*," she corrected Rashelle's misstatement. "No body was ever found. That's why it is referred to as a mystery." She pressed on. "And didn't he say she was lying on the ground, not the porch, when he ran outside to see how she was? The porch didn't exist on that building until renovations were done to convert the school into an inn."

"Liz! What if you're right?"

"Well, it would mean we have solved the mystery of the student's disappearance, but we still have a present day mystery to solve. We may not be finished yet." She looked directly at Rashelle. "We need to find the chief. This is not over. The Hutchins' girl may still be alive."

They found Chief Austin on the phone at the front desk in the lobby. They stood off to the side of the lobby to wait patiently for him to finish. They could overhear part of his conversation even though he was obviously trying to be discreet. "...and you're sure it was from his boat...no survivors?...okay...alright...thanks... yeah...okay...thanks..." Elizabeth was feeling a little sorry for Chief Austin. He was definitely out of his league and she was sure it was a bit humiliating to have the state police swarm in and take over in his jurisdiction. He finished his conversation, hung up the phone and turned toward Elizabeth and Rashelle, who had made their way across the lobby toward him. They were each resting an elbow on the reception desk counter, like bookends.

The chief beat them to the punch. He looked like he was anxious to change the subject from his phone conversation.

"Rashelle...just the person I need to speak with." He made his way out from behind the counter and into the lobby to confront Elizabeth and Rashelle. They turned to face him when he emerged from the office door.

Elizabeth examined his face and watched for any body language to see if he meant without her, but the chief kept going. "Were you the staff person who was on duty when the Hutchins checked in?"

"Yes..." she answered cautiously. She wasn't sure where this conversation was headed.

"Did they show you any ID when they registered?"

Rashelle knew she needed to tread carefully here and choose her answer wisely. She didn't need Chief Austin turning the tables and blaming her for any of this. She was beginning to think he was getting desperate and just needed someone to pin something on. "No, they paid in cash and so I didn't need any ID. I only need to verify ID if they are paying with a credit card or personal check."

It was clear that the chief was trying to keep his cool. "So you don't really know if they really were Mr. and Mrs. Hutchins, or anyone else for that matter." The pace and volume of his voice were escalating.

She took one step closer to him, looked him in the eye, and held her ground. "Until now, we have never had a reason to question the identity of the guests who walk through our doors. We welcome them with open arms and treat them like family. That's the way we do business here. Amelia wouldn't have it any other way. And until I have been instructed otherwise, I will continue with this procedure." She held her gaze for effect.

Elizabeth had goose bumps! She was proud of her friend. Rashelle was a relatively new employee, yet she just demonstrated incredible loyalty to Amelia and the entire Pennington Point Inn family and staff. She held herself back from giving her a hug. Another time, perhaps.

Austin seemed pushed off his stance. He stammered, "Uh…
well, it certainly seems that it might have helped in this situation."
He was struggling to regain his composure.

"What do you mean? They aren't who they said they were?
They are not the Hutchins?" Elizabeth chimed in.

"Well, I didn't say that. We are still trying to confirm their
identity in West Hartford, Connecticut, which is where they said
they were from. The address they gave when they checked in is
coming up as invalid. Of course, it could be a new address. I can't
very well accuse the distressed parents of a missing girl of giving us
a fake address. Unfortunately we also haven't been able to search
for a daughter named Kelsey in any schools in the area since it's
the holiday weekend. Seems that the superintendent of the public
schools is away for the weekend and there are quite a few private
high schools in the surrounding area so it will take some time to
contact the administrators of each one. Of course, if we don't have
a valid last name…we will have to keep working on that piece."

Lizzi and Shelle were puzzled. They couldn't keep themselves
from asking, alternately, "What does this mean? Why would they
give a fake name?"

He gave them both a stern look "Who knows! We don't know
that they did yet." He didn't seem to have any patience left. "We
don't really have any answers yet." His voice had turned gruff and
he sounded thoroughly frustrated. They were practically back
on square one with a hurricane barreling down on them. He
pushed between the two of them brushing both with his shoulders. They spun around and watched him disappear through the
front doors of the inn. Their heads swiveled back to look at each
other. Suddenly, Elizabeth's observation of the inconsistencies in
Renard's story seemed rather unimportant now. She would catch
up with the chief later. Nothing was making sense right now.

Chapter 19

Elizabeth and Rashelle were left standing alone in the lobby of the inn, but not for long. Soon they could hear footsteps heading up the porch steps toward the front door of the inn. The door was opened by an unidentified hand that held the door while Amelia stepped inside. She was soon followed in by Kurt.

"Girls! There you are. Kurt has some information for us. I thought you would want to hear, too." As Kurt started to explain, Amelia discreetly left and headed toward the dining room.

"Ladies, I was just telling Amelia about the man found dead in the kitchen." Lizzi was not sure she wanted to know any more about him. The less she knew the better. But he continued anyway. "Rashelle had told me that he had registered as Joseph Stevens with his wife, Suzanne, from New Canaan, Connecticut. This all checks out. He is an accountant, a CPA, with clients in the Tri-state area; greater New York City, New Jersey and Fairfield County, Connecticut. I spoke with one of the partners in his firm who knew he was heading up to Maine for a long weekend but was, of course, shocked when I told him what had happened to him. He couldn't think of anyone who would have had a grudge against him. I also asked him about any extra-marital affairs he might have had that could have caused a very angry husband to get revenge. He referred me to another partner who was closer to him. I haven't been able to reach her. In the meantime, I've asked for a complete client list so we can get started trying to find a possible connection there.

"State police ran the prints found on the knife and only Tony's were identified. Unfortunately, we can't eliminate him just yet. Before Mr. Stevens passed out he was able to type a few numbers into his cell phone. We are still trying to identify what the numbers mean."

Elizabeth was following along very closely. "What were they?" She felt she could help solve this as much as the next guy. *Bring it on.*

Mitchell examined her face to see if she was serious. Upon realizing she was, a discreet smile pushed up slightly on one side of his face forming a dimple in his left cheek. He looked pleased she had asked. "Let's see." He looked closely at his notes and then to her from across the clipboard.

She was starting to feel uncomfortable again. He was taking too much time to answer the question. *Can we get on with it already?*

"8, 7, 0, 7….8707."

"Well, it's not a seven digit number like a regular phone number."

"No, it's not." Mitchell agreed.

"Maybe it's just part of a phone number because that was as far as he could get before he died."

"Could be."

"What about the letters on a phone that represent each number pad? Maybe he was trying to spell out something." Rashelle joined in and was thinking out loud.

Elizabeth wrinkled her forehead. "That would have taken a tremendous amount of concentration to spell something out while he was busy dying."

Rashelle shrugged her shoulders. She was just trying to help.

"It had to be something he felt comfortable with, something he has done many times before. It was second nature to him." Elizabeth was staying focused.

There was a moment of silence while everyone tossed around those last couple of thoughts. Finally, Lizzi's face lit up. "Rashelle, you have an adding machine in the office, don't you?"

"Yes, it's right on the desk." She led the way to the door into the business office, behind the front desk, with Elizabeth following behind her. Lizzi pulled her cell phone out of her pants pocket and flipped it open. She looked from the phone to the adding machine and back again several times. The other two waited in silence while she sorted through her thoughts.

"That's odd…"

"What's odd?" Rashelle took the bait.

She turned and looked directly at Rashelle. "Did you ever notice that the keypad on the adding machine is backwards from the keypad on any phone?"

Mitchell and Rashelle looked at each other and then at Elizabeth, with looks that indicated they had never made that observation.

"See…the top row on the phone is 1, 2, 3. But the top row on the adding machine is 7, 8, 9. Think about it. This was an accountant. He was probably quite familiar with the adding machine. It was a tool in his trade. But he probably also used his cell phone a lot, too. What if he was trying to leave a clue as to his killer's identity but did it as if he was using an adding machine instead of a cell phone, even though he was using a cell phone? After all, we should cut him some slack. He was dying and he probably knew it."

"Okay," Kurt was willing to play along. "So what are the equivalent numbers on the adding machine?"

"Let's look." Elizabeth quickly compared the two. "2…1…0…1." The three thought on this for a moment. No one was coming up with anything obvious.

"Maybe it's a date.2/1/01. That could be a significant date to this man." Rashelle offered. Elizabeth and Kurt nodded as they considered this idea.

"February 1st, 2001…or could it be 1901?" Kurt added.

Lizzi threw in her two cents. "What if the first two numbers are the day and the last two digits are the month? Sort of in European order. That would make it January."

"Or it could be that it's not a date at all." Kurt was turning the discussion upside down. "Could it be part of a license plate or a room—?"

"Miss Pennington!" The lieutenant's voice boomed from behind them. He stood at the reception desk counter. "You need to come with me."

"Wh-what?!"

"I'm afraid you are coming with me. This is the end of the road for you."

Rashelle sprung to life. "Lieutenant! What are you talking about?"

"I need you to come out from around there." He had his eyes focused on Elizabeth.

Rashelle followed Elizabeth out to the lobby in time to see Perkins pulling his handcuffs off of his belt. "OH MY GAWD!!" Her accent shone through in her excitement. "WHAT ARE YOU DOING? YOU DON'T NEED TO DO THIS!"

Amelia couldn't help but notice the commotion in the lobby and came running from the dining room. "What is going on?" She saw Elizabeth standing there with her hands behind her back. Perkins was behind her clamping on the cuffs. "Lieutenant! What are you doing? This is not necessary! Take those off of her! What do you think she has done? Take them off! They are not necessary!" Panic was in her voice and terror in her eyes.

"I'm sorry ma'am. There is too much evidence against her to just let her stay here—" Elizabeth figured that Perkins must be getting pressure from a superior to get someone in custody and get the situation under control. He was only making the situation worse.

"Evidence?! Your evidence is WRONG!! She hasn't done anything! You are taking the wrong person! For God sake, take off the handcuffs. She is not a criminal!"

Perkins had heard his fill so he turned away from Amelia, grabbed Elizabeth by the arm, and started heading for the door.

"NO! NO! Lieutenant, you listen to me!" Amelia was approaching hysteria at the thought of her granddaughter being dragged away like a criminal. "There is no need for this…if you are going to take her, at least take off the cuffs. Who is the bigger person here? Look at her. Do you really think she could overpower you? Please! I beg of you!"

Her comments must have hit a nerve with him. His shoulders dropped and he reluctantly shoved his right hand into his uniform pants to retrieve the handcuff keys. Skillfully he slipped the key into the cuffs and he popped them off quickly. Elizabeth took a moment to massage her wrists where the cuffs had been while he replaced them on his belt. Then he guided her through the front door and to the right side of a waiting squad car without looking back. He opened the back door and motioned for her to get in. Looked like she was going to find out what it was like in the rear of the car after all. Amelia was at their heels with Rashelle right behind her. "Where are you taking her? For God sake, please don't take her! She hasn't done anything. I need her here." Amelia continued to implore him.

The lieutenant closed the door on Elizabeth and then turned around to address Amelia's hysteria. Once again Elizabeth was alone in the squad car. She took a deep breath. This couldn't be happening. Leaning back, she remembered she had shoved something into her back pocket to look at later. She reached behind her and pulled out a magazine, a random snatch from the Hutchins' coffee table. She unrolled it, flipped it over to the back cover, and gasped. Quickly, Elizabeth shoved it back into her pants pocket. She needed to get out of the car!

While the lieutenant was still tied up with her grandmother, she quickly slid across the seat to the other side of the car, away from Perkins and Amelia. Thank goodness Amelia had convinced Perkins to let her out of those cuffs. Suddenly she realized she needed a flashlight. The trooper must have one somewhere in the vehicle. She peered through the cage separating the back seat from the front and scanned from right to left, noting a sturdy metal flashlight tucked neatly in the pocket on the driver's door. Quietly she let herself out on the left side of the car, crouching to stay out of sight. She didn't close the door tightly, so as not to alert them of her escape. She grabbed the handle on the driver's door and listened for conversation on the other side of the car.

"We will bring her back just as soon as we can." His voice was suddenly getting louder. He was rounding the back of the cruiser. In a desperate move, she hit the ground and rolled under the car. She held her breath. Listening closely, she could tell he had opened his door, but hadn't entered the vehicle.

"WHAT THE HELL!"

Not much gets past him.

"WHERE IS SHE?! DAMN IT!" Footsteps led away from the car. Elizabeth lay as still as she could muster, listening for voices. After what seemed like an eternity of quiet, she scooted back out from under the car, looked around for any movement. It seemed clear. She still needed the flashlight. Perkins had left the driver's door ajar so she pulled it open just enough to reach the flashlight on the door. She reached in slowly, trying not to set off the overhead light in the cruiser. On a gray overcast day like this, she couldn't be too careful of having anyone notice the light. She was getting closer. Her fingertips touched the end of it. She pushed her arm further. She could almost reach enough of it to grab it. One more inch and she would have it. Finally! She had the tips of her fingers around the flashlight. She looked up and realized the light was on inside the car. It wouldn't matter how much more she opened the door, the light would still be on. She opened it wider, grabbed the flashlight, and then returned the door to its original position, hoping no one had noticed the light at all. She had to get moving. She kept low and headed straight for the woods.

Elizabeth knew she had lost precious time retrieving the trooper's light, but she would need it later. Her feet carried her swiftly to the woods, allowing the trees to swallow her up and hide her from all of the police she had left behind, scattering at the inn. By now everyone was aware of what had happened outside the front of the inn. She needed to redefine the word "disappearance."

Once in the woods, she pushed through the trees with both arms out in front of her. Her feet were moving quickly, small steps, one in front of the other. Her eyes were focused on her feet so as not to trip over an errant root, glancing up periodically to avoid running head long into a tree. Twigs were snapping beneath her feet. The further into the woods she went, the darker it became, as the daylight was waning. The woods became very thick soon after entering. Her feet came to a stop and she listened to the woods for a moment, becoming aware that she was the only one making any noise. A silvery gray mist hung in the air. The woods were eerily quiet, like something evil had happened or was about to happen. A shiver ran down her back. The thought of going deeper made her stomach turn over. She had no choice. She couldn't retrace her steps. She had to put as much distance as possible between her and the commotion behind her. She took a deep breath and started to move her feet again, glancing left to right to detect any unexpected movement.

Escape while in custody. Elizabeth tried that on for size. A bit of a sticky situation, but she couldn't worry about that right now. *One foot in front of the other.* She had to keep—thud! Her right hand, which held the flashlight, hit a tree. The light was knocked loose and landed in the brush below. "Shit!" She dropped to the ground on her hands and knees groping for the flashlight. It had to be right there. Did it bounce? She widened her circle. Her hands patted the ground frantically. It was prickly with dried pine nee-dles, sticks, and pine cones. Where was the light?! Panic was creep-ing into her mind. She stretched further to reach under a big, old pine and hit metal. She found it! "Yes!" Grabbing it tightly, she backed out from under the conifer and stood up into someone's arms behind her. A hand clasped firmly onto her mouth, letting out only a muffled scream. She quickly surmised that it was a man who had her in a tight hold. He was very strong. She struggled to pull free. She heard the flashlight make contact with the ground for a second time. So *much for using that as a weapon.* She kept trying to scream and wriggle out of his grasp. Her muffled shrieks drowned out her captor's words. Finally she stopped struggling and took a breath.

"Elizabeth!" His voice was barely above a whisper. Her eyes opened wide. It was Mitchell. "Shut up already…hold still and I will let go of you!" Her body relaxed and she stopped trying to scream. Kurt stood there with his arms around her and one hand over her mouth. "Okay? You've calmed down? Remember I'm on your side."

Elizabeth wasn't so sure about that but she was willing to pretend if it meant he would let go of her. She nodded her head. Slowly he removed his hand from her mouth, paused, then slowly released his vice grip from around her upper body, keeping one hand on her upper arm as insurance that she wouldn't run.

"Alright, already. I'm not going anywhere!" Her voice was barely a whisper. She jerked her arm out of his grasp. If it wasn't so dark in the woods she would have seen a red spot on her arm where his large hand had been. She rubbed it to relieve the pain. She turned and pretended to spit to her side. "And where has that hand been, for God's sake! Wash them once in a while!"

"What the hell are you doing?! You were in custody! Perkins will be having a canary about now."

"A canary? Kurt, no one says that anymore." She didn't really give a damn about Perkins right now. "Mitchell, I need to get back into the tunnels. And I can't help my grandmother if I'm in custody. I don't care how mad Perkins is. I've just got to steer clear of him for the moment."

"Well, the tunnels would be a good place for that. Let's go." He grabbed her arm again.

"Wait!" I need the flashlight."

Mitchell pulled a miniature light out of his pocket and snapped it on. Elizabeth was relieved to see it shed a narrow band of concentrated light. Kurt scanned the ground around their feet until he located the larger light. She reached down and snatched it up.

"Good, that will come in handy." He turned and headed deeper into the woods. She followed behind, wondering what he was up to. Was he actually going to help her or was he leading her right back into Perkins' custody?

Chapter 20

Elizabeth and Kurt stopped short of emerging from the woods near Acadia House. She searched his face to see if she could tell what his intentions were. She wasn't sure she should trust him. He turned to her. "There is an opening to the tunnels just to the left of the steps going up to the back door to the Hutchins' room. We need to get to it without anyone seeing us."

He looked around, and then stepped out of the safety of the woods. "C'mon." They stayed low and headed across the grass toward the end of the building. Elizabeth followed behind Kurt as he approached the first set of steps in the back of the building. He passed the steps and went directly to the left of the steps, into the bushes, that were evidently concealing the entrance to the tunnel. She watched as he reached into the greenery and yanked on a hatchway door. It seemed to open fairly easily as if it was used regularly. Odd for a tunnel that had been sealed off for years. "Ladies first." He motioned for her to enter. Oh, how she hated the tunnels. Curiously, she wondered what she would find starting from this end. At least she had a decent flashlight this time. Cautiously she descended the steps. Just as she reached to switch on the lieutenant's light, she heard a voice approaching. She stood still.

"Mitchell!" It was Perkins. Had he seen her? Her feet were frozen in place. "What are you doing?" She held her breath.

Kurt swiftly closed the door behind her with a loud thud. "Just checking the tunnels, making sure the access points are secure."

She heard the latch click into place on the hatchway door. She was locked in! "That Bastard!" she yelled in a whisper. She *knew* she couldn't trust him! "Damn it!" The tunnel was suddenly darker than any darkness she had ever seen before. She waited for her eyes to adjust but the absolute darkness remained. She stood still, barely breathing, listening to hear if they were still there. She didn't dare turn on her light yet. She couldn't afford to be detected by Perkins. Wouldn't he be happy if he did? She listened as the voices trailed off. Somewhere off in the distance in the tunnel there was a dripping sound. The familiar damp, musty air of the underground permeated her nose. She waited until she couldn't stand the dark any longer and pushed the switch so the flashlight came to life. Taking a moment to let her eyes adjust, she glanced around her. Nothing unlike the other end of the tunnel. She took what comfort she could from that. Well, she had wanted to get back down into the tunnels and she did have a good flashlight with her this time. But she was locked in. Maybe Mitchell had her right where he wanted her. Suddenly she wanted to get out of there. Her cell phone! She could call Rashelle to come to her rescue. Her friend could come and let her out. All she would have to do would be to break the lock on the hatchway…Of course, calling her would be very risky. They were probably monitoring her cell phone on GPS. One call and more than just Mitchell would know where she was. "Alright, Elizabeth. Think." Her voice was barely a whisper. It sounded odd to her. The tunnel suddenly seemed colder and wetter and emptier than before. She shined the flashlight down the tunnel shaft and listened. It was quiet. She put her free hand on the back of her hip while she thought for a moment. Should she attempt to find her way to the main building of the inn? What would she do once she got there—if she found her way there? It didn't look like she had much choice. There was no leaving through the hatchway. She would have to devise a plan as she went. Then she realized the hand on her hip should have brushed the magazine that she had swiped from the Hutchins' room. It wasn't there! Had she dropped it in her haste to get down the hatchway? Did Mitchell slip it out of her pocket? She didn't want to think about either possibility. It was time to start moving. If she was going to be a target, it would be better for her to be a moving target.

Taking a deep breath, she started hesitantly down the dark, dank tunnel. The trooper's light was of much better quality that the two rusty cast-offs that Rashelle had rescued from the desk drawer of the office. She was fairly confident that this one might actually stay on. Elizabeth made her way slowly down the tunnel, taking small steps and stopping periodically to listen. Oh, how she hated the tunnels. It's no wonder why she was forbidden from exploring them as a child. She was barely a few feet from the hatchway when her cell phone came to life in her pocket and made her jump. "Shit!" She plunged her hand deep into her pants to retrieve the noisy offender. One glance told her it was an area code of 917. Drescher again. He was certainly persistent. She had to give him that. Probably the last person she wanted to speak to right now. She just flipped opened the phone and closed it again. She acted quickly enough so that it only rang twice. Was it enough for them to detect where she was? Elizabeth didn't have time to think about it. She quickly shut off the phone and shoved it back into her pocket.

Elizabeth pressed on, shuffling her feet a few dozen yards, until she noticed the reflection of a light, bobbing along the wall. She quickly extinguished her light and watched the reflection. It was gradually getting brighter and closer. Someone was in the tunnel, coming right toward her. There was nowhere to hide. Nowhere to go. All she could do was to wait until the person reached her. Her breathing quickened. Her palms became damp. She had to focus on not dropping her light. The person was shuffling his or her feet. Almost on top of her. Suddenly there was a light shining in her eyes. She quickly turned on her light and pointed it at the intruder. "M-Mrs. Leibowitz? W-what the—What are you doing here?" Elizabeth couldn't believe her eyes. There, standing in front of her, in the dark, damp tunnel, was none other than one of the inn's regular guests, Mrs. L. She stood there in Elizabeth's light like they were casually meeting in the hall of the inn. Of course, in reality, no meeting with Mrs. Leibowitz was casual. Then Elizabeth noticed she was holding something down at her side. She moved the light lower to get a better look. "A bottle of wine? Mrs. Leibowitz, you're sneaking a bottle from the inn's wine cellar?" Elizabeth was incredulous. A long-time guest was using the old tunnels to pilfer wine. She moved her light back up to Mrs. L's face, looking for a response.

"Bah!" Her free hand gestured as if to say, "no big deal." "The wine you had sent up earlier was of questionable quality so I thought I would help myself and make my own selection." Elizabeth couldn't believe her ears. She had obviously done this before and knew right where to go to find the inn's wine cellar. Before she could wonder how long this had been going on, the defiant guest pushed past her and headed for the end of the tunnel Elizabeth had just left. Mrs. L. called back to her as the darkness quickly swallowed her up, "I'll just leave the unopened bottle in my room to be picked up." Elizabeth watched as her light bobbed for a few seconds and then disappeared out of sight.

"What a bitch!" Her voice was barely a whisper. Elizabeth just stood there alone in the dark shaking her head with her mouth opened slightly. She wasn't about to do her any favors and tell her the hatchway was locked. She would see her on the rebound. Her feet starting moving again.

Several minutes passed while Elizabeth shuffled her feet, making her way toward the wine cellar below the main building. She couldn't shake her encounter with Mrs. Leibowitz, but she really needed to be focusing on other matters right now. What or who was she going to find when she got to the cellar? Would Perkins and/or Mitchell be there to greet her? She felt trapped like a rat. She had no choice but to keep moving. Her feet proceeded at a steady pace. Then she smelled it. It hit her in the face like it had before. The odor was so strong, it almost made her eyes water. She slowed her feet until she was nearly standing still. She wasn't so sure she wanted to see where the odor was coming from but she kept moving. Slowly she crept closer. A few steps at a time. The smell was very strong now. It couldn't be too much farther. A few more steps. Then her light shined on something dark in the middle of the tunnel. She stopped dead in her tracks. What was it? She held her breath. She took a few more steps closer, squinting her eyes to make out the lifeless form on the floor a few feet in front of her. A few more steps closer. Then she noticed the fur. It was just an unfortunate animal that had met its match in the bowels of the inn. Not a very large animal. Hard to tell what it was and what did it in because it had obviously been there decomposing for a while. She was relieved that the carcass was not human, though. Gingerly, she stepped over it and moved on. The more space she could put between herself and that smelly mess, the better.

Elizabeth picked up her pace as much as she dared, but kept her feet as close to the ground as possible to avoid slipping and falling on the damp, dirt floor. She pressed on, further into the tunnel. Oh, how she just wanted to get out of there. Her thoughts went back to Mitchell. She couldn't decide if she could trust him. Did he have the Hutchins' magazine? If so, what was he going to do with it? Would he give it to Perkins so he could use it to charge her with breaking and entering? Oh, she wished she could call Rashelle to ensure someone was going to be on her side when she exited the tunnel. Elizabeth hated to think about what kind of a welcoming committee would be there to great her. She decided to just put it out of her mind for a while and keep going. Suddenly she became aware of her feet. She felt as though they had sped up while she was deep in thought so she reached out with her free hand to run it along the wall. It was cold and damp. All of a sudden the air in the tunnel felt very cold. A shiver ran down her spine. She felt so alone down below the ground. The urgency to get out of there was stronger than ever, but she stopped for a moment to listen. It was too quiet.

"Get out!" The voice startled her. It was a whisper in her ear. She jumped and turned her head back and forth trying to determine where the sound came from. It was a woman's voice, but not one she recognized. It certainly wasn't Mrs. Leibowitz's. She couldn't decide if the voice had originated from behind her or in front of her. It almost seemed like it was all around her.

Elizabeth decided to heed the warning just the same and she resumed her trek toward daylight. Her feet started to move at a pace that was flirting with the danger of slipping on the wet ground beneath her, but her desire to escape had never been stronger.

She had covered a few yards when the hand that was running along the wall felt a subtle vibration, which made her stop and listen again. What was that? She took a few tentative steps, keeping her hand on the wall, stopping to listen again. Somewhere near her there was a creaking sound, like a heavy weight was causing something to give under the pressure. Elizabeth blacked out before she saw what happened next.

Chapter 21

Elizabeth was struggling to open her eyes. She became acutely aware that the back of her head ached like she had never felt before. She moaned as she started to stir from her prone position on the floor of the tunnel.

"Liz!! Are you alright?" Elizabeth was vaguely aware that she was hearing a familiar voice. "Lizzi! Oh my gawd, are you all right? Tawk to me." As Elizabeth slowly regained her consciousness, she strained to see her friend. There was a bright light in her face that was hard to see past.

A gruff voice barked directions to someone. "Get the light out of her eyes, for God's sake. Give her some room to breathe!" Elizabeth suddenly realized who was speaking. Perkins had found her. *Was he responsible for the throbbing in her head?* Her stomach turned over and she suddenly felt nauseous. She struggled to remember what had happened and was frustrated that she couldn't. She knew this couldn't be good.

"Liz. What happened? Are you all right, girlfriend? Tawk to me. Can you sit up?" Rashelle was desperately trying to help Elizabeth. She grabbed onto one of her arms and tried to encourage her to move.

"Whoa, Miss Harper. Give her a few minutes to gather herself. She'll be fine. Just give her some time." *What is Perkins up to? He was sounding entirely too compassionate.* Elizabeth wondered exactly who was hovering over her. She was becoming aware of several people. It seemed like a crowd that gathers at a car accident. She kept blinking to clear her eyesight while squinting to try to see past multiple flashlights. She wished she knew what had happened. Damn, she could use some ice and several hundred milligrams of ibuprofen. Elizabeth reached with one hand to the back of her head to perform a tactile examination. She felt a large lump that was excruciating when she touched it and her hand felt wet when she pulled it away.

"Take it easy, Miss Pennington. You've suffered quite a blow to the back of your head. Take your time. If need be, we can carry you out of the tunnel. Suddenly, she felt the need to sit up and get out of the limelight of a half a dozen flashlights. She tried to sit up and the whole world started to spin.

A very firm hand latched onto her left upper arm to steady her. There was a new voice. "Elizabeth, you heard the lieutenant. There's no rush. Take your time." It was Mitchell. She guessed she shouldn't be surprised that he was with Perkins. But Rashelle?

She took a deep breath and exhaled. "I know, I know. I just would like to get out of here. What happened?"

"We can fill in the details in time. Let's first get you safely out of here."

What is Mitchell up to?

"Do you feel that you can stand up?"

"Let's give it a try. I really want out of here." There was a real sense of urgency in her voice.

Another unidentified voice broke in. "Actually, sir, we really should vacate the tunnel. It's not as stable as it once was. We don't know how long we really have." As if on cue, Perkins and Mitchell reached down and each grabbed onto her forearms.

"Ready, Elizabeth?"

She nodded her head. "Let's do it."

Slowly the two men lifted her into a standing position. Her knees started to buckle so they held onto her until she was steadier on her feet. Her head was swirling after all that movement, but she was so glad to be upright and on her feet. She had had enough of the tunnels. She wanted out. Slowly they made their way toward the exit. Elizabeth pushed herself as hard as she could. She plodded along forcing her feet to move. She was acutely aware that Mitchell was on one side and Perkins was on the other. She wondered if they were taking her into custody. She almost didn't care. She just wanted out of the bowels of the earth and hoped she never saw the tunnel walls again.

After several yards of shuffling her feet, she felt absolutely drained and started to slow down. The back of her head started to throb. The pain was unlike anything she had ever felt before. She felt very light-headed. Things started to spin again. She started to black out again on her way to becoming a heap on the cold wet floor. Someone scooped her up and headed toward the way out.

Chapter 22

Elizabeth came to, for a second time, in the familiar territory of the sitting room off the lobby of the inn. Someone had applied a bandage to the back of her head while she was unconscious. The pain was unbearable, but she was just thrilled to be above ground again. She could sense there was a lot of commotion out in the dining room. She tried to sit up and see what was going on. As soon as she moved, she knew she needed to take it slowly. A stabbing pain shot through her head. Her body was saying, "SLOW DOWN!" Unfortunately, she needed to push it beyond the edge of the envelope right now. Her body flopped back down on the worn out floral couch that didn't seem to be near the fireplace where she and Rashelle had talked late into the evening on the first night of her arrival. The room seemed to have been rearranged. It was very different. Even though she was curious about the sitting room, she really wanted to find out what had happened down in the tunnels. Perhaps it was more important to find out what was happening at the inn at the moment. Elizabeth struggled to sit up. She listened closely to the din nearby.

"Elizabeth! The sound of her grandmother's voice felt wonderful.

Oh, how she wanted to reach out and hug her, feel her warmth inside and out. "Nana! What's going on? What happened?"

"Are you alright? You look awful. You poor thing! The tunnel you were in had a cave in. You are lucky to be alive!" Amelia was pleased and grateful to see that her granddaughter was going to be okay.

"Nana, I'm okay…I'll be fine. Don't worry. What is going on?"

"Liz, the hurricane has taken a turn. It is heading inland… right for us. We need to start evacuating the inn."

"What about the missing girl?"

"Oh, the officers seemed to think they have—"

"Excuse me, ma'am." Perkins was speaking directly to Amelia. She turned abruptly toward him. "We really need to get going with the evacuation of the guests."

"Yes, yes! Of course. I'll be right there." She turned her attention back to her granddaughter. Perkins lingered next to Amelia, looking directly at Elizabeth. "I have to help the officers. You need to rest. You stay put and I'll be back as soon as I can."

The lieutenant finally spoke in his stern voice. "Elizabeth, if I didn't have more pressing issues to address, you would be back in custody for running off like that. As it stands now, though, the investigation just took a turn which seems to get you off the hook… but I still want to talk with you later."

He and Amelia turned toward the dining room and disappeared before Elizabeth could open her mouth to ask a question. She felt as though she had been gone a long time and that a lot had happened while she was down under. The throbbing in her head made her wish she could take an ibuprofen or two or three. She decided she needed to go find some. Everyone else seemed so busy. She would just do it herself. Slowly she sat up again. This time the room didn't spin quite so fast. She considered that a huge improvement over her attempt a few minutes earlier. Resting on the couch in a sitting position, she gathered all the energy she could muster to try to stand up. She looked around the sitting room. The furniture was definitely different. She squinted and thought about it for a while and then realized that things had not only been rearranged, several pieces were added. Then she noticed that the furniture had been pushed to one side to make room for the furniture and bikes off of the front porch.

Gingerly she eased herself off of the couch into a standing position. She hung onto the arm of the couch for a while to make sure she wasn't going to take a nosedive. So far, so good. She started to take little steps toward the registration desk. Rashelle must have something strong stashed in one of the drawers. She got as far as the old, round, wooden table in the foyer, with the large vase of flowers on it, when the world around her started to spin again. Lunging for the edge of the table, she was just in time to grab hold to steady herself until things cleared in her head. Finally, she felt strong enough to do a bee line for the front desk. She let go and fast-walked to the counter, a little crooked, and grabbed on for dear life again. Taking a deep breath, she pulled herself across the counter to see if there was anything obvious on the desktop below. She hung on for a moment while her head throbbed. She blinked, trying to see things more clearly. It looked like there might be something resembling an ibuprofen bottle next to the phone, but she couldn't be sure. She would have to make her way around to the inside of the office to check it out. That would take some effort. She waited a while to gather her strength, and then skirted around the corner, running both hands along the walls to steady herself. Reaching the office door, her body hit it with a thud. *Oh, that didn't feel very good.* She fumbled for the doorknob and managed to turn it enough to release the catch and allow the weight of her body to push open the door. The momentum carried her into the tiny office where she aimed for and landed in the desk chair. She took a few deep breaths and surveyed her surroundings. The drawers. There had to be something in one of the drawers. She swung the chair around toward the desk and started to pull out drawers and look deep into the back of them. She was in luck with the second drawer. A well-worn bottle of pain reliever rattled around inside the drawer when Elizabeth gave it a good tug. She was so relieved. She snatched up the bottle, opened the top, and poured half a dozen gel caps into the palm of her hand. Wondering what she was going to wash them down with, she quickly scanned the desk and noticed a bottle of water sitting on the far side. Under any other circumstances, she would have been totally repulsed by the idea of drinking out of someone else's water bottle. She had no idea whose it was, but she was desperate and didn't have time to find out. The six ibuprofen slid down her throat without delay. She longed for them to take effect immediately. She closed her eyes and tried to will her body to rid itself of the pain that was still throbbing in her head. Without realizing it, her body weight eased the chair into a semi-reclining position. Her body shut down for a third time under the stress of her injury. There she lay in the relative quiet of the tiny office. Meanwhile, the rest of the inn was in chaos as the staff and troopers labored to reach every guest and instruct them as to evacuation procedures. A couple of local schools had opened up, even though they weren't scheduled to start classes for a few more days, to take in evacuees of the impending storm. The meteorologists were suddenly concerned about certain towns along the Maine coast, and Pennington Point was one of them. There was talk of the hurricane maintaining a category four label. Such a strong storm had not hit Maine for as long as even the old-timers could remember.

Chapter 23

Elizabeth awoke to her cell phone ringing. She lurched forward in her chair and grabbed the phone out of her pocket out of habit, before she was fully conscious. "Hel…hello!" Elizabeth was trying to clear her head while listening to the voice on the other end. Suddenly she realized it was Vera. *Oh my God, why did I answer the phone?* "Yes…Yes. Vera is that you?"

"Well of course it is me! I have been trying to get a hold of you for quite a while. I think Drescher has too. What the hell is going on?"

Elizabeth was regretting answering the phone while still semi-conscious. It was bound to happen, though. She had been dodging Vera since she arrived. This was not the responsible Elizabeth Pennington, the professional interior designer that Vera knew and loved…well, knew.

"Vera…I'm sorry! Things are a little crazy here right now."

"I don't want to hear that! I've got Drescher on my back looking for design ideas for his new building. He wants to meet tomorrow afternoon! What am I supposed to tell him, Elizabeth? Sorry, my top designer was busy over the weekend and couldn't be bothered to spend time for our most important client?!"

"What?" She couldn't believe what she was hearing and she certainly didn't have time to deal with it.

"Look, Elizabeth! I need your designs!"

"Vera, there is a hurricane headed our way! We are currently conducting a complete evacuation of the—"

"Fax me what you have!"

"I can't right now! I have to go!" Lizzi flipped her cell phone closed. She could not believe that Vera was being such a bitch about this. *Is New York City that far away that she and Drescher had no idea what was happening in Maine?* She sat for a moment to reflect on the brief, but ridiculous conversation. She conceded to herself that it was probably grounds for dismissal. She may have just lost her job. Elizabeth had had enough of her boss and she really needed to focus on the inn and the impending hurricane at the moment. She needed to help with the evacuation. Lizzi struggled to her feet and headed for the door. Her head was starting to spin so she grabbed onto the door frame for support and took a moment to gather herself. Then it hit her that she had turned off her phone when she was down in the tunnel. She wondered how it could have gotten turned back on.

Chapter 24

Elizabeth stepped out into the lobby and could sense the commotion in the dining room. She peeked in and it became clear that the room had been turned into central dispatch. Everyone wanted to make sure that everyone got out safely and that no one was left behind. She listened in to see how things were going.

"We tried that door. No one answered. How are we supposed to know if they have already left?"

"Amelia has the master list of guests checked in for the weekend. She is also maintaining a tally of who has left, when they left and who has yet to check out. Let's ask her to give us a list of those who are still here and what rooms they are in, so we can divide and conquer. We need to accomplish this as quickly as possible."

Sounded like things were under control, even under the circumstances. Elizabeth could certainly lend a hand, though. She decided to head outside. It wasn't clear if she should still steer clear of Perkins. Better to play it safe. The fresh air would do her good.

Once at the bottom of the porch steps, she took a deep breath which felt so good. The sea air was always refreshing to her. A light rain was falling. Heading around the side of the inn, she figured she would aim for Moosehead to start knocking on doors. She would just have to keep track in her head who she was able to reach and which doors were unanswered.

She was approaching Acadia House when she realized that she wasn't thinking clearly. She didn't know what the evacuation instructions were. That bump on the back of her head must really be affecting her. She slowed her steps to think for a moment. She could at least direct the guests to central dispatch in the dining room; she wanted to be of some help. Resuming her pace, she rounded the back of Acadia House and started up the sidewalk between the back of the building and a long narrow strip of pines that ran parallel to the building. Before she got to the end of Acadia she started feeling lightheaded and decided to grab onto the nearest stair railing, taking steady breaths. The rain had become heavier. The drops on her face felt good. They were helping to clear her head, but she also knew they were just the beginning of a tremendous storm that was barreling toward them. She was tempted to sit on the back steps for a moment, but didn't dare. She knew it would be difficult to get up again.

Behind her was the sound of a door latch. She turned to see who it was. Suddenly she realized where she was standing—at the bottom of the back steps leading to the Hutchins' room. "Oh, you must be Mrs. Hutchins; I didn't mean to disturb you. Surely you are aware that the hurricane is—" Someone had grabbed her from behind. Strong hands had pulled her arms behind her so tightly that they ached. She felt something sharp at her throat. A soft gasp escaped her mouth. She could still see Mrs. Hutchins standing at the top of the stairs looking down at them. Her face remained motionless. She couldn't understand why she wasn't reacting to what was happening to her. She had to know the person who had grabbed her. Elizabeth was convinced from the strength that the person was exerting on her, it could only by a man. She was guessing it was Perkins…or Mitchell, depending on whose side he was on at the moment. She didn't have the energy to struggle this time. "Okay, already. You don't have to be so rough. Ease—"

"Oh, yes I do. All the other tactics don't seem to be working."

Elizabeth's eyes got wide. She didn't recognize the man's voice but it wasn't Perkins or Mitchell.

"For God's sake, Elizabeth, why did you even come up here? Everything was going swimmingly into turmoil and then you arrived to save the day."

She looked to Mrs. Hutchins for a response. Still no reaction. She swallowed hard. It was hard for her to breathe. The man's hand, with what she imagined must be a knife, was pressing hard against her neck. Elizabeth struggled to speak. "Wh-what are you doing? What is going on?...How do you know who I am?"

Perkins had appeared from around the corner at the end of the building where Hutchins room was, with his gun drawn, facing Elizabeth and her unknown assailant. "Hold it right there." The man tightened his grasp and pulled her closer to him, the knife still pressed to her neck.

"Don't come any closer! I will slit her throat with your next step!"

"Hey, just take it easy." His voice was assertive and deliberate. "You don't have to involve Eliz—"

"*I* don't have to involve Elizabeth! She already has herself involved." Elizabeth didn't like the sound of his voice. He sounded desperate. "She should have left well enough alone and stayed in New York City. After all, she does have enough work to keep her busy for a while. But she chose to put that all on the back burner and run to her grandmother's rescue."

Elizabeth was trying very hard to figure out who had her by the neck.

"So...you may have underestimated how close she and Amelia really are. Obviously the bond of love shared by these two is very strong. But you planted evidence on her just in case she did decide to head up to Maine to try and stick her nose into things." Perkins was fishing, hoping to elicit a response that would provide him with information he needed.

"Evidence?" Lizzi could barely utter enough sound to make the word heard. She was gasping for air. The man's grip was getting tighter.

"Yes, Miss Pennington. There was a package planted on you before you left the city."

Elizabeth racked her brain to think. What package? Then it dawned on her. She had all but forgotten that Lenny from the mail room had brought a manila envelope to her just as she was pulling out of the parking garage.

"It was still on the front passenger seat when we impounded your car. So we took the liberty of opening it for you. In the process, we were able to lift prints from the packing tape used to seal the box. It was a long shot, but we decided to give it a try and run them through the FBI's database. Inside the box was a girl's necklace, the description of which the Hutchins' had given to us with the description of their missing daughter. We were disappointed not to find any DNA on the necklace, but our disappointment turned to suspicion when the jacket found on the breakwater, didn't have any DNA on it either." We should be hearing back from the FBI very soon to verify who is involved in this mess. But we did determine that the couple who had checked in as Mr. and Mrs. Hutchins are really James and Ann Rizzo. Isn't that right, Rizzo?"

Elizabeth listened intently to the Lieutenant. Rizzo was the addressee's name on the magazine she picked up in the Hutchins' room. Elizabeth was very scared. The man's grip tightened as Perkins talked. She took shallow breaths to keep from passing out. The rain was starting to get heavier. The wind was picking up.

Perkins continued. "Alright Rizzo, it's over. Give it up. This is the end of the road."

"Oh, no...." His voice was still remarkably calm, but firm. He spoke as if he was the one in control. "This is certainly not over, is it Elizabeth?" He pressed his face up next to hers which gave her the creeps. Her stomach turned. How did he know her? She thought she was going to get nauseous. This just couldn't be happening. She needed to get out of his grip. His knife was starting to cut into her neck. This was a nightmare. God help her.

Suddenly, the man's arm pulled away from her neck and she was knocked to the ground. The world was spinning again. She blinked her eyes and shook her head, struggling to stay conscious. She could sense a scuffle on the ground next to her. It was Rizzo being tackled by Mitchell. Kurt easily overpowered him long enough to slip on a pair of cuffs, and then pulled him up to a standing position. A couple of beat cops rounded the corner on a dead run and came to a screeching halt when they stumbled onto the scene. Two more followed behind them. Elizabeth looked up to the landing where Mrs. Hutchins/Rizzo had been standing. Perkins had her in cuffs and was leading her down the steps into the custody of the first two officers to arrive. The other two officers took Rizzo from Mitchell. Elizabeth struggled to her hands and knees. Rizzo had to have the last word. "Oh, and Elizabeth. I took a look at your initial sketches of the lobby. They are disappointing, at best. Definitely not your best work. Too bad you hadn't stayed in the city where you could have stayed focused." The two suspects were swiftly led around the corner, presumably to waiting squad cars.

Kurt immediately kneeled next to Elizabeth. "Are you alright, Liz?" He firmly grasped her shoulders and lifted her slightly to look into her face. "Talk to me!" He noticed the gash on her neck from Rizzo's knife. It was glistening with blood. "Are you okay? Lizzi?" The wind was starting to pick up in gusts.

She was finally catching her breath. Kurt had rescued her from an uncertain fate. God, she was so thankful to him. She was beginning to like him after all. "Yeah, Kurt. I'm okay…or at least I will be. Just help me up, please." She stood up on her own two wobbly feet with his help. She rubbed the front of her neck and noticed a smear of blood across the palm of her hand. There didn't seem to be too much damage. She dismissed it with a swipe of her hand down her pants' leg. It felt good to have the Rizzos, or whoever they were, out of her sight. "What the hell just happened? What is going on?" Suddenly, Amelia and Rashelle appeared around the same corner from which the officers disappeared with the bad guys. They were a sight for sore eyes. Elizabeth desperately wanted to run to her grandmother and give her a hug. Unfortunately, there were more pressing matters, like getting out of there before the full force of the storm hit.

"Alright Lieutenant, we have checked and double checked every room." Amelia had to shout over the wind and rain. "All guests have been evacuated. The only staff left are the ones you are looking at. Everyone else is safely at the shelter or is on the way."

Perkins looked relieved. The stress of the past couple of days was starting to show in his face. "Right, then. Let's get out of here! Mitchell, you see that Amelia and Rashelle get to the shelter. Elizabeth your car has been returned to you. It's parked out front where you left it. Are you up to driving or do you need someone to take care of that for you? I'm assuming you wouldn't want to leave your car here, with the hurricane coming."

Elizabeth had never let anyone drive that car before this and she wasn't about to let that happen now. It was bad enough that the police had snatched it out from under her nose without her consent. There had better not be a scratch on it. "No, I'm good. I'll drive. Thanks." In frustration and confusion she asked, "But could someone explain what just happened?"

"Miss Pennington, I'm sorry. That is just going to have to wait. We will rendezvous at the shelter and debrief you then. Okay? Let's move out!"

Elizabeth could feel her frustration building. Everyone else seemed to be clued in. She couldn't stand it, but she was going to have to wait to hear the details. She wanted to know if the girl had been found and if she was alive. She couldn't bear the thought of leaving her behind. The last five people at the inn headed around to the front of Acadia building toward the main building of the inn. Mitchell and Rashelle led the group. The two Pennington ladies were in the middle. Perkins brought up the rear. As they were walking, Amelia put her arm around Elizabeth. "Are you sure you are alright, honey?" She was yelling to be heard above the roar of the wind. Elizabeth nodded her head in response. "Are you okay to drive?" She nodded her head again. "Alright, well I'm going to go with Kurt and Rashelle. I will meet you at the shelter. Okay?" Amelia never had felt comfortable in Elizabeth's little sports car.

"Okay, Nana." She was yelling back at her grandmother. "No problem. I will see you there." She lunged forward and grabbed Mitchell's arm in front of her, stopping him momentarily on the walkway to the inn. He turned back toward her and Rashelle stopped to see what was going on, too. "You take care of her. Do you hear me? Take care of my grandmother."

"Got it, Liz. She's in good hands. Now let's get out of here before it's too late to leave." They all picked up the pace. They were almost jogging when they reached the front of the inn. The wind off the ocean was incredibly strong. It hit them right in the face. They had to lean forward to walk against the wind. In the semi-circle in front of the inn were three cars. Mitchell's very modest Honda something or other was located furthest down the drive, with Lieutenant Perkins' squad car and Elizabeth's Z4 closer toward the front porch of the inn. Lizzi was thrilled to see her pride and joy again. She couldn't wait to get in it and become free again. She glanced over to see Amelia walking between Kurt and Rashelle toward his car, their ticket out of there. Apparently, Rashelle had wrapped her car around a tree during the summer on her way back from a night out at a local bar. She had to rely on others for transportation until she could get a new one.

Elizabeth suddenly gasped. She turned to Perkins who was behind her. "Lieutenant! There is one more guest left at the inn!"

"What!?"

"Yes! I am absolutely certain! Come with me! I'll need your help."

Elizabeth set out on a dead run with the lieutenant right behind her. She led him around the corner of the Acadia House back to the spot from where they had just come. Perkins was getting very anxious. She had better be right. They were running out of time. Elizabeth ran right up to the hatchway that Mitchell had locked behind her earlier. She turned to Perkins. She had to shout for him to hear her over the wind. "Mrs. Leibowitz is still in there.

I passed her in the tunnel when I was heading toward the main building of the inn. She was walking in the opposite direction. The hatchway was locked so she couldn't have gotten out, but she couldn't have made her way back to the inn because of the cave-in." She stopped to take a breath. Perkins was considering everything she had just yelled to him.

He knew there was a possibility that Mrs. Leibowitz had perished in the cave-in. No one knew the extent of the damage in the tunnel. On the other hand, she could have been spared any injuries and was down there trying to figure out how to get out. There was one way to find out. Without wasting any time, he drew his revolver out of its holster and took several shots at the lock on the hatchway. Elizabeth cowered behind him to avoid any shrapnel. She opened her eyes to see him opening the door. There, sitting halfway up the steps, was Mrs. L holding an empty bottle of red wine. The neck of the bottle had been broken so she could access the wine. The front of her shirt showed evidence that she had missed her mouth a few times. Lt. Perkins grabbed her firmly by the arm and helped her quickly up the steps. She was obviously feeling no pain. She was walking like she couldn't feel her feet. When she reached the top, he snatched the bottle out of her hand and threw it aside. Slamming the door to the hatchway, he shouted to the ladies that they needed to clear out quickly. Elizabeth grabbed onto Mrs. Leibowitz' other arm to speed up the process. They started to make their way back to the last two cars in the circle in front of the inn. She was a little wobbly on her feet, but they got her through the wind and sleet to the circular drive in front of the inn. They loaded her into the back seat of the cruiser. Perkins slammed the door and turned around to address Elizabeth.

Lt. Perkins grabbed her by the forearm and pulled her closer to his face. He spoke urgently. "YOU HAVE TO GET OUT NOW. NO ONE STANDS A CHANCE WITH THIS STORM! GET OUT NOW!!" He loosened his grip and she pulled away from him. He quickly turned away. He had done his duty and he was leaving.

Elizabeth took one last look around while the state trooper headed around to the driver's side of his squad car. They were the last three remaining at the inn after a mandatory evacuation that had started a few hours earlier. She could tell the storm had strengthened significantly since they started the sweep of the inn's guest rooms. Sleet stung as it hit her face. The wind and rain were whipping her hair into her face. She kept wiping wet strands from her eyes and pulling them out of her mouth. The wind was getting so strong that it was becoming difficult to stand in one place without getting pushed to the side.

She really needed to get out of there before it was too late. Elizabeth found it hard to leave her beloved childhood home, though. She didn't want to think about what it might look like after a category four hurricane had plowed through it. She turned and watched Lt. Perkins disappear down the driveway of the inn. It was her turn to leave, too. Her eyes welled with tears. She reached for the door handle of her car and gave it a pull, but it didn't budge. She tried it again and a look of horror crossed her face. The state police had returned her car to her, but had neglected to give her back her keys. Were they inside? The rain was hitting the window so hard that she couldn't see in. She banged on the window with her fist and it didn't give. Even if she was able to break the window, it wouldn't do her any good unless the keys were inside. Panic was starting to take over. A strong gust of wind pushed her to the side so she had to shuffle her feet to keep them under her. Her eyes were wide and she was desperately looking around her, trying to get herself out of this mess. She was going to have to wait out the storm here. *But where is it safe?* She shuddered at the idea of the tunnels. Before the cave-in she would have considered the tunnels a safe place to wait out a storm, but not anymore. Then she remembered her cell phone. She headed for the porch of the inn, hoping for a little refuge from the storm, while she slipped her phone out of her pants' pocket. As both feet landed on the porch, she flipped it open. She could call ahead to Rashelle and they could come back to get her. One glance at her phone told her she had no service. The storm had probably already taken out cell towers along the entire East Coast. She had no way to call for help. What about the phone in the inn? She grabbed the knob on the front door. Through the windows she could see the porch furniture and the bicycles stacked up inside so they wouldn't become flying projectiles outside in the storm. She tried to turn the knob and it didn't move. Her eyes grew wide and she stubbornly tried again and again, shaking the knob and trying to force it to turn. "NO!" She pounded her fists on the door. She had no way to get in. This couldn't be happening. She had nowhere to go. For the first time, she felt that she was in real danger…she was all alone…she was going to die alone.

She turned around and pushed her back up against the door, slowly sliding down into a crouching position. Tears fell down her cheeks and melted into the rain drops that were already there. She began to sob. She couldn't believe it was going to end like this. She rested her bottom on the welcome mat in front of the door and hugged her legs with her arms. Her whole body was shaking from her sobs. She bowed her head, resting her forehead on her knees. This was it. Amid regrets that were crossing her mind, she had an irrational thought that she wished she had gone to the lighthouse one more time. She didn't get a chance to go back up into it after she got interrupted by Renard when she had first arrived. She loved that lighthouse. It always made her feel safe—

THE LIGHTHOUSE!! She would be safe in the lighthouse! She just needed to get there. She would need to get down the cliff and across the breakwater. It would be very treacherous. Unfortunately, she didn't have much choice. The lighthouse was her only hope. She gathered all the courage she could and headed down the front steps, across the front lawn. She started to run toward the path through the woods, the wind blowing in from sea and nearly knocking her off her feet. She did not even bother to take one last look at her car. She felt as if it had been a traitor to her. It wasn't there for her when she needed it most.

Elizabeth reached the narrow path in the woods and was relieved that the trees provided some shelter against the strong wind.

She moved as quickly as she dared, taking little steps in rapid succession. She needed to get to the lighthouse as quickly as possible before the storm got much worse, but she would need to do it without falling and getting hurt. She kept going, one foot in front of the other, little steps. Finally, she reached the lookout on the bluff where the path took a turn. Elizabeth slowed down enough to navigate the turn on the muddy path. Just as she thought she was clear to speed up, her foot slipped out from underneath her and she almost went down. She caught herself after some uncoordinated acrobatic maneuvers with her arms flailing and she headed to the steeper part of the trail. Slowing her pace, she cautiously proceeded. The wind was getting stronger in her face because the trees were thinner at this point on the trail and would be all the way down to the end of the path. She held onto tree branches to keep her balance, trying not to go too fast. She thought of Nana, Rashelle, and Kurt. She hoped they had made it safely to the shelter. Hopefully they weren't worrying about her. She wished she had a way to get in touch with them. She wished she had a way out of there.

After an excruciatingly long climb down the path, going from tree to tree, she reached the bottom. She looked out in front of her at the lighthouse; her refuge. *Not much farther now. Almost there.* She was trying to convince herself. There was no turning back anyway. The shed was her first stop. She reached in to grab the key off the nail.....it wasn't there. "OH MY GOD!" she screamed into the wind. There was no one around to hear her. Why wasn't the key there? What did that mean? Was there someone already in the lighthouse? Elizabeth had no idea what the answers were to those questions. Her eyes grew wide again. She was desperate to figure out what to do. Maybe whoever had the key had left the door to the lighthouse unlocked. Should she take the chance and cross the breakwater? She watched as the wind was whipping the waves over the huge rocks, her path to safety.

She had to risk it. She was out of options. She took a deep breath and headed toward the lighthouse across the rocks. The wind was directly in her face so she had to lean forward to keep from being blown backward. The sleet stung her face. She tried to focus on each step, on her usual technique for crossing the jagged surface. One foot in front of the other, pushing through the wind. She felt a wave crash on the rocks just behind her. She didn't dare look. That was too close. *One step at a time.* A wave crashed just in front of her. Was she next? She couldn't let that thought occupy her mind. One step at a time. It couldn't be much farther. Then she made the critical mistake of looking up to see how close she was. The wind caught her in the face and pushed her backwards. She was forced to take two or three steps backwards and her foot missed its mark on the last one. Her left shoe wedged down into a crevice between two large rocks. She felt a sharp pain in her ankle that was twisted at an awkward angle. At that moment, a wave crashed over her. Her wedged foot kept her from getting knocked into the frigid water, but the wave did manage to push her onto her side. She hit hard and she lay there with her hip throbbing. She was so cold. She wasn't winning the fight and she didn't know how much more she had in her. Her whole body ached from getting thrown onto the rocks. She just lay there with the storm thrashing all around her. She considered just staying there and letting Mother Nature do her will. She was breathing hard. Another wave crashed over her. She held her breath until the water subsided. How much longer could she take this? *Elizabeth, you have to get up! Don't just lie there. Get up!* It took everything she had left to pull herself up into a sitting position. She needed to save her own life. She yanked and yanked on her foot stuck between the rocks. It wouldn't come out. This can't be it. She couldn't die out here on the rocks, all alone. Her grandmother would be so sad when they found her...if they found her. She thought about her grandfather and how he had fought the storm and didn't win. She wondered if this was how he had felt. Another wave crashed over her hitting her hard on the side of her face. Water slammed into her nose and mouth. She was so overwhelmed she couldn't even cough at first. After a few seconds, her body went into panic mode and fought to get the water out of her nasal cavities. She coughed and choked and gasped for air until finally she could start to breath in air. *Lizzi, get up! Get out of here!* Thankfully the waves gave her enough of a reprieve so she could catch her breath. Then another wave. This one knocked her sideways again, but she kept herself from hitting the rocks. She was desperately trying to save herself. She had to get her foot out from between the rocks. In all her struggling, fighting the waves, it felt as though the foot was wedged further into the rocks. She had to get out of there and get to the lighthouse. That was her only hope. She had to get her foot out from between the rocks...her foot, but not necessarily her shoe! Quickly she loosened the ties and pulled out her bare foot, leaving the shoe between the boulders. She could tell she was running out of time. The waves were getting higher and more violent. She bowed her head to the wind, held her breath, and started to run toward the lighthouse, perhaps a foolish act but she had nothing left to lose. Finally, she reached the large wooden door. She threw herself against it. Fortunately it was on the side of the lighthouse opposite the wind so she had a momentary break. The door was heavy so she had to give it a good tug. As she was pulling, she noticed her hands and arms were all scraped from fighting the waves on the rocks. She didn't realize it, but her legs looked even worse. The door didn't move. She tried again, this time she used so much force that her wet hands slipped off the handle and she catapulted backwards and landed on her rear end. This couldn't be happening. It can't be locked! She picked herself up and flung herself at the door, banging on it with both fists. "GOD, PLEASE HELP ME! YOU ARE MY ONLY HOPE! PLEASE LET ME—"

She thought she could feel the door pressing toward her. Could it be? She stepped back but grabbed onto the door handle for stability. She couldn't believe her eyes. In the doorway of the lighthouse, with a look of fear and shock, was none other than her sweet, elderly grandmother. Amelia reached toward Elizabeth, grabbed her by the upper arm, and firmly pulled her inside, slamming the door behind them. "What are you doing here?! For God's sake Lizzi, you could have been killed trying to get down here!"

The volume of her voice was approaching shouting. She was scolding. "Why didn't you leave when you could?!" She reached over and locked the door behind Elizabeth.

"Nana!" She was shouting over the driving wind and crashing waves. It sounded like the ocean was starting to swallow the lighthouse. "What are *you* doing here?" Her emotions overcame her shock. "Oh, I am so glad to see you!" She hugged her grandmother with all her might. She loved her so much. She couldn't believe she had found her in the lighthouse. They could only pray that the fortress that had stood strong and tall for so many decades would carry them safely through this storm. It was a strong one. Elizabeth was still scared of the hurricane, but felt so much better now that she was with her grandmother. They lingered in the warmth and comfort of each other's arms.

Finally Amelia pulled away, taking a step backwards, and looked directly into her granddaughter's eyes. "Let's find a place to sit this one out for a while." They headed over to the wall on the far side of the lighthouse. It was the side that the wind was coming from. A couple of old blankets were already in a heap on the floor. They tried to make themselves as comfortable as possible. The wind raged just outside the walls. They held each other and prayed. The waves relentlessly crashed against the wall on the other side of them. *Please hold strong. You've stood for all these years. Please protect us from the storm.* For over an hour, they held each other and listened to the force of the hurricane outside. They could only imagine what it looked like on the other side of the fortress walls. The winds continued to whip the water against the lighthouse. The century old structure creaked and groaned with the battering to its front. Grandmother and granddaughter held onto the hope that they would survive the storm.

Chapter 25

The winds were dying down a bit. Sounded like the eye of the storm was approaching. It was a time to catch their breaths, but it would only be a brief reprieve. The tail end of the hurricane would soon follow. Amelia thought it was time for them to have a little chat.

Amelia turned toward Elizabeth. "Lizzi, there is something I need to tell you, once and for all. You should have heard this a long time ago and if I don't tell you now…well, it's time you finally knew what happened to your parents."

Elizabeth quietly gasped. Finally, and in the middle of a major hurricane, she was going to get to hear what she has been dying to know for years.

"And I know that we all have kept this from you over the years, thinking we were protecting you from the pain. But I imagine not knowing was just as painful." She paused to gather her thoughts. Elizabeth was all ears, anxious and fearful to hear the truth. "Your parents loved you so very much. I don't think I saw two people who got as much joy from being with their child as your mother and father did with you. You meant the world to them. The three of you were inseparable. You did everything together. When one was helping to run the inn, the other was with you.

"Your mother was so good at handling the day to day operations at the inn. The guests and the staff loved her. She was so sweet. Your father was more of a "big picture" kind of guy who ran things from more of a backroom operation. Also, a very sweet guy. They made a great team and the inn was quite successful under their reign." She paused again, perhaps to catch her breath, and then continued. "You were so happy while they were alive. You loved to be where your parents were. All of that changed one day. You were little, about four years old. You and your father had taken a walk down to the lighthouse one afternoon, as you loved to do so often. It became dinner time so your mother took a walk down to fetch you two. It had been particularly windy that day, the fringes of an offshore storm, so the water had been unusually rough. No one could have predicted what happened next. Your mother had nearly reached where you and your father were sitting on the breakwater, and to her horror, she watched as a rogue wave crashed on top of you. She ran to try to help you. When the water receded, your father was nowhere to be found, but she could see you clinging to the rocks below at the water's edge. You were half submerged in the cold water. Frantically, she ran to pull you out of the water. There was no one else around to help. She picked you up and carried you part way up the rocks when another wave knocked her down from behind—"

"She fell and the force of the wave knocked me out of her arms," Elizabeth continued. Her grandmother looked at her, eyes wide in disbelief. "She was able to keep me from getting sucked in by the sea. But she wasn't so lucky. She was pulled into the water as my father had been."

"How did you know?" Her voice was breathless. Amelia was incredulous. She thought she was the only one that knew the details of the horrible tragedy. "Who told you?"

"No one. I saw it all in a dream, one that I will never forget." She looked as though she could see the dream in her mind's eye quite vividly. "It was many years ago and, at the time I wasn't sure what to make of it. I will never forget it, though. So it was my parents…" Elizabeth was lost in her thoughts and holding her breath. Her poor parents. Then she thought for a moment of Amelia's con-

196

nection to the event. "…but how did you know what happened to them?" She hadn't been there.

"I also had a dream. Could have been the same one as yours. I think it was your mother trying to show us what actually happened. She knew we were agonizing over it. You know, loved ones who have passed on have different ways of communicating with us. One way is through dreams. It is their way of helping us deal with our grief."

Elizabeth just looked at her grandmother in disbelief.

"It's true, dear. If you can resist becoming frightened when these things happen, they can be quite comforting."

Elizabeth went back to the images on the rocks in her dream. What an awful way to die…so the newspaper clippings she had dug out of the old desk in Cecelia's room were about her parents. But one of the articles had a headline about three people being swept off the rocks, not two.

Amelia continued. "At first, we thought all three of you had perished off the breakwater. You evidently were a little dazed after the incident, but somehow found your way back up to the inn. You slipped through the lobby unnoticed by anyone and went and hid in a closet in the rooms you shared with your parents. It took a while before anyone found you, so they were originally searching for three people. Someone from housekeeping finally opened the closet door and found you all bloody from your head lacerations and in a bit of shock." As an aside she added, "We never did figure out why you hid in the closet so often."

Elizabeth was staring forward, looking like she was in a trance. "Aunt Cecelia."

"What?" She wasn't sure she had heard correctly.

"Aunt Cecelia." She turned her head and looked directly into her grandmother's face. Suddenly, her eyes filled with anger that had built up over the years. Her voice became firm and loud. "I hid in there because I felt safe… safe from Aunt Cecelia. She was always yelling at me when I was little. I hated it. I tried to stay away from her, but she always seemed to find me. The closet was my refuge from her."

Amelia was stunned. She wasn't sure how to respond. "Lizzi… Cecelia is dead…She died before you were born."

Elizabeth eyes grew wide as she tried to understand what her grandmother was saying. "W-what?"

"Cecelia died a long time ago. She wasn't a very happy person to begin with, very bitter at the world, very self-conscious, suspicious of other people. She never married. She got sick one winter and she got really ornery. Her body never recovered. She was gone before spring. It was probably pneumonia. We didn't really have all the medical resources back then like we do now. That was back in 1969."

This just wasn't making any sense to Elizabeth. "How can this be?"

"Well…I have heard that some of the guests over the years have reported seeing a ghostly figure of a woman from time to time. I thought perhaps that it was the young girl who died at the school. I suppose it could have been Cecelia."

Elizabeth's mind was reeling. She was having trouble grasping everything her grandmother was sharing with her. She took a deep breath. Her great aunt was just a ghost? Her parents had died on the very rocks she had crossed so many times as a child and, yet, she had somehow survived? It didn't seem fair. But then again, so many things in life weren't.

"Elizabeth, I am so sorry. I know this must be so hard to hear. I never knew when the right time would be to tell you so I kept postponing it. I'm sorry." She gazed at her beautiful granddaughter whom she had raised from an adorable preschooler to a beautiful, young woman. She was as proud of her as if she were her own daughter. She just wished she wasn't racked with guilt over Lizzi's less than joyful childhood and the years it took her to tell her the truth. At least, now, it was out in the open and she would just have to try to help her accept it.

Elizabeth was finally able to speak. "Nana, I love you so much. I know that it was hard for you to tell me." She swallowed hard, almost choking on her emotions. "It was a bit of a shock to hear." She took hold of both of her grandmother's hands and looked deeply into her eyes. Her face looked drawn and worried.

The strength of the wind was picking up again. It was time to brace for the other half of the hurricane.

"Thanks for telling me, Nana." She hugged her grandmother like she had never hugged her before. Amelia needed that.

Then Elizabeth had a thought. "Nana…why did you come down to the lighthouse instead of going to the shelter?"

"Oh, Lizzi. You were supposed to go off to the shelter and not worry about me." She looked sideways at her granddaughter. "I couldn't imagine leaving the inn even if a hurricane was coming. I thought I would stay with the ship, like your grandfather had done, and go down with it, if necessary. I had never left it before. I've seen this place through good times and bad. And there have been a lot of bad. I told Kurt and Rashelle that I would get a ride from you—"

"And you told me that you were going with them." She was starting to get annoyed with her grandmother.

"Precisely." She wasn't going to let her Lizzi give her a hard time. This was her decision. "I realized that the safest place for me to ride it out would be here. So I managed to get down here before it got too rough." She thought for a moment and then admitted, "It was a bit scary until you showed up!"

Elizabeth couldn't believe her grandmother was willing to die with the inn. Of course, that thought made her feel hypocritical. Thank God she had been there. It would have been certain death for her if her grandmother hadn't been at the lighthouse to open the door for her.

Elizabeth and her grandmother settled in again to weather the tail of the storm.

Chapter 26

The Pennington duo huddled close together as the wind howled loudly outside. Suddenly, there was a thunderous crash against the wall of the lighthouse behind them. It made them jump. Sitting on the floor across from the sturdy wooden door, they watched in horror as water started to seep under it. Quickly, grandmother and granddaughter jumped to their feet, gathering the blankets that had been cushioning their seat on the floor, and scrambled for the circular stairway. Elizabeth helped guide her Nana up the first few steps. Amelia ascended slowly, trying to be careful not to lose her footing. The old steps can trip you up very easily. They got narrower the closer you stepped toward the center column and if you weren't keeping an eye on where you were placing your feet, you could take a misstep that would be very painful.

Water rose quickly on the ground level. Before Elizabeth could reach the first step, she was ankle deep, one sneakered foot and the other one bare. Amelia and Elizabeth climbed a dozen or so steps before they turned around and sat down on the narrow planks of wood, a couple steps apart from each other, on the widest part of their steps. They huddled with the blankets around their shoulders, watching the water rising up the steps. After a while, it seemed to be receding, but the next big wave against the fortress brought more water inside. How far would it rise? Would the lighthouse remain steadfast in the storm? Amelia and Elizabeth were praying it would.

———————————

After nearly a half an hour of being perched on the narrow steps of the circular stairway watching the water rise and recede, Amelia spoke, "Lizzi, there is something else I need to tell you." She looked as though she couldn't wait any longer to get it off her chest. Elizabeth turned her head upward, looking expectantly at her grandmother. *What else could she have to say? This can't be good.*

"Lizzi...there may be a problem trying to hang on to this place."

"What?!" Elizabeth's gasp was drowned out by the roar of the storm. She banged the back of her head against the metal railing as she reeled back. The knot she had received earlier in the tunnel started to throb again. She rubbed around it to relieve the pain.

"Elizabeth, I may not really be a Pennington." Amelia was looking down at her feet as if ashamed.

Elizabeth could scarcely comprehend what her grandmother was trying to tell her.

"You see, when I was little—and that was so many years ago. I was probably around four or five." She looked into Elizabeth's eyes, "...about the age you were when you lost your parents." Elizabeth felt a nasty tug in her abdomen. "Well my parents, evidently, were having trouble getting along. I don't remember much of it. I just remember a lot of yelling. Finally, they decided that the three of us would be better off if they split up. I don't even know if they ever got divorced. That just wasn't very common back then. So, I imagine, they argued about who would have custody of me. In all their wisdom, they decided I would decide who I would live with. A tremendous burden to put onto a small child. To do this, they took me for a ride to the shore, to the Pennington Point Lighthouse. Back then, the public could access the trails to the lighthouse during the summer months when school wasn't in session. There were more trails back then, including one through the woods that brought you out further down the access road.

So my parents decided to walk down to the bluff with me and leave me there. I was to decide who I was going to leave with. One waited at the top of the trail through the woods and the other waited at the top of the only trail that exists now. I was to decide and walk to the top of the trail where that parent was waiting. I must have agonized over the decision and took too long because neither parent was there when I got there. I don't remember which one I tried first, but neither was waiting for me. Each must have figured I had chosen the other and given up."

Elizabeth couldn't believe what she was hearing. "Oh, Nana, how awful." A small, warm tear rolled down her cheek.

Amelia looked down at her granddaughter, not really acknowledging her reaction, "So I must have wandered the property searching for my parents. It got dark and I ended up spending the night in the woods. By morning, I was in shock, partly traumatized over the whole situation." Amelia's eyes started to fill with tears. "I've often wondered if they really just abandoned me."

"Oh, Nana! No!" Elizabeth jumped up and hugged her grandmother with all her might. "That isn't true!" They embraced while the wind howled and the waves crashed outside.

Finally they pulled apart and Elizabeth sat back down on the narrow step, taking a moment to glance at the water creeping up the steps. It had crept a few steps closer to them. Amelia pulled the blanket tighter around herself and continued. "Evidently the couple who owned the school, the Penningtons, found me and took me in. I don't know if I could even tell them my name. They pieced together my story from what I could tell them. They probably searched for my parents, but if they had gone their separate ways thinking I was with the other parent, they wouldn't have realized I was missing." She paused to gather her thoughts. She let out an inaudible sigh before continuing. "So when I say they took me in, that's what they did. They took care of me. I used the last name of Pennington because they never knew what my real name was. But they never really officially adopted me." She let her last comment sink in for a minute.

Elizabeth was getting it. If Amelia wasn't really a Pennington, then neither was she. Perhaps neither of them possessed legal claim to the property. She felt as if the ground was collapsing beneath her feet.

Amelia went on. "The Penningtons were such nice people. They had two children of their own. A boy and a girl, both were a few years older than me. After we were all grown, I grew very close to the Pennington boy."

Elizabeth thought she knew where this was going.

"Things ran their course and, eventually, we fell in love. He asked me to marry him. I couldn't imagine doing anything else. Of course, there were people who thought we were brother and sister when, in fact, we were no relation at all. We just happened to live under the same roof for many years. His sister was one of those people who opposed the marriage—always has."

"Aunt Cecelia…"

"Yes, Cecelia." Amelia looked like she was thinking carefully before she continued.

Suddenly a thought crossed Elizabeth's mind. "But, Nana, if you were married to the Penningtons' son, then doesn't that make you a Pennington, at least by marriage?"

"In theory, yes. Unfortunately, I haven't been able to find a copy of our marriage license and the files at town hall don't go back far enough. No one seems to be able to put their hands on a copy. This *was* an awful lot of years ago."

"So, why do you have to worry about that? You know you were married to him. Isn't that enough?"

"Not when this real estate attorney says he has proof that I don't rightfully own it."

"What!" The howling winds and the crashing waves were taking a back seat to their conversation.

"He claims that he has definitive proof and that I would be better off selling the property to him at a reasonable price than to lose it outright."

"Nana, this guy sounds like an extortionist. He can't have anything on you. This is absolutely ridiculous!"

"Well, I have no proof that I do own it." Her head hung low. She looked exhausted and defeated.

"Nana, don't you worry another minute about this. I will figure out a way to get this guy off your back. You certainly *do* own this inn."

Amelia perked up a bit. She sat up straighter and a slight smile crossed her face. "Well, let's see if we even have one after this storm passes through." She managed a little chuckle. So much was out of her control. Everything was slipping through her aging, frail fingers. She was trying very hard to fight back the tears. She didn't want her granddaughter seeing her falling to pieces. She wrapped her arms around herself, closed her eyes, and took deep breaths. Her little Lizzi sensed she was trying to be strong, so she scooted up as close as she could to her on the step above and put her arms around her wonderful grandmother. She had been carrying a lot on her shoulders all her life and even more so lately.

The two Penningtons stayed cuddled in this position for what seemed like an eternity, as if the clocks of the world had stopped, but the wind and the waves were going to go on forever. Amelia had switched roles with Elizabeth. Once the strong matriarch of the Pennington family, now she was feeling her strength waning and her granddaughter was stepping into her shoes. She had every confidence that Lizzi would take care of everything. Liz had always been a strong, young lady, who went after what she wanted, and had grown into a young woman who usually got what she wanted.

Elizabeth held tightly to her grandmother. Her head slid onto Lizzi's shoulder. She just smiled. She was going to take care of her. She would make it all better. Amelia's eyes opened. "Lizzi, I love you. You have grown into a wonderful, beautiful person. Your parents would be so proud of you. *I'm* so proud of you." Liz struggled to hear her soft voice. "Thank you for everything you have done… everything you will do."

Elizabeth looked down on her like a parent looks upon her young child. Amelia's eyes were getting too heavy. She was struggling to keep them open. This whole ordeal had been too much for her. Slowly her eyes closed. Elizabeth figured she could use the rest. Amelia's body suddenly got very heavy for her to support. It was hard for her to hold her onto the step.

"No…Oh, Nana, no!" Elizabeth couldn't believe this was happening. A large tear ran down her cheek. She didn't think she could feel any sadder. At that moment, she felt a gentle squeeze on her shoulder. Someone knew she needed some shoring up. It was going to take everything she had to hold onto her grandmother through the rest of the storm.

Chapter 27

E lizabeth slowly opened her eyes to the stillness that filled the dimly lit lighthouse. Sunlight pierced through the small dirty windows that punctuated the walls. The storm had finally passed. It was a new day. She turned to look to the step below and realized her grandmother wasn't there. Trying to hold onto her throughout the entire night had proven too difficult for Elizabeth. At some point, she must have let go when she lapsed into inevitable sleep, unaware that she had lost her grip. In the cruel reality of daylight, she turned her gaze toward the bottom of the stairway and looked in horror. There was Amelia in a lifeless heap on the lighthouse floor. Elizabeth leapt to her feet.

"Nana!" She stumbled down the stairs landing awkwardly at the bottom, her legs sore and stiff from perching on the steps for so long. Her knees started to buckle so she gave into them and knelt next to her grandmother. Fortunately the water had receded from the floor of the lighthouse, but it was still wet and slippery. "Oh, Nana. I am so sorry I let you fall! I just couldn't....I'm sorry." An image of her grandmother rolling down the stairs started to cross her mind so she shook her head to clear the thought before she actually saw her land at the bottom. She reached out and gently touched Amelia's arm. She couldn't believe she was gone. "I'm so sorry...." Elizabeth pressed her eyes closed for a moment.

Elizabeth's mind was racing, trying to figure out what to do next. She needed to get them both out of there. She needed to get help. But since there was no one at the inn, help was a long way away. Leaning over, she kissed Amelia on the cheek. It was not the soft, warm face that she was used to feeling when they embraced. It made her pause. She took a deep breath and let it out, trying to shore up her emotions. Gingerly she stood up and hobbled toward the door. Elizabeth knew it was going to take everything she had to open it, so she put the left side of her body against the old wooden door and pushed. At first it didn't give so she moved her feet slightly away from the door to give her more leverage. Another heartier push made the door move outward, letting sunlight flood into the base of the lighthouse. Elizabeth turned for one last look at her grandmother and then slipped through the opening, her eyes squinting against the bright sun. She paused for a moment as they adjusted to the extreme change in light. Then she thought of the uncomfortable bulge in her pants pocket. She wondered if her cell phone could have survived her treacherous trip out to the lighthouse at the beginning of the storm. Sliding her hand into her pocket, she struggled to pull it out of her still soggy pants. It looked like it was unscathed. She willed it to work and then flipped it open. Nothing. No lights. No sounds. It was dead. Elizabeth's heart sank. Getting help was going to be more difficult than she had thought. Disgusted, she shoved the phone back into her pocket and started her trek back across the rocky breakwater.

It was a remarkably beautiful day with a clear blue sky. A pleasant breeze was blowing in off the water. Elizabeth had no idea what time it was, probably mid-morning, but the air was warm and the sun already strong. It felt good on her face. Knowing she had to be careful, she placed her feet methodically on each boulder as she made her way, one at a time. Each wave that crashed gently near her made her gasp and stop momentarily, as she remembered the powerful waves that Mother Nature had unleashed the day before. Eventually she got used to the movement and was able to make steady progress. Reaching the shed, Elizabeth allowed herself a sigh of relief that she had made it that far. She wondered what was in store for her on her climb up the hill, through the woods. She pressed on.

Immediately she could see the narrow path was quite muddy and littered with branches. She deliberately kept her eyes on her feet and hung onto branches to steady herself while stepping over small branches and climbing over larger ones. The climb up the hill was much more challenging than usual. She was breathing heavy, but didn't slow her pace. In spite of the impediments she reached the bluff in due time. She stopped to glance out to the lighthouse. It stood there appearing as it had for so many years, belying the fury of the storm from the day before and the sadness that remained within it. Elizabeth closed her eyes. A tear escaped and ran down her cheek. She turned away. There was no time to waste so she continued up the hill.

The top half of the path was as cluttered as the bottom, forcing her to climb over more branches littering the path. She slipped in spots that were particularly wet. Elizabeth reached the top, huffing and puffing, but did not linger. She started toward the inn but then stopped in her tracks. Her beloved childhood home had clearly taken the brunt of the storm. She gasped. Her eyes welled with tears and she swallowed hard. The inn still stood majestically on the precipice, but it was damaged with broken windows and shutters hanging by a thread. Her car was nowhere in sight. Slowly she turned and walked toward the access road. There would be no reason to go to the inn. She couldn't get in anyway, but now it might be dangerous to try. She felt so alone. It was as if she were the only one who had survived the storm.

The access road had its share of trees and branches strewn across it. Elizabeth realized that would pose a challenge for emergency vehicles to get back down the road. She kept walking, trying to think of the nearest place to find a working phone. There were a couple of houses near the entrance to the inn's access road. She would start there. Elizabeth looked down at her feet and laughed. There was no point in having just one shoe on so she took the lone shoe off of her foot. Winding up like she was pitching at an MLB game, she hurled the shoe into the woods and listened for the soft thud when it landed. She smiled slightly and then started down the access road. Pennington Road. She wasn't sure exactly how long it was but if she were to take a guess, she would say it was about a mile. Maybe a mile and a half. It seemed so much longer on foot. Especially barefoot. The partially graveled dirt road was not easy to traverse with no shoes on. She was beginning to regret discarding her only shoe. Too late now. She wasn't turning back for a shoe, especially one that was now lost in the woods. She kept walking.

Elizabeth was trying to keep her head clear of thoughts and just stay focused on her task. It seemed eerily quiet as she made her way back to Route 72. Her bare feet made no sound on the road. They were becoming sore. The occasional sharp rock protruding through the packed dirt cut into her feet and made her yell out. She thought of her grandmother and kept walking. Her feet were becoming dirty and gritty. Since she was scanning the woods on both sides of her as she walked, she didn't notice a particularly sharp object lodged in the road and stepped directly on it with her right foot, which absorbed the weight of her body. It was too much for her to recover from. She winced, yelled out for no one to hear, and fell forward into a heap on the dirt road. The fall knocked the wind out of her so she lay there gasping for air. Panic started to creep into her mind. She kept trying to get air and finally the panic subsided when she realized she was going to be fine. She took one deep breath, picked herself up, and started down the road again, oblivious to the cut in the bottom of her foot. There were small tracks of blood forming a staggered line behind her.

Finally Elizabeth could see the end of the access road where it met Route 72. There was no sound. No cars passing by. This was not a usual day in Pennington Point. She turned left onto the main road and headed toward what she hoped would be civilization and help for her grandmother. The road turned from dirt and gravel to hot pavement. Elizabeth was relieved to have something smoother to walk on. She walked about a hundred yards when she came upon a little cottage on the right side of the road. Just the sight of the driveway made Elizabeth's heart flutter. It would be a relief to get off of the hot pavement. She turned into the driveway and made her way to the front door. She noticed there were no cars in the driveway but she reasoned that they were in the detached garage. There was a screened-in porch on the front of the dwelling so she opened the door and took a few steps to the front door. It was rather quiet but Elizabeth remained optimistic that there was someone inside. She opened the screen door and banged with her fist on the door. Silence. She listened for footsteps or hushed conversation. Nothing. She breathed in and banged even louder and then listened in silence to see if she had aroused anyone. Nothing. Her heart sank. She decided that the owners either were at a local shelter or had closed up the cottage for the season and headed back to Connecticut, or wherever they were from, and called it a season. She thought about breaking in, but figured even if she did, the phone probably wasn't working anyway.

She stepped back and let the screen door slam. Making her way back across the porch, she did her best to talk herself into believing that she would find someone home at the next house. She let the porch door slam behind her as well and headed across the lawn. Onto the next house.

Elizabeth continued down Route 72. Her feet were becoming so sore that she began to limp. The sun was now directly above her and very strong for early September. Perspiration beaded up on her forehead. Her body was heating up and she was starting to feel dizzy. She couldn't remember the last time she had anything to eat or drink. Fighting to stay focused, she pressed on to find the next house on the road. She walked in the eerie silence until she noticed she was having trouble walking in a straight line. The yellow line was at her feet. She paused, shook her head, and then adjusted her direction to return to the right side of the road. The pavement was so hot, though, so she decided to try to walk in the weeds along the side of the road. Not very comfortable on her feet, but certainly much cooler. Off to the right of the pavement, she noticed yellow Dandelion blossoms, delicate Queen Ann's Lace and light blue

Bachelor Buttons that dotted the embankment as it dropped down and away from the road. It was taking everything she had to keep putting one foot in front of the other. Her throat became parched. It was difficult to swallow. She paused again as dizziness started to overcome her. Her knees buckled and the last thing she saw before she passed out was the faded white line on the side of the road. Her unconscious body landed in the weeds next to the road, but gravity took over and forced it to roll down the embankment into the gulley. She was on her left side, her arms and legs splayed at awkward angles. She lay there, out of view from passing motorists, in the hot, late summer sun.

Chapter 28

Darkness. A muffled voice. More darkness. Elizabeth tried to open her eyes. Her lids were unusually heavy. The voice again. "Elizabeth." It sounded familiar. "Elizabeth. You have to wake up. Elizabeth!" She managed to open her eyes slightly and moan. The sun was so bright that she closed them again. "Elizabeth! Stay with me." She tried again. This time the man who was speaking to her was shielding her eyes. She got them open but her vision was blurry. She tried blinking and then squinting. Finally she understood who was knelt over her.

"Kurt." Her voice was barely audible. Her mouth felt like sandpaper.

He put his arm around her shoulders and lifted her into a sitting position. She groaned. "Here. Drink this." He put a clear plastic water bottle to her lips and she drank eagerly, water dripping down her chin and onto her shirt. He pulled it back after she had taken a couple of gulps. A puzzled look crossed her face. "Not too much at once," he explained. "We need to get you out of the sun. Let me help you up." Without another word, he swiftly lifted her to her feet." She was still groggy and a bit dizzy so she couldn't support her own weight. He scooped her up in his arms, like a groom carrying his bride over the threshold, and headed up the embankment to the side of the road where his car was parked. He opened the passenger side door and carefully placed her on the seat. Once he was sure she was in safely, he closed the door. Still holding the water bottle, he quickly ran around to the driver's side, pulling the keys out of his pocket as he went. He jumped in, revved the car to life, and turned the air conditioner to high. He turned to Elizabeth and offered her more water. He needed to get her cooled down and hydrated.

The fog in her head was starting to clear. She wasn't exactly sure what had just happened. "How did you find me?" She remembered walking down the road but wasn't sure how she had ended up next to it in a ditch.

"Well you didn't exactly make it easy for us."

"Us?"

"Yeah. When you didn't show up at the shelter yesterday, we were all worried about you. You and Amelia. Where were you?"

Suddenly the events of the last several hours came flooding back to her. "Oh Kurt, Amelia is gone. She died in my arms last night." She burst into tears and relayed the story of how she got locked out of her car and the inn so she sought shelter at the lighthouse, only to find her grandmother when she finally got there. Absentmindedly, she wiped her tears with her scraped and filthy hands and left streaks of dirt on her face, turning her tears to mud.

Kurt filled in the rest on his own and realized Amelia's body was still in the lighthouse and would have to be extricated. "Alright." He glanced at the water bottle that she was holding with both hands. "You stay put in the cool car. I'm just going to make a phone call." He stepped out into the hot sun and pulled his cell phone out of his pants pocket, closing the car door gently. He thought this conversation needed to be out of her earshot. While he waited for the person on the other end of the telephone to pick up, he leaned his back side up against the car door and used the back of his free hand to wipe the sweat from his forehead. After a few seconds he stood up straight.

"Lieutenant, we're going to need the medical examiner."

Chapter 29

Acool, stiff breeze was blowing in off the ocean pushing Elizabeth's hair across her face. She watched as
two men, with black, short-sleeved shirts stamped
with MME on the back, loaded the stretcher into the medical examiner's white commercial van. On it was her grandmother's lifeless body, covered by a black cloth. A sharp pain stabbed at her
stomach. Her eyes stung with tears that were welling. She didn't
think she had felt so miserable in her entire life. Amelia was gone.
Forever. Elizabeth was alone for the first time ever. She felt lost....
like the young girl who had been a guest at the inn and had not
been found before the hurricane hit. Surely she had perished.
Or had they found her? Her mind was racing with images of the
events that had occurred during the past few days. The back doors
of the van banged shut in succession, startling Elizabeth out of her
thoughts and refocusing her on the pain of losing her dear grandmother. Dizziness crept into her head, causing her to take a step
to the side to shore up her balance. As the van pulled away, her
emotions completely took over. She began to sob uncontrollably.
Overcome by her grief, she barely noticed the warm touch on her
arm and then the tender, strong arms that wrapped around her,
pulling her toward his chest. She welcomed the refuge and put her
arms around him to hang on. Her whole world had fallen apart.
She was desperate to hang onto whatever was left. His strong hand
started to rub her back. She was completely lost in his embrace,

not wanting it to end. She was glad Kurt was there. He was turning out to be one of the good guys after all.

With her sobbing under control, Elizabeth stepped back and looked into his eyes. She whispered a grateful thank you.

He nodded with a concerned look on his face. "You need some rest, Elizabeth. You've been through so much, and not exactly unscathed." He glanced down at the scrapes on her battered legs. She was still barefoot. "We should get you checked out by a doctor, then let you get some much needed rest."

"Oh, I'm alright. Don't worry about me. Really. I'm fine....I probably could use a little sleep though. I am a little tired," she conceded. Elizabeth took a moment to glance toward the inn. The devastation left in the wake of the hurricane was daunting. The pain in her stomach turned to nausea. Not able to take in any more, she turned away.

"I'll give you a ride to the hotel where a bunch of us are staying in town. If there are no rooms left, you can have mine."

"That's really nice of you, but you—"

"I insist."

She didn't protest any further.

They rode in silence for the ten minute drive to a local chain hotel. Elizabeth watched as the pine trees along the road zipped past the car. It was starting to make her feel dizzy. She felt exhaustion washing over her, which she fought with everything she had left in her.

When they arrived, Kurt pulled the car into the circular drive and directly up to the double doors in front. Elizabeth decided to stay put. After the night she had just had, she was sure that she looked rather disheveled. She watched as Kurt approached the entrance to the hotel where he grasped the handle of the door on the right side and then stepped back to hold it for a young mother struggling to steer a stroller through the door while hanging onto the hand of a toddler. Elizabeth smiled slightly. Someday.

She had just enough time to start dozing off when the sound of Kurt opening the passenger door startled her awake. In his extended hand was a card key. He had been able get a room for her. She took it from him with a sigh of relief.

"I bumped into Rashelle in the lobby and she is going to stop by your room to drop off some clean clothes for you."

Elizabeth nodded in acknowledgment. Clothes and a shower might go a long way to lift her spirits. Time would tell if any of her things were intact back at the inn. She would cross that bridge another time. Kurt took her hand to help steady her while getting out of the car. They left the car where it was parked. Kurt stayed at her side as they entered the hotel so he could be sure she got to her room safely.

Crossing the lobby, she averted her gaze from the staff at the reception desk. If they were looking her way, she could just imagine the looks on their faces. Better to just avoid the situation altogether. She set her sights on the elevators.

The ride up to the seventh floor was quiet. Thankfully no one had joined them in the elevator from the lobby and they did not have to stop on the way up to let in any other passengers. The doors opened to the antiseptic smell of cleaning supplies mixed with stale cigarettes. Kurt held onto Elizabeth's arm as they headed down the carpeted hallway so he could guide her past two large housekeeping carts parked on opposite sides of the hall, a few feet away from each other. They were piled high with clean sheets and towels, unopened boxes of tissues, personal sized soap, and shampoo. Further down the hall was a room service tray, left over from the night before, on the floor next to one door. Kurt yanked her arm just in time before she caught a toe on a water glass that was still half full. At the end of the hall on the right was the room they were looking for. An exit sign hung from the ceiling and pointed toward the doorway across from her room. She slid the card into the slot next to her door and a small red light turned on. She sighed. She just wanted to lie down for a while. She tried three more times, losing patience with each attempt, varying how quickly she inserted the card and how long she left it in before removing it. Each time the red light appeared. She double checked the room number listed on the small cardboard folder that came with the card and looked up at the number on the door. She was so tired that she wouldn't have been surprised if she was trying to open the wrong door. It was the right one, however. Before she could try the card again, Kurt spoke.

"Would you like me to give it a try?" he offered, trying not to offend her.

She smiled. "Sure. Thanks." She just wanted to get inside.

Kurt slid the card in and the green light came on immediately. He stifled a grin.

Elizabeth just shook her head. "Whatever." She was too exhausted to get annoyed. "Damn card keys." She took the card back from him and squeezed it in her hand.

He pushed open the door and held it for her. "Give me a call once you've had a chance to get some sleep and we'll grab a bite to eat. I'm in room 321." He closed the door quietly behind her and stood for a moment in the silence of the hallway. He was obviously relieved he had found her.

Her accommodations were set up as a modest two-room suite. The door to the room opened into a sitting room with a pull-out couch, small desk on the wall across from the couch, coffee table, two end tables, and a kitchenette opposite the windows. The adjoining bedroom held a king sized bed and the bathroom. The décor was tasteful and the room was functional. She flopped on the couch in the seating area and quickly drifted off to sleep, but was awakened by the sound of Rashelle's voice and a pounding sound. Elizabeth forgot for a moment where she was. She dragged herself from the couch and staggered to the door. Her feet had never been so sore. When she opened it, Rashelle had her right arm raised and her hand formed into a fist as though her knocking had been interrupted.

"Oh! There you are. I've been knocking for quite a while. Are you alright?"

Rashelle's voice was a little too loud for her liking. Elizabeth paused for a moment and decided to ignore the question. She glanced down at the clothes tucked under her friend's left arm and the shoes dangling from two fingers on her hand. "Thanks so much for letting me borrow more of your clothes. I really appreciate it."

"No problem. I am so sorry for everything you are going through, Lizzi. I'm so sorry about Amelia...your grandmother. And sorry about the inn." She squeezed Elizabeth's arm with her free hand. "Oh and I thought you could use this, too." She bent down and picked up a bottle of white wine. She must have been carrying it with her right hand and had to put it down to pound on the door.

"Thanks kiddo. You know me too well." Elizabeth took the clothes and wine from her friend. "My cell phone isn't working." She patted a front pocket of her stained pants. "I'll catch up with you somehow. I'm just going to grab a little nap and get cleaned up." She hoped it didn't sound like she was trying to get rid of her, but she just wanted to crash for a while.

"Sounds good. See you then." Rashelle turned and started down the hallway toward the elevators.

Elizabeth let the door swing shut behind her. She placed the bottle on the desk on her way to take a shower. She put the borrowed clothes on the top of the toilet, dropped the shoes on the floor, and then turned around to go back out to the sitting room. She had changed her mind about the wine. A little Pinot would taste good. She rummaged through the drawers in the kitchenette looking for a corkscrew with no luck. Then she glanced at the top of the bottle and discovered it was a screw top. "Of course, it's Australian," glancing at the label. "They don't seem to mind screw off tops down under. Good thinking Shelle." She quickly twisted off the top and looked around for a glass, figuring it would probably be clear plastic and wrapped in plastic. She was pleasantly surprised to see that there were four drinking glasses and four wine glasses arranged upside down on the counter, each resting on a plain, white paper doily. She selected a wine glass and noted that it wasn't of the finest quality, certainly not what would have been used at the inn, and not very large, but it would do. She filled it as close to the brim as possible. After placing the open bottle on the counter next to its cap, she headed to the bathroom for a nice hot shower, taking a sip from her glass as she walked.

Slipping out of her soiled clothing felt slightly cathartic. She had worn them far longer than any clothes were meant to be worn. They were so tattered and stained that the only option was going to be throwing them in the nearest trash can. Not even the local charity would want them.

While the shower was warming up, Elizabeth continued to sip her wine. It tasted better than she remembered wine ever tasting. It started to warm her inside as it trickled down. A quick glance in the mirror made her gasp. She looked worse than she had imagined. A female version of Albert Einstein. Her head started to spin again as the events of the last twelve hours started to replay in her mind. She shook her head, left her wine glass on the sink, and slipped into the warmth of the pulsating water, wincing as the water hit her cuts and scrapes.

Elizabeth turned and stood with her back to the shower, enjoying the invigorating sensation of the pulsating spray on her skin. She wanted to stand there forever, but the heat was starting to make her feel sleepy. As she started to relax, she began to think of her poor grandmother. Tears welled in her tired eyes. She grabbed onto the stabilization bar meant for handicapped guests. Her whole body started to shake as she sobbed uncontrollably. Her knees buckled and she landed in a heap in the tub. The warm water continued to rain down on her as she tried to gather herself. After several deep breaths she grabbed the bar again and pulled herself up to a standing position. She hung on until she felt comfortable standing on her own. She started to sob again, but hung onto the bar until she could pull herself together. She needed to bathe quickly and get out of the shower before she drowned herself. She washed with the little bar of soap that housekeeping had left in the soap dish, being careful to give gentle attention to the scrapes and cuts on her legs and the bump on the back of her head.

After drying herself off with a towel that the staff at the inn wouldn't have called a bath sized towel, she slipped into Rashelle's clothes, grateful that she and her friend were about the same size. Ignoring the shoes for the time being, she opened the bathroom door, grabbed her wine glass from the sink, and drank the last of the glass. She headed straight for the bottle in the other room and refilled her glass. Taking a couple of sips as she walked, she made a beeline for the king-sized bed. She placed her glass on the bedside table and then went to the windows to close the curtains. Returning to the side of the bed, she noticed that the clock on the table read 3:00. It meant nothing to her. She had no sense of time at the moment. Her head was in a fog. She sat on the edge to quickly drink the rest of her Pinot and then slipped under the covers. Her wet hair dampened the pillowcase. Quickly she dropped off to sleep.

Chapter 30

Elizabeth awoke from a fitful sleep to the sound of the telephone next to her bed. It took her a few seconds to realize exactly what the sound was. The room was so dark that she had to fumble to find the phone, knocking the receiver onto the table. Once she managed to get the phone to her ear she could hear Kurt's voice.

"Elizabeth? Are you okay?"

"I was until the phone rang." She winced when she realized how rude that sounded.

"I'm sorry, Liz. It has been several hours and I thought you could use—"

"What time is it?" she interrupted.

Kurt paused, apparently to check his watch. "It's a little after nine."

"p.m.?" She was struggling to make sense of it, her head still hazy from being awakened.

"Yes, p.m. I thought you could use a little food by now."

Elizabeth's body was awake enough to send her hunger pangs. "Yeah, I could eat." She still sounded groggy. "Give me a couple minutes and I'll meet you in the lobby." She tried to rub the sleep out of her eyes.

"Alright, see you then."

She fumbled again to replace the receiver on the base of the telephone in the dark. Then her fingers groped until they found the light on the bedside table. Closing her eyes tightly, she turned the switch. Slowly she opened her eyes, adjusting gradually to the bright light. She let out a groan and started for the bathroom. This time she avoided looking directly into the mirror and went straight to the task of splashing water on her face. Then she realized she had no make-up to use and had no idea what room Rashelle was staying in. She couldn't borrow from her this time. She also didn't have a comb or brush so she just wet her fingers at the sink and ran them through her hair, hoping to improve her appearance as much as she could so it wouldn't be so obvious that she had just rolled out of bed. She glanced in the mirror and sighed. Hopefully he had a sense of humor. There wasn't much else she could do. She quickly slipped on Rashelle's shoes that resembled black ballet slippers, noting that they weren't really her taste, and headed downstairs.

When the elevator doors opened, she could see across the lobby and into the bar. There was Kurt with his blond, wavy hair perched on a stool sitting sideways so he could easily watch the big screen TV and glance to the elevators from time to time. She got about halfway across the lobby when he turned his head and smiled. He stood up and walked toward her.

"Hey, Elizabeth. Good to see you. The restaurant has closed for the night, but we can grab a bite at the bar, if you don't mind." He didn't seem to notice how horrible she looked. She figured he was just being kind. She was grateful.

"That's fine with me." Then it occurred to her that she didn't have her purse. Everything was back at the inn....at least she hoped she would find it when she got back there. "Uh, Kurt, I don't have any cash on me, or credit cards for that matter."

"Oh, hey, don't worry about it. I've got it covered." Gently, he took her arm and led her toward the bar. He motioned for her to take the stool next to the one he had been sitting in. The bartender dropped a couple of menus in front of them without a word and then returned to restocking glasses in the overhead rack. Elizabeth noticed that Kurt had a drink in front of him. It was an amber colored liquid on ice in a short, wide glass. Jack Daniels, she guessed.

The two sat in silence as they perused the short bar menu. When the bartender returned, they both ordered burgers, hers medium and his medium rare. Elizabeth also asked for a glass of white wine, which he poured right away and delivered it to her before putting in the food order. Did it look like she needed it that badly? She supposed that she did.

After a few minutes of sipping drinks and listening to the din of the bar, Elizabeth finally spoke, "So, can you fill me in on what happened back at the inn?"

"There's really no rush and there's not a lot I can tell you at this point." He had a look of concern for her.

"Oh, yes there is. I'm going to need to get back to work at some point, that is, if my boss hasn't fired me already. The last time she called me, I hung up on her."

He decided not to address her comment. "The investigation is ongoing, but I can tell you what they know so far." He examined her face to see if he should continue. She was clearly exhausted and probably numb from the death of her dear grandmother. Yet, in spite of it all, she was still absolutely beautiful in his eyes. But he needed to keep it professional and stick to the task at hand.

Elizabeth rubbed her forehead, trying to relieve the tension. "Oh, just go ahead and spill it. How much worse can it be after the last couple of days?"

Kurt chose not to answer that question directly. That would have to be for her to decide. "Let's start with the Hutchins. The piece of the puzzle that was solved before the hurricane hit was that the Hutchins had given false names when they checked in and are really the Rizzos. Why they chose to do that is unclear at this point, but they are in custody and have a lot of explaining to do. The poor gentleman that you found on the kitchen floor, Joseph Stevens, the accountant, seems to be connected with Hutchins because of the numbers he punched into his cell phone before he died. 2, 1, 0, 1 are the numbers you came up with when you translated from the cell phone keypad to the calculator keypad. Two is the building number for Acadia House and 101 is the room number, the Hutchins' room. Mr. Stevens would have dialed 2101 to reach him on a room phone."

"You mean Rizzo."

"Ah, yes. Rizzo. At this point it looks like he was Rizzo's accountant, but there is no obvious motive for murdering him so the investigation continues."

Mitchell looked up to acknowledge Rashelle approaching them.

"Hey, guys. How's it going?"

Elizabeth turned and examined Rashelle's face. She smiled, stood, and hugged her good friend who was now an unemployed inn manager. "So good to see you." She turned to include Kurt in the conversation. "Kurt was just starting to explain what they have figured out so far that happened at the inn before the hurricane hit." She revisited the image in her mind of the inn's devastation from earlier that morning. It hadn't really sunk in yet that it would take a tremendous amount of rebuilding to restore the inn to its former stature.

"You don't mind if I join you, do you?"

"Of course not. Pull up a seat." Rashelle grabbed the stool next to Elizabeth's and pulled it closer to her. "Okay, so go on." Their focus was back on Kurt.

Then Elizabeth remembered who she was speaking to. "I just have one question, Kurt. How is it that you got so involved in the investigation and know so much about what went on? Was that in your job description as the tennis pro?" She had a twinkle in her eye.

At that untimely moment, the bartender appeared to take Rashelle's order. She went for a lobster roll and glass of wine. He returned quickly to deliver her wine on a small, white cocktail napkin. She took a sip and turned to Kurt to acknowledge that she was listening.

Kurt glanced at Elizabeth and back again to Rashelle. Both were sporting blank but expectant expressions. A smirk came across his face. "Good question." He paused for effect and seemed to be enjoying the suspense he was creating. "I was hired by your esteemed assistant manager," he nodded toward Rashelle, "upon the urging of your grandmother. I actually work for the FBI." Elizabeth's and Rashelle's mouths dropped open. Kurt smiled in amusement.

Elizabeth found her voice first, "What?" She hadn't seen that coming.

Kurt chuckled. "Well I'm glad to hear I didn't blow my cover."

"So why were you there?" She didn't see the connection.

Kurt knew he couldn't tell her much more during an ongoing investigation so he had to do his best to tactfully refrain from revealing any additional information. "I'm sorry, ladies. There isn't really anything more I can tell you at this point. But as soon as the investigation is complete, you will be the first to get briefed on the outcome."

"What about the girl who was missing? Kelsey."

"I'm sorry, Liz. I can't."

Elizabeth's face clearly showed she was disappointed in his response, almost shocked. She had been hoping for so much more. She felt so uncomfortable not knowing the fate of the young girl. Elizabeth was quickly becoming angered. She could feel it building up inside of her. It was difficult suppressing it. She desperately wanted answers and was very frustrated that Kurt was not willing to give them to her.

At that moment, their burgers arrived and the bartender reassured Rashelle that her order was on the way. Rashelle and Elizabeth exchanged looks of disgust and then turned away. The three became silent as Kurt and Elizabeth started in on their late dinner. Elizabeth was so hungry; it was all she could do to maintain her table manners. God help anyone who got their fingers near her food.

Before long Rashelle's lobster roll arrived and she ordered another glass of wine. Elizabeth and Kurt ordered another round as well. The three ate in silence as they devoured their late night meals. The sounds of the bar's televisions and the loud chatter of the bar's patrons filled their ears. Elizabeth found herself longing for a quiet corner.

Chapter 31

In the days after the hurricane, while they were waiting for the authorities to perform an autopsy on Amelia's body, Elizabeth and the staff did their best to clean things up a bit at the inn. Lizzi also kept busy making phone calls, determining priorities, and coordinating outside contractors who were performing the repairs necessary to keep the inn and outbuildings water tight. One of her calls was to her boss to let her know she wouldn't be back to work right away. She made sure to place the call late one evening when she could be fairly sure that Vera would not be in the office. She left a message for her and it was comforting to know that Vera had no way to return her call. There was something very liberating about that.

Elizabeth thought her grandmother would have liked the idea of having her memorial service at the inn, right next to her garden. Unfortunately, even on a beautiful, sunny, September afternoon, the inn seemed so sad. Broken windows were boarded up for the time being until Elizabeth had a chance to decide what her long term plans were for the property. The front of the main building had taken the brunt of the storm. There wasn't much of a porch left. Acadia Building was so heavily damaged that there was talk that it should just be leveled and rebuilt. Moosehead Lodge seemed to be in much better shape. Some minor repairs should put it back into working order. All of those decisions would be made in time. At the moment, the focus was on saying good-bye to beloved Amelia.

One by one, the staff and local neighbors stopped on their way out to speak to Elizabeth as she stood like a sentry at the gate to Elizabeth's garden. Everyone had warm, comforting words to share with her. They all seemed to love Amelia. She would be sorely missed. The inn just wouldn't be the same…well, it wouldn't be the same physically because of the storm, but it also wouldn't be the same without Amelia at the helm. The future of the inn was up in the air.

After most of the crowd had passed by Elizabeth, Kurt Mitchell approached her tentatively. "Elizabeth…I am so sorry about your grandmother." She looked into his eyes and could only shake her head. A tear escaped her eye and traveled down the side of her face. He wrapped one of his long arms around her shoulders and held her tight. No words were spoken. This was what she needed. She was lost in his thoughtful touch for several moments. They stepped apart and she felt instantly cold. A shiver ran down her spine. She desperately wanted to grab hold of him again but she really didn't want to appear as desperate as she felt.

Kurt noticed Chief Austin making his way toward them. "Hello, Chief."

"Hello, Mitchell. Miss Pennington." He tipped his hat. Elizabeth thought he looked rather humble. "Sorry to interrupt." The chief extended his hand towards Elizabeth. "I just wanted to offer my condolences to you."

"Thank you very much." She took his hand. He gently pressed his left hand on hers in a sweet sign of compassion.

"Elizabeth, you should know that Chief Austin was instrumental in identifying the Hutchins as the Rizzos. He made a huge discovery when he did a search of the Hutchins' room and uncovered a magazine that had their correct name on it. It was the break we needed in the case. After that, it was relatively easy to put the pieces together."

Elizabeth looked at Mitchell for a moment and then realized what he was trying to do for the chief. She decided to play along.

"Chief, nice work."

"Just doing my job, ma'am."

"Well, we certainly appreciate it. Nice job."

"You are so welcome, Elizabeth. I'm just sorry that it all turned out the way it did. You and your grandmother didn't deserve any of it."

"Thank you." Her face was sad and drawn. She turned her face away and looked at the ground.

"Oh and there is some good news in all of this." Elizabeth looked up and searched his face. "The lobsterman, Slater, and his passengers were rescued not far off the coast well before the hurricane hit. We may never know if there was a connection with that mishap and the mess at the inn. But at least that part had a happy ending."

Elizabeth forced a smile at this news. "That is wonderful news. Thank you."

"Well, I will leave you to carry on. I must get back to the station to see if the state boys need any more assistance." He gave a quick tug at the waist of his pants with both hands, as if to ensure it was secure, and then tipped his hat as he turned to take his leave.

"Thanks again, Chief." There were nods and waving hands all around as they watched him stride toward his squad car, a little more spring in his step than he'd had lately. Elizabeth was impressed that Kurt had returned the chief's self-esteem to him. What a thoughtful and sweet thing to do. She turned back to him.

Kurt looked into her eyes. "There is something else I need to talk to you about, Liz." He hesitated as if trying to decide how to proceed, pointed toward a garden bench for them to sit on and then continue. "The medical examiner released your grandmother's autopsy report." Their eyes met as they sat down and he looked to her for approval to continue. Her eyes told him she was quite weary but expected him to go on. "Elizabeth, Amelia's autopsy showed she had a high level of a drug called Zoloft in her blood stream when she passed away that suggests ingestion over an extended period of time. Zoloft is an anti-anxiety drug that causes drowsiness. Her doctor told us that he had never prescribed that or any other similar drug for her. Do you have any idea where she might have gotten something like that? He waited to see if Elizabeth had a response.

She wrinkled her forehead and shook her head. Her grandmother never liked to take any kind of drugs, over-the-counter or prescription. This certainly didn't sound like something she would have done on her own.

"The fatigue she was experiencing from the drug put an additional burden on her body that was hard for her to handle. With everything going on, she didn't have time to slow down and rest. The medical examiner concluded that the Zoloft contributed to her passing." Kurt paused as he knew she would need to process that information.

Tears welled up in her eyes and she turned away slightly. The evening in the lighthouse came rushing back to her. Her poor grandmother had been through so much before she arrived on the scene to help. Elizabeth feared that having to shoulder the burden of running the inn on her own also contributed to her grandmother's passing. A wave of guilt crashed over her. She wondered what kind of granddaughter lets that happen. She should have checked in with her more often. All she could do was to shake her head. A tear rolled down her cheek and dropped silently in her lap. She wiped the tear trail from her face.

Kurt looked up to see Rashelle making her way over to the two of them. She quietly approached Elizabeth's side of the bench and put her arm around her friend's shoulders. Her face was drawn with concern. Elizabeth reached up with one hand and squeezed the hand resting on her shoulder. Her gaze rested far off the shore on the distant horizon. No one spoke. Time just passed in silence.

Finally Elizabeth found her voice. "What does all this mean? Was my grandmother…murdered?" Her eyes were wide and her facial expression showed she expected an answer. Rashelle looked from Elizabeth to Kurt and back again.

Mitchell paused and tilted his head slightly, "It's possible. We can't be sure. Hopefully we will have more answers soon."

Kurt's response didn't help her. She needed answers. Silence took over the conversation as they thought about what had been revealed and the questions still unanswered.

Elizabeth finally came to life and threw out a random thought. "I wonder what happened to my portfolio of drawings."

"Well, I do remember seeing a portfolio in the Hutchins' room. I don't know what shape it might be in after the storm. But we can certainly look." He looked at her closely, surprised that she was at all concerned about something that seemed so trivial, at least to him.

"It's not that big of a deal. I just thought that perhaps I could get it back." Artists can be quite possessive of their work.

"We will certainly try," he reassured her, pressing onto the next topic. "The room that the Hutchins requested just happened to be the same approximate location that the missing student from the school had disappeared from. This was either a tremendous coincidence or somehow someone knew."

Elizabeth's face looked doubtful. "I don't see how."

"Well, anyway, Renard's confession does fit if we put it into the right time frame. Looks like we solved that age old mystery of the student's disappearance. But now he is looking at prison time. Apparently, the situation of the missing guest brought back too many memories, ones that he had pushed to the back of his mind. With them came a flood of emotions, including tremendous guilt. Unfortunately, he was afraid his brother would snitch on him and he felt compelled to silence him. He agreed to show us where he had buried both bodies so we could exhume them. There won't be much left to the girl, but if we can contact the parents, I'm sure they would want some closure."

Elizabeth had a good idea of where at least one of the bodies was. Things were not right in the section of the woods where

Mitchell had caught up to her when she escaped from Lieutenant Perkins' squad car. It was just too quiet there. Hopefully Renard will remember where they are and show the officers. Elizabeth's head was spinning. Questions kept popping up. So much of it didn't make sense.

He paused to let everything sink in. "And that's about the long and short of it at this point. That's certainly enough for now." Kurt looked at Elizabeth, who was staring straight ahead as if in a trance. He wondered if she had heard him during the last few minutes. Finally she spoke.

"So, what happened down in the tunnel...to me? I know there was a cave-in, but was it caused by human hands?"

"It would take an engineer to determine if it happened naturally or if someone's deliberate actions caused it. Looked like you got grazed on the back of the head by a support beam. Fortunately, you did not receive the brunt of the force. A couple seconds difference and you might not have been sitting here right now.

Elizabeth rubbed the back of her head, which was healing nicely, and took a deep breath. She remembered the voice. Someone had saved her life. "I guess I have lived to design another day." She allowed herself a little humor.

Rashelle chimed in at last. She suddenly looked rather awkward standing in front of her friend. "Lizzi." She took a deep breath. "I need to apologize...I haven't been completely honest with you and I'm very sorry."

Elizabeth turned and looked into Rashelle's eyes. Her dear friend. Whatever had she done?

"Well before everything else that started going on around here, I started a little affair of my own." Elizabeth raised her eyebrows. "I am so sorry, Liz. I guess I wasn't prepared for the abrupt change in lifestyle coming here from the city. It is so quiet, especially at night. After a while I couldn't stand it anymore. There was nothing to do. I needed a little excitement in my life and I certainly wasn't going to find it at the inn. So I started to head into town on my nights off to do the bar circuit, meet new people, maybe find a new guy. Well, I did meet a guy who I was absolutely crazy about. Once he knew where I worked, he was perfectly honest with me and told me he had been fired as the tennis pro not too long ago." Elizabeth gasped but Rashelle seemed to take no notice and continued. "At first, I was shocked and taken back. I didn't know what to do. I felt like I was cheating. Unfortunately, that made our relationship that much more exciting. It was like we were having an extra-marital affair without hurting our spouses. It was so exciting. I hadn't felt that exhilarated in a very long time. I know that probably sounds a bit silly...immature. Because of the excitement, I let it keep going even though I knew we shouldn't, and I am so sorry, Lizzi. I had no right to do that. I know Aaron wasn't supposed to be anywhere near this place after his dramatic removal from the grounds last spring. After I wrecked my car, though, he had to pick me up. I think it was fun for him, too...I'm sorry, Liz."

She just gazed into her friend's eyes. Even though what Rashelle did seemed trivial in comparison to the big picture and Elizabeth had already put the pieces together, she still felt betrayed by her good friend. She was at a loss for words. All she could do was look out at the horizon and shake her head slightly.

Rashelle backed away from the bench where Elizabeth was seated. "We'll talk later when everything else is all sorted out. I am sorry to have added to your burden. Not a very nice thing for a friend to do, I know...I am truly sorry." Her face was very somber, quite uncharacteristic of her. She walked away towards the circular driveway where a rental car was parked; a black, four-door Nissan of some sort. Elizabeth couldn't bear to watch as her friend drove away, down the access road away from the inn. A single tear rolled down her cheek. She felt so hurt.

Mitchell couldn't stand seeing her so sad. He needed to wrap up the conversation and get her out of there, "The state police have Aaron Gabeau in custody and are interviewing him to see if he has any connection to all of this. They will also be speaking with Rashelle." The silence that hung in the air was palpable. "Liz, why don't we head out of here? I imagine you could use a change of scenery about now."

She looked around and saw that there were no more mourners lingering. A few of the loyal staff were cleaning up from the service, stacking chairs to be picked up by the rental company. "Well, I'm at your mercy until I can get another car. I guess I'll have to pick up a rental somewhere. I've got to head back to the city and see if I can pick up the pieces of my career."

The sound of a truck engine and its wheels crunching on the gravel driveway made their heads turn toward the unexpected arrival to the inn. Kurt turned back to look at the expression on Elizabeth's face. It was a flatbed truck with a delivery. Lizzi's face lit up when she saw it was none other than her beautiful silver Z4. "What the—?"

Kurt smiled. "Your car had suffered some body damage, but it looked fixable. The wind had pushed it up against the bushes along the woods, which may have served as a cushion for it. It was out of sight from you when you returned to the inn after the storm. There were much more pressing priorities at that point so you overlooked it, and rightfully so. We scooted it out to a local auto body shop and asked if they could put a rush on it."

Elizabeth allowed herself to smile slightly. She looked up to see that the truck driver had parked on the circle and was walking up to Kurt. His arm was extended toward him with a key dangling from it. He took the key and immediately turned around and handed it to Elizabeth.

A tear rolled down her cheek. This time, a happy tear. She was all choked up so it took a great deal of effort to speak. "Thanks, Kurt. This means so much to me. Thanks so much for doing this. I just can't thank you enough." She put her arms out and hugged him tightly. He hugged her back. She could feel her heart starting to mend. With time, everything would be all right again. She had to believe it.

Mitchell glanced over at the circular driveway. The delivery guy was quickly unloading the car. "Why don't you take a closer look?" She looked up into his eyes. He smiled and nodded.

Elizabeth turned and admired her prized sports car. A grin spread across her face. She turned back to Kurt with a twinkle in her eye. "Would you like to take a ride with me?"

He was tickled she had asked. "Of course! Let's go!" He put his arm around her and they started across the lawn towards the driveway. His arm felt so right around her. She felt as if she was melting. It had been a while since she had felt this good. It was going to be fun to take her car for a little spin before she had to hit the highway back to the city.

They climbed into the car, Elizabeth in the driver's seat. She looked around. It was incredibly clean and there was a new lavender air freshener dangling from the rear view mirror. "Cute." She inserted the key and the engine sprang to life as soon as she turned it. The car's engine sounded like a cat purring in her ears. She pushed the gear shift forward into first, eased off of the clutch while pressing the accelerator, and started down the driveway. Elizabeth slowed down long enough to take one more look back before leaving. It looked like her great aunt was standing in the window of one of the front rooms, her room, watching her niece go. She was sure that Cecelia would always be watching over the inn.

Chapter 32

Elizabeth was moving a little more slowly than usual this morning. She had driven straight though without stopping the night before and had arrived at her apartment rather late. It had been difficult to leave her childhood home in the condition it was in after the hurricane's powerful wrath, but she really needed to get back to work. She also had such unsettled feelings about the human tragedy she had left behind. She didn't think she would ever recover from the heartbreak of losing her grandmother and it really bothered her that she didn't know if the young girl had been found. It was so frustrating that Mitchell couldn't divulge anything about the investigation. All she could do was to remain optimistic and believe that they were doing everything they could to resolve the situation.

She hadn't realized how much she missed the inn until she arrived the previous weekend. Now that she was back in the city, she already missed the comfortable familiarity of it, the salty sea air, and the warmth of her grandmother's smile. The corners of her mouth turned upward when she realized she was going to miss seeing Mitchell as well. She hoped he would get back to her soon and fill her in on what exactly went on at the inn before the storm and, more importantly, why.

Elizabeth had been away from her office for several days, far longer than she had planned. Mentally and physically drained, she dragged herself out of bed and headed toward Loran Design. She had no idea what was in store for her or what mood Vera was going to be in. A second cup of coffee seemed like a good idea so she stopped into her favorite coffee shop on the walk from the parking garage. She took a deep breath as she entered to take in the pleasing aroma. The familiar surroundings were somewhat comforting to her. It was a local, family owned shop, not a high-priced national chain. Elizabeth felt good about giving them her business. She thought the husband and wife made a cute couple who looked a bit Italian, maybe Greek. They were always behind the counter, side-by-side, working long hours day in and day out, starting very early in the morning by preparing their fresh-from-the-oven, home-made pastries and muffins. She couldn't really place their accents because her conversations with them were brief. Business was usually brisk so they stuck to the task at hand, trying to please their customers by getting them in and out as quickly as possible. She had been stopping in so often over the last few years that they always acknowledged her when she approached the counter. The wife smiled warmly and said "good morning" and the husband winked and said "hello."

With a warm, aromatic coffee in hand, she continued her walk in the morning sunshine, happy to be walking next to and through groups of people she had never met before. It looked to her like every other person was on a cell phone. It became more apparent at each corner as a group of people would form, waiting for the light to change so they could cross the street. She always found it interesting that so many people walking toward each other could navigate so that no one ran into each other, at least not directly. It was like a well-choreographed ballet. New York's hustle and bustle never got old to her. She slowed her pace to take in the sights and sounds of the city, which she never wanted to take for granted, and to postpone the inevitable. Seeing Vera face to face.

She kept rewinding the video in her head to the part where she hung up on her boss. Elizabeth feared Vera would just fire her on the spot for insubordination, but was trying to be more optimistic than that. Eventually she reached the revolving doors into the lobby of her building and she pushed the nearest glass panel that was slowing from the last person who had entered. Starting through the motion of a half circle, it crossed her mind to just keep going all the way around and exit again out onto the street. She rolled her eyes and sighed. *Just do it, Elizabeth.* She exited the revolving doors and headed across the lobby.

Surprisingly no one else entered the elevator with her so she ascended to the twenty-second floor alone with her thoughts. The doors opened into the lobby of Loran Design. It was uncharacteristically empty. She took in a deep breath and exhaled. No one was at the front desk and no one was in the waiting area that was furnished in ultra-modern, off white leather seating. Elizabeth took it all in and then turned right to head directly to her office. Fortunately she did not have to pass Vera's office on the way. A few minutes to herself would be ideal to gather her thoughts and finish her coffee. Vera could wait.

As Elizabeth made her way down the hall, she could hear a male voice in the conference room that was coming up on her left. She slowed her pace when she recognized that it was Drescher. Her eyes widened when she realized she had not remembered to grab her portfolio before she left Maine. She had nothing to show him. Nothing to prove she was working hard on his new project even while she was away. Panic was rising up inside her. As she quickened her pace to get past the conference room, she heard him say, "You and I both know that this is going to happen the way I want it to. We also both know that there will be serious consequences if it does not." Elizabeth wasn't sure exactly what he had meant by that but she kept walking, with her eyes forward, without hearing the rest of the conversation. She desperately hoped that he hadn't noticed her walking past the doorway. Once inside the security of her private office, she turned her attention to the stack of little pink phone messages on her desk.

Her office was decorated with a modern, updated feel. Since it was not on an outside wall, there were no windows, but it was still bright and airy with light-colored grass cloth wallpaper. A light wood desk and credenza with sleek lines took up most of the space. There was also a small round work table framed by two chairs in one corner. Abstract prints were tastefully hung on three of the walls. An open concept shelving unit occupied the fourth.

Once her laptop booted up, she busied herself with picking up emails. As she scrolled through the long list of unopened mail, it dawned on her that one of her first priorities needed to be replacing her cell phone. It had been a welcomed relief not having one since the hurricane. No calls from a persistent client and, better yet, no calls from her obnoxious boss. But she knew she needed to get one as soon as possible now that she was back in the city and back to work.

Just when she had decided it was probably time to go check in with Vera, Sara, the receptionist, stuck her head in the doorway. "Elizabeth, so glad to see you are back and I was sorry to hear about your grandmother. Not what you were expecting from a weekend away, I'm sure. Listen, I can't hold her off any longer. When you get a chance…well as soon as you can, Vera would like to see you in her office."

Elizabeth looked intently into her face, shaking her head slightly. "How the hell did she know I was here already?" She turned away, not expecting an answer. They both new that Vera had this uncanny sense of what went on at Loran Design. It was almost creepy. Elizabeth's stomach turned over. She couldn't procrastinate any longer. She swallowed hard and nodded to Sara. "Okay, I understand. I'll be right there." She closed her eyes and bent her head toward her desk, resting her elbow on the surface and rubbing her forehead with the fingers on her left hand.

She stood, took a deep breath, and headed for the door of her office. She tried to walk down the hall as tall and as confidently as possible. She had to pass the conference room that Drescher was occupying and then make her way through the lobby to get to Vera's office, but she held her head high. She entered Vera's open doorway, raising her fist to knock lightly on her open door. She looked in and, to Elizabeth's surprise, she could see that Vera was not at her desk, but decided to wait for her anyway. After all, she had garnered the courage to approach her so she wasn't going to waste the energy that had taken. She glanced around the dark and somewhat depressing office. The venetian blinds were turned upward which minimized the amount of outside light that entered the room. The furnishings were modern but dark. Vera's deep mahogany desk was the focal point in the room and was facing the door. There was a matching credenza behind it, up against the wall. There were a couple pieces of artwork on the walls that were post-impressionistic prints and a small sculpture on a pedestal in front of the two windows that looked out onto the streets of Manhattan. Elizabeth noticed one of Vera's skinny, brown cigarettes smoldering in a cheap black plastic ashtray on her desk. A wisp of smoke snaked its way upward, disappearing five or six inches above its source.

On the credenza was Vera's purse. It was a signature satchel bag by Louis Vuitton and was partially open. A small brown container sat next to it. Elizabeth's eyes grew wide. Without looking around, she headed past Vera's desk. It was a prescription bottle with a small white child-proof twist off cap. Her heart started to beat faster. She picked it up and turned the bottle in her hand so she could read the label. Zoloft. She turned when she heard Vera's voice.

"Hello, Elizabeth. So good to see you. I was so sorry to hear about your grandmother." Vera was sporting a mauve-colored suit in raw silk, matching two-toned stilettos, and the customary bulges in the jacket pockets that were her pack of cigarettes and lighter.

Elizabeth turned to look into her boss's face, still holding the bottle.

Vera's eyes moved to the bottle in her employee's hand and then back to her face. Her eyes narrowed and her brow furrowed. "Can I help you with some—?"

"It was you!" Elizabeth couldn't believe her boss was involved with what just happened at the inn.

Vera look puzzled. "Whatever are you talking about Elizabeth?"

"You know exactly what I mean!" She couldn't believe her boss was denying her involvement. Elizabeth was breathing rapidly as she walked directly toward Vera, holding the prescription bottle out in front of her. "How could you? What the hell was in it for you?" Her voice was getting louder with each sentence. "You murdered my grandmother." Elizabeth's face was so close to her that her boss was becoming very uncomfortable. For once, their roles were reversed.

Vera's mouth fell open. If she was feigning surprise, she was a very good actress. "Elizabeth, I can assure you I have no idea what you are talking about!" Her voice matched the volume of Elizabeth's. "Think about what you are saying." Her voice became much quieter and gentler, which was uncharacteristic for Vera. "I know you must be very upset about your grandmother and I'm very sorry that it happened. Truly I am. But I don't think you really know what you're saying right now. Maybe you came back to work too soon. If you need to take more time, take it. We'll just forget this whole conversation happened." She paused and searched Elizabeth's face for any clue as to what she was thinking. A look of concern spread across her face.

Elizabeth took a couple steps back. She was overwhelmed with emotion. Her head was spinning. The situation had turned surreal. She had just made an incredible, unthinkable accusation. She rubbed her forehead with the fingers of her empty hand. Without acknowledging she knew what she was doing, she placed the prescription bottle on Vera's desk and started moving toward the door, brushing past her boss as she went. Her eyes were glazed and fixed on the door. She staggered slightly and put one hand out to steady herself in her boss's doorway.

Vera remained quiet, watched her gather herself, and then head through the doorway.

Elizabeth's head was pounding as she walked down the hall with a purpose. She needed to put as much distance between her and her boss. She was in such a fog, she didn't notice if Drescher was still in the conference room when she passed. Once inside her office, she closed the door behind her and braced herself against it. She wished the door had a lock on it. Her mind was racing and she was feeling terribly alone. She wasn't sure what to think, where to turn or what to do next. Suddenly the phone on her desk started ringing. She jumped and her eyes widened. She wasn't sure if she should answer it. It rang just a few times but it seemed like it went on forever. Elizabeth was frozen in place at the door. Finally, the ringing stopped. She took in a deep breath and let it out. It crossed her mind that her office phone was her only means of communication with anyone on the outside since she didn't have a cell. She couldn't decide what her next step should be. The clock on her credenza was ticking loudly in her quiet office. It seemed to echo like it had never done before. She needed to think. She was paralyzed by indecision. Finally, only one thing came to mind. She pulled herself away from the door, turned and pulled it open slightly so it was ajar, flipped the light switch into the "off" position and then walked around to the other side of her desk. She pulled her chair part of the way out and slid herself into place under the desk and then pulled the chair back in as far as it would go. She settled in with her back up against one side of the desk, with her legs pulled up to her chest and arms wrapped around them. It was a dark, but familiar place.

───────────

Kurt closed his flip phone. His forehead was creased. He was worried because he really needed to reach Elizabeth, but could not. Her cell phone was ruined and there was no answer at her office extension. He was afraid that she could be in danger. He tossed his phone onto the passenger seat and climbed in behind the wheel.

Chapter 33

Elizabeth was trying to keep her breathing steady and quiet. She didn't know how long she could stay where she was but she needed time to think. Time to get her head straightened out. What had just happened in her boss's office seemed more like a nightmare than anything real.

Suddenly the light was switched on in her office. She jumped and held her breath, listening for footsteps. Someone was walking around her office, not making much noise at all on the carpet. Elizabeth watched to see if any feet came into view from her perspective down under. Finally a shoe came into view. It was a man's shoe. Black. It took everything she had to stifle a gasp. Then the second shoe moved next to the first. They were pointing towards her credenza. Elizabeth was holding her breath. She placed her hand over her mouth and nose to help her keep from making a sound. She had a feeling that she knew who the shoes belonged to and was hoping he would just leave her office. Then came the voice from the doorway.

"That's Elizabeth and her grandmother." It was Vera. She sounded like she was standing in the doorway. Elizabeth surmised that the male she was talking to must be looking at her photos on the credenza. Then she heard the sound of the frame being returned to its original location. She felt so uncomfortable that someone was handling something of hers that was so personal. The photo had been taken many years ago when her grandmother attended her college graduation, a very special occasion that she felt so fortunate to have been able to share with her.

Then came the second voice. "Very sweet."

This confirmed her suspicion that it was Drescher with Vera.

Finally, the shoes left her field of vision and made their way back to her office door.

"I'm sure she hasn't gone far."

"Well, her office was dark so maybe she has already left."

"She just got here! She better not have left already. Especially if she didn't tell me first!"

Elizabeth cringed at hearing Vera's voice. She was starting to perspire. She was feeling trapped, totally unsure of what was going on.

Someone extinguished the light in her office and their voices continued down the hall out of range of her ears. She held her breath again.

She waited and listened. No sounds. No lights. No voices.

It was so quiet that she felt like she was the only person in Loran Design. The only person in the building. Finally, she felt brave enough to scoot out from under the desk slightly. She peered over her desk to see if she could see anything in the hall. Nothing. She crawled back under the desk and waited some more. No one knew she was there. Still no sound except for the clock on her credenza. *Tick. Tock.* It was so loud. It sounded like the ticking was in her head. She wanted it to stop.

Chapter 34

She dozed in and out of sleep for a while. It was still dark in her office when she became lucid. She had no idea how long she had been there. Even if she could see the clock on her credenza from where she was, it was too dark to make out the time. She listened. She wasn't sure what to do, although she was beginning to feel the need to escape her close quarters.

She felt a nagging feeling that she needed to leave and find an alternate way out of the building, that someone would stop her if she took the usual route. She stood in her office, trying to think what to do next and decided that the safest way to exit would be down the back fire stairs. There was a main set of stairs but she really wanted to try to get out without anyone seeing her.

She reached the door to the back stairs and quickly pushed it open. There were twenty-two stories to get down. This wasn't the lighthouse at Pennington Point, but she had to get down to the bottom anyway.

Elizabeth had to focus on getting to the bottom of the stairs safely. She hung onto the railing and kept her eyes on her feet as she descended the stairs. Her shoes made a clicking sound as she went. There were no other sounds in the stairwell. She kept going, watching the signs on the doors as she passed which displayed the floor number. 21…20…19…18…17…16. Even though she was moving with gravity, her legs were starting to get sore. She just ignored them and kept moving. 15…14…13…12. She had to stop briefly and catch her breath. Her legs felt wobbly. It crossed her mind that someone her age should not have trouble with this. It was time to make the gym a priority.

Elizabeth pressed on. 11…10…9…8. She stopped again to take a breath and give her legs a break. She listened for a moment because she thought she heard a noise. All was quiet. Nothing. Then she heard it again. Footsteps above her. She gasped and started her feet again. She had eight stories to get down. She had to do it as fast as possible. She didn't need to find out who was in the back stairs with her.

7…6…5…4…3…So close to the bottom but she could hear the footsteps even louder. Who was in the stairs with her? She didn't want to find out. She forced her legs to keep moving on to the second floor and finally the first. She pushed open the exit door and burst into an alley. Her feet stopped. She looked up and down. No one else had exited recently. No one was in sight. There were dumpsters scattered throughout the narrow passage that ran between her building and the one behind it. Frantically trying to think which way to go, she knew she needed to head toward Lexington Avenue. She looked in both directions again and finally decided to turn right. She ran as fast as her legs would take her. Halfway up the alley her left foot landed in a pothole and she started to roll her ankle. She pulled up on her right foot enough to catch herself and resume running. She thought she heard the exit door slam again, but didn't take the time to look back.

When she hit the sidewalk on Lexington, her eyes scanned the street looking for a taxi. She ran to the curb, waving her arm and whistling. A yellow cab pulled right up. A light rain was falling but she didn't notice. She opened the back door to the cab and started to climb in. Suddenly there was a hand grabbing her arm. She gasped and tried to pull away.

A familiar voice said, "Elizabeth, it's me."

She stopped trying to pull away and instead, turned her body around, landing with her back against the side of the taxi. She looked into his eyes.

"Kurt." It took a few seconds for it to sink in that he was really standing there. She was so glad to see him. "What are you doing here? You're a long way from Maine." She smiled slightly.

"I thought you might want to hear how our investigation turned out...and I wanted to make sure you're okay." There was genuine concern in his eyes.

Elizabeth looked up at him and smiled more broadly. Her suit jacket had spots of water on it and her hair was tussled from her run down the stairs. Kurt appeared amused by her unkempt look. So uncharacteristic for her.

Elizabeth could sense he was noticing her unusual appearance and quickly became self-conscious. She ran her fingers through her hair to try to put it back into some sort of mediocre coiffure.

Mitchell's amusement turned to concern about her being wet. Elizabeth reassured him that she was fine. He gave her his jacket anyway. She started to protest but he insisted. She thought he was sweet.

They walked across the street to a neighborhood bar, one that Vera and Elizabeth had visited on a few occasions, when her boss was trying to prime her with alcohol and find out what made her tick. It was Friday, barely midday but New York City was known for being alive any time of the day. Stir was a bar with an uptown, metro feel with contemporary lighting and seating. It was dark wood paneled with stools at the bar running along the left side of the room and small square tables scattered throughout which were mostly empty. Not quite up to a standard of fine, white table linens, but still a few steps up from the trashy McLendry's Irish Pub a few doors down. The air was a bit stale, but tolerable and the canned music had a jazz flavor to it, which was not really her taste, but she could ignore it. They found a relatively quiet corner and ordered a round of drinks. The bar was known for its martini menu, but they stuck with their usuals, Pinot Grigio for her, Jack Daniels on the rocks for him. The standard basket of pretzels and dipping sauces were delivered along with the drinks. Elizabeth was exhausted but anxious to hear what Kurt had to say and happy to leave behind whomever was in the stairwell with her.

They shared small talk between sips of their drinks but Elizabeth was anxious for him to get started. She pulled his jacket up closer around her shoulders and looked to him to begin the debriefing.

"Elizabeth, you may find this hard to believe…" He found it difficult to just blurt it out.

"Go on." She was impatient and didn't understand his hesitation. Her eyes implored him to continue.

"Your client…" He took a deep breath, buying himself some time to choose his words carefully. "Your client, Jack Drescher, was involved in all of this." He paused to allow her time to let that sink in.

She sat back in her seat as if to put distance between her and something she couldn't wrap her mind around. "What? Kurt, what are you talking about?"

"Elizabeth, evidently he had some business dealings that had gone sour recently and was not doing well financially. Actually, that's probably an understatement. Apparently, he was so over-leveraged that he was desperate. His accountant, who turned out to be the now deceased Joseph Stevens, had refused to sign off on a set of financial statements that he had prepared in the hopes of securing additional financing. Stevens refused to have his name associated with the statements because they were not only misleading, but downright false. Completely fabricated. So, without the CPA's blessing, the bank refused Drescher any additional credit. As a result, he became insolvent. He had no liquid assets to work with on a day-to-day basis and his business came to a grinding halt. In his mind, the inn was his last hope. He actually started several months ago harassing poor Amelia about selling the place."

"He was the real estate attorney who wouldn't leave her alone?" Elizabeth was following right along, but she couldn't believe her ears.

"Yes. He pretended to be an attorney in the hopes of coercing her into doing what he wanted her to do, sell it for next to nothing. This place could have meant millions to him. A prime piece of coastal Maine real estate. We think that initially his plans were to build luxury condos. But when cash became a problem he switched his plans to buying it cheap and selling it quickly to the highest bidder. That could have solved his financial problems in one transaction."

"Oh my God! But how would he even have known about our inn? I know he and I never talked about it. Our discussions were strictly professional." She looked at Kurt and furrowed her brow. "Vera!"

He shrugged his shoulders and tilted his head in a gesture of "could be."

Elizabeth could imagine Vera chatting away with Drescher over drinks and inadvertently passing on personal information about her.

"Right. Well, most of the harassment came in the form of phone calls, but then he took it up a couple notches and started sending letters, very professional looking letters from this fictional attorney he was portraying. Your poor grandmother must have been so stressed out.

Elizabeth let out a heavy sigh. Had she been there sooner maybe she could have been of more help. She wished her grandmother had called her sooner. She wished she had thought to call her. She had had no idea of what was going on. She would have to live with that one.

"We had been tracking Drescher's movements for quite some time in his business dealings throughout New England when we made the connection between him and Pennington Point Inn. As the tennis pro for the inn, I was able to maintain a good cover while I kept an eye on things up close. We knew it was just a matter of time before he slipped up and we could nail him. He is now facing a laundry list of charges against him including extortion and murder. Somehow, the financial problems that started all this seem so trivial in comparison."

"Yeah. Seems like things really got out of control." Elizabeth looked like she was in shock. A client she had admired and respected had done the unthinkable.

"I'll say. He tried to convince Amelia that she didn't rightfully own the property."

"Yes!" Elizabeth remembered her conversation in the lighthouse. "My grandmother told me she couldn't find her copy of their marriage license at the inn and had no luck at town hall."

"Well, we didn't give up on that. We put some people on it. I think the town clerk was just too lazy to go into storage when Amelia asked. But it's amazing how motivated she became when we flashed an FBI badge. The oldest records had never been put on microfiche or any other type of long-term storage. They were just thrown into boxes and stored off site when they moved into the new town hall. It was a minor miracle that they still existed and could be read. We located a copy of her marriage certificate and the deed to the inn. Case closed on those questions."

"Thank God." Elizabeth heaved a sigh of relief. "If only she were around to hear this."

"Oh, I think she knows." He tried to comfort her with a pat on the shoulder.

Elizabeth fixed her gaze on a focal point across the room. She was trying hard to process what he was saying. She couldn't help wonder if this had anything to do with all the times she had rejected Drescher. She shuddered.

Mitchell continued. "Evidently Amelia wasn't caving in like he wanted her to. So he decided to pump up the pressure by making things miserable on a daily basis for her and the entire staff to the point that no one would want to stay or work at the inn. His brother owed him a favor or two so he coerced him into checking into the inn for the weekend to really stir things up."

"Hutchins." Elizabeth was catching on.

"Exactly. Bill and Sara Hutchins were really James Rizzo, Jack's brother-in-law, and his wife, Ann. Ann is Drescher's sister."

Elizabeth was fighting back her anger toward the Dreschers, every last one of them.

"The Rizzos pretended to have a daughter who went missing."

Elizabeth turned away from Mitchell. He had to lean in to hear her speak. "So there was never a Kelsey Hutchins who was missing and feared dead?" Her teeth were clenched in anger.

"No. That was merely an elaborate distraction for us and another black mark on the inn to dissuade potential guests from booking reservations there."

She turned abruptly toward him. "They had half the Maine State Police out looking for that girl!" Her voice was elevated.

"Well, don't worry. They, too, will be prosecuted to the fullest extent of the law. They have racked up filing a false police report, obstruction of justice, interfering with a police officer, aiding and abetting a felon. The list goes on.

"On top of it all, Drescher lured his accountant, who wouldn't sign off on his financials, to the Pennington Inn under the pretense of burying the hatchet, so to speak. Instead, Drescher buried the hatchet in him, probably thinking he could pin it on Tony, if he used his knife, or you and Rashelle by videotaping you finding the body, which he accomplished by hiding in the wine cooler."

The package that we found in your car, that supposedly contained the missing girl's necklace, was actually from Drescher. It was originally a token of his affection for you but when you left unexpectedly for the weekend in Maine, it suddenly took on a whole new purpose.

Elizabeth was staring intently at the floor. She breathed in deeply and let it out slowly. "Somehow, whatever they get just doesn't seem like it's enough for what they've done."

"I know. But they all will certainly see prison time. Drescher also had his nephew involved in this mess, too."

"Armand."

Mitchell raised his eyebrows at her. He was definitely impressed. "Yes, again. He got himself hired as an all-around handy guy, helping in all areas of the inn's operations, wherever he was needed. He got his foot in the door by first befriending Slater."

Elizabeth's eyes got wide upon hearing this.

"He asked Slater to recommend him for the job. So since his job took him all over the inn, he was able to slip in and out without anyone getting suspicious or asking questions. Drescher had him distributing those handwritten notes asking about the missing girl. His intention was to further stir up the pot and to legitimize the search."

Elizabeth realized she wasn't the only one receiving the mysterious notes. "I never thought I could feel this much hatred toward someone."

"I understand. That wasn't all he was distributing..." He waited until he had her undivided attention.

She looked at him, squinted her eyes slightly, and tilted her head as if trying to figure out what he was going to say next.

"From what we can tell, Armand was also the one who was delivering Zoloft to Amelia...your grandmother."

Elizabeth's eyes took on the look of a tiger.

"He apparently brought drinks to Amelia under the guise of delivering refreshments from the kitchen and they were laced with the drug."

Elizabeth jumped to her feet slamming her hands on the table. "That BASTARD!!"

Kurt rose to his feet, skirted around the table and grabbed onto her arms. He knew she was very vulnerable right now. She burst into tears and he pulled her into his arms. She sobbed uncontrollably for a while with her face buried in his chest. Finally, she lifted her head and looked into his eyes. She was having trouble accepting what he had told her. It was bad enough before when it looked like someone might be slipping her grandmother the drug. But somehow, it was so much worse hearing who actually did the dirty deed.

Suddenly she started to feel faint and her knees were feeling weak. Kurt grabbed her around the torso and eased her into the nearest chair. "Breathe, Elizabeth, breathe. In through the nose, out through the mouth. Breathe." He looked intently at her to see if she was doing what he was telling her to do.

Her head bobbed a couple of times and then stabilized. She blinked to try to stay focused and took deep breaths. He kept his arm around her back to support her. She raised her hand as if to say she was all right. He pulled his arm away, but kept it within a safe distance and watched her carefully. She seemed to be recovering nicely. Perhaps the wine wasn't such a good idea but he thought she was a very strong woman, particularly under the circumstances.

"I'm sorry. I don't know what came over me."

"Oh, Elizabeth, don't worry about it. You're fine. I know this is a lot to take in."

Her head was still feeling a little light headed so she reached out and held onto his arm for a moment. She needed something or someone to hang onto. She was so glad to see him again, even if he was the bearer of bad news. She released his arm again.

He kept his eye on her and an arm within reach of catching her but she seemed to quickly come around so he pulled back and returned to his seat.

She looked into his eyes with a smile and shook her head slightly. "So Vera was never involved?" Elizabeth cringed when she thought back to her conversation in her boss's office earlier that morning.

"It doesn't appear so. Zoloft is a pretty common drug. Readily available. We have FBI agents tailing Armand and should have him in custody shortly."

She smiled. Even so, she didn't know if she could really trust Vera again. "It's amazing how screwed up things can get, especially when you have no control over them." She looked to see if he had a response.

"I think a very wise person once said that it's not what happens to you that matters, it's how you handle it that makes a difference."

She considered his words of wisdom and sat silently for a while. She realized that at some point she would be able to understand that he was absolutely right. It would take some time, but she knew that eventually she would be able to accept what had happened at the inn during the last couple of weeks and also so many years ago with Renard and the missing student. She needed to move on. And maybe that meant moving on from Vera as well.

He glanced down at his cell phone and pressed a key to retrieve a text message. He looked up with a smile. "We just took Drescher into custody."

Elizabeth thought about that for a moment, stood up from the table and moved around to the side of it. She smiled, took a deep breath and then leaned over and kissed him on the right side of his face, bushing the left side with her hand. She stood up straight again, looked directly into his eyes and said, "Kurt, I hope to see you again. Thank you for everything you have done. I really appreciate it." She pulled his jacket off of her shoulders and draped it over the chair she had just vacated and turned away, leaving a half a glass of wine on the table.

A look of surprise came across his face. "Elizabeth…are you okay?" He was suddenly concerned about her leaving alone.

She lowered her head for a moment as if she was deep in thought and then smiled slightly. She turned back and looked into his eyes with one side of her mouth curled upward and said, "I'll be fine."

He watched as she turned, walked toward the door, and out onto the streets of Manhattan.

Glancing across the street to her building, she got a glimpse of Drescher being led out of her building with his hands in cuffs behind him. He looked rather humble between two uniformed New York City police officers. Half a dozen plain clothed men wearing black wind breakers followed behind. She assumed they were FBI agents. Several unmarked black Surburbans were waiting at the curb along with two New York City patrol cars with lights flashing.

He turned his head toward her and made eye contact.

She turned away from him and headed in the opposite direction down Lexington Avenue in the light rain.

About The Author

Ms. Goetjen resides in Connecticut with her husband and their three children.